The Diva
Cooks Up
a Storm

Krista Davis is the author of

The Diva Cooks Up a Storm

Krista Davis

KENSINGTON BOOKS
www.kensingtonbooks.com

KENSINGTON BOOKS are published by

Kensington Publishing Corp.
119 West 40th Street
New York, NY 10018

All Kensington titles, imprints and distributed lines are available at special quantity discounts for bulk purchases for sales promotion, premiums, fund-raising, educational or institutional use.

Special book excerpts or customized printings can also be created to fit specific needs. For details, write or phone the office of the Kensington Sales Manager: Kensington Publishing Corp., 119 West 40th Street, New York, NY 10018. Attn. Sales Department. Phone: 1-800-221-2647.

Kensington and the K logo Reg. U.S. Pat. & TM Off.

First Kensington Hardcover Edition: June 2018

ISBN-13: 978-1-4967-1470-1 (ebook)
ISBN-10: 1-4967-1470-9 (ebook)
Kensington Electronic Edition: June 2018

ISBN-13: 978-1-4967-1469-5
ISBN-10: 1-4967-1469-5
First Kensington Trade Paperback Printing: March 2019

10 9 8 7 6 5 4 3 2

Printed in the United States of America

To Amy Norwood Wheeler
with love and gratitude

Acknowledgments

It's such a pleasure to be back in Old Town with Sophie and the gang in this book. Huge thanks to my agent, Jessica Faust, and my editor, Wendy McCurdy, for keeping the divas alive. And special thanks to all the readers who love the divas and asked when the next book would be out. I hope you'll enjoy it.

As always, a lot of research went into this book. If I have anything wrong, it's my own fault entirely. The Revolutionary War spy John Dixon really did exist and is said to haunt a house in Old Town. They say he was so upset about the revolution that he was exceptionally unfriendly to a visitor from England who toured the house he haunts. I have, however, taken great liberties with his family tree. That part is pure fiction, as is the young widow who hosted dinner parties for spies. While there are records of women passing communications, her character is entirely fictional.

While there are several libraries in Alexandria, Virginia, and at least one in Old Town, the library in this book is entirely fictional and a figment of my imagination. It has no connection whatsoever to an actual library anywhere.

My friend Amy Norwood Wheeler was a huge help to me in the writing of this book, and I will be eternally grateful. Those of you who notice the connection to Nina Reid Norwood's name will understand that I cannot omit thanks to Elizabeth Nina Strickland and Susan Reid Smith Erba as well.

And I thank my writing friends Ginger Bolton, Allison Brook, Peg Cochran, Kaye George, Daryl Wood Gerber, and Janet Koch, who are always there with support and encouragement, just a quick e-mail away.

Cast of Characters

Old Town Residents
Hollis Haberman
Kelsey Haberman, Hollis's wife
Gavin Haberman, Hollis's son
Cindy Haberman, Hollis's ex-wife, Gavin's mother
Angus Bogdanoff
Madison Jenkins (husband Gage)
Trula Dixon
Parker Dixon
Dr. Jay Charles

Sophie's Friends
Francie Vanderhoosen
Nina Reid Norwood
Bernie Frei
Humphrey Brown
Lavinia Brown, Humphrey's mother
Mars Winston
Alex German
Natasha

Chapter 1

Dear Sophie,
I met a very cute guy recently. We went out once and now he has invited me to an "underground dinner." He doesn't know where it will be, what will be served, or who else will be there. This sounds very suspicious. I don't want to end up under the ground! Is this a real thing?
Trepidatious in Lick Fork, Virginia

Dear Trepidatious,
Underground dinners, also known as pop-up dinners, are all the rage right now. An undisclosed but well-known chef prepares a surprise menu in a location that isn't revealed until the last minute. Tickets are typically bought well in advance. Underground dinners are a lot of fun, but you'll have to decide whether this is what the new boyfriend actually has in mind.
Sophie

At ten in the morning on the first day of my summer vacation, a bloodcurdling scream pierced the tranquility of my neighborhood in Old Town Alexandria. My hound mix, Daisy, had been sniffing around my backyard while I enjoyed a mug of coffee.

Daisy barked once and ran for the front gate. Dogs have far better hearing than humans, so I trusted her inclination about the direction of the trouble and followed right behind her.

A man ran toward us on the sidewalk, his gait awkward and ungainly. He waved his hands madly around his head and continued screaming.

By that time, my neighbors Nina Reid Norwood and Francie Vanderhoosen had emerged from their homes.

At first blush, the man appeared to be deranged. But as he neared, his dilemma became readily apparent. Angry bees buzzed around him and more followed.

I seized his hand. "Quick. Into the house!"

Daisy snapped at the bees as we ran. Nina and Francie brought up the rear. We rushed into my kitchen and quickly closed the door behind us.

A few bees made it inside. Nina and Francie grabbed sections of the newspaper and swatted at them while Daisy continued to chase and snap at them.

Meanwhile, I sat the man down. Thirtyish, I guessed. His green T-shirt bore the hound face logo of The Laughing Hound, a local restaurant. His jeans were dusty, as though he'd been doing lawn work in them. He was having trouble breathing. Red welts had already formed on his face.

"Do you have a bee allergy?" I asked.

"Doh. Gihzzy." He opened his mouth for some deep breaths. There was no mistaking the swelling of his tongue.

I grabbed the phone, dialed 911, and handed it to Nina while I wet a kitchen towel with cold water. I had no idea whether that was the right thing to do, but I held it against his face.

Francie seized the beautiful pink begonia from my bay window, pulled it out of the pot, and scooped up dirt in her hands. "Scoot over, Sophie."

She packed the dirt against his face. One of his eyes was swelling shut.

"Will you look at that?" asked Nina. "Bees are still buzzing around your kitchen door."

Some of the bees outside were even hitting the glass window in the door as though they were angry that they couldn't come inside.

Moments later, the reassuring wail of an ambulance soothed my nerves. Allergic or not, this guy needed medical attention. I ran to the front door and opened it. In moments, the ambulance had parked, and emergency medical technicians walked inside calm as a serene lake.

An EMT asked the man, "What's your name, sir?"

"Anguh Guhanhoh." His speech was so garbled that none of us could understand it.

"You ladies know him?"

The three of us looked at one another and shook our heads.

"He came running down the street with bees buzzing all around him," I explained.

The EMT felt the man's pockets for a wallet and extracted it while another EMT asked what was on his face.

Francie beamed when she said, "Dirt. It's an old home remedy. Soothes the stings."

The EMT shook his head in obvious disbelief.

The one with the wallet said, "I don't see any allergy alerts in here. You're Angus Bogdanoff?"

The man nodded.

"Got any allergies?"

"Doh." He shook his head.

They administered a shot of epinephrine, put him on a stretcher, and wheeled him out to the ambulance. We trailed along, feeling helpless. We couldn't even notify anyone for the poor guy.

When the ambulance departed, Nina, Francie, and I returned to my kitchen. I took lemonade and iced tea out of the fridge to make Arnold Palmers.

"I'd suggest sitting in the garden," said Francie, "but we probably ought to let any lingering bees dissipate."

"Not to mention that it's already getting warm," Nina fanned herself with both hands. "I swear this is the hottest summer I can remember. I try to stay indoors until six in the evening. Thank heaven the underground dinner tonight doesn't start earlier. They'd have people fainting all over the place."

"Everyone is too pampered these days. We didn't have air-conditioning when I was growing up." Francie sipped her Arnold Palmer. "I remember my daddy sitting outside to read at ten o'clock at night because it was too stuffy in the house. And no one had air-conditioning in their cars, either. We kids sat in the back with the windows rolled down and hung our heads out like dogs. Mom and Dad made ice cream with an old crank machine and cream. Can you imagine? It had fat it in! Best ice cream ever. It was such fun running around the neighborhood, catching fireflies in the dark. Now *that's* how summer ought to be."

Nina shot her a sideways glance. "I bet you wouldn't go without air-conditioning today."

She'd caught Francie, who laughed. "I bet I could weather it better than you."

I suspected that might be the case. A true outdoorsy Southerner, Francie had reached the age where she said what she thought, even if it might sting. She made no effort to tame her dyed-yellow hair that looked as brittle as straw, or to hide the wrinkles she had earned from years of gardening and bird-watching in all kinds of weather.

"What do you know about bees, Francie?" I asked. "Why would they chase Angus like that?"

"Bees can be ornery little buggers. They're focused on protecting the hive and the queen. My guess is that Angus accidentally stumbled onto a hive and disturbed it. I've heard they'll chase a person up to half a mile."

Nina shuddered. "I love honey, but bees scare me."

I was perusing the fridge for a snack when someone knocked on the front door. Daisy accompanied me to open it.

Hollis Haberman, who lived on the next block, stood on my stoop. A respected criminal attorney in his fifties, Hollis liked to eat and had long ago given up any sort of exercise. His face was flushed from the heat and the short walk to my house.

"Hollis! Come on in out of the sun. Could I offer you an Arnold Palmer?"

"That would hit the spot. Sorry to disturb you, but my yard man vanished, and I'm told he was seen headed this way acting kind of strange."

I closed the door behind him. "Angus was working for you? Come into the kitchen. Nina and Francie are here. It was the strangest thing. Angus was being chased by bees. You'd better be careful in your yard."

Hollis touched my arm ever so gently. "Could I have a private word with you out here first?"

"Sure." I frowned at him. "What's up?"

Hollis's belly heaved when he took a deep breath. He lowered his voice to a whisper. "Do you know of a way to test food at home to be sure nobody poisoned it?"

Chapter 2

Dear Sophie,
My husband, who likes to pull my leg, says there's
such a thing as a zombie bee. He claims they fly
around at night! I always thought I was safe from
bees at night.
    Spooked in Beebeetown, Iowa

Dear Spooked,
Alas, while the name "zombie bee" sounds humor-
ous, the situation is not. A parasitic fly injects eggs
into the bee. The baby flies feed off the bee, killing
it. If you see a "zombie bee" at night, he'll proba-
bly be lurching around near death.
    Sophie

My first thought was of Hollis's new and much younger
wife. "Hollis! If you suspect someone is poisoning
you, then you need to talk to the police."

His lips bunched together. "I'm not quite ready to do
that. What if I'm wrong? I'd like to keep this on the q.t."

I understood the problem. It would destroy his marriage.

The Haberman divorce had been the talk of the town. Rumor had it that Hollis's lawyer buddies had chewed up his wife Cindy's lawyers like a wood chipper, leaving her with a tiny pile of shredded mulch. As an event planner, I had seen Cindy frequently at local society affairs in the past. Sadly, the divorce had put an end to her life on the party circuit. The new wife, Kelsey, a woman barely touching thirty with long blond hair, too much eye makeup, and a knockout figure, had replaced Cindy.

Hollis hadn't been married to Kelsey very long. "You think Kelsey is trying to poison you?"

"I did *not* say that." Hollis's face was purple.

Poor guy. He probably suspected her of poisoning him but wasn't ready to admit it. "My friend Humphrey Brown is a mortician with a lot of connections. I can check with him."

"I would be very grateful, Sophie. I don't mean to push you on this, but obviously, the sooner the better."

"In the meantime, I believe I'd only eat takeout."

"Sophie, please don't breathe a word of this to anyone. No mentioning my name, okay? That's why I came to you. I know I can trust you to keep this under your hat."

I took a deep breath. "Hollis, I still think you should speak to a cop. I don't want to see anything happen to you."

Hollis smiled at me. "I appreciate that. Now, how about that Arnold Palmer? I'm parched. Think the hospital would give me an update on Angus?"

He accompanied me into the kitchen. "Good morning, ladies. I hear you helped rescue poor Angus."

After a brief exchange, he asked us to which hospital the ambulance had taken Angus and called from my kitchen phone.

The three of us listened shamelessly while I poured him a cold drink.

The hospital confirmed that Angus was being treated

there, but had no information regarding his condition. Hollis hung up. "Those aggravating HIPAA laws. Well, if you don't mind, I'll enjoy your hospitality for a few minutes, then head over to the hospital to see him."

"Does he have any family to notify?" asked Nina.

"Not that I know of. I believe he's single. Nice young fellow." Hollis took a seat on the banquette with Francie and Nina.

I handed him an Arnold Palmer. "Will we be seeing you at the underground dinner tonight?"

"Wouldn't miss it!" He eyed me. "Have you got the inside scoop? Know what they'll be serving?"

"I don't know anything more than you do."

"Don't believe her!" cautioned Nina. "I sent them to Sophie when they couldn't find a location. But do you think she would tell me where it was going to be? She kept that secret for six months. I couldn't get it out of her."

"That's one of the things we all admire about Sophie. She knows how to keep a secret." Hollis winked at me.

I felt a little sick. Hollis's secret wasn't the kind I liked to know. I excused myself for a moment and hustled back to my tiny home office to phone Humphrey.

I punched in his number. Humphrey Brown had had a crush on me when we were children. At the time, I had been too self-absorbed in my own childhood insecurities to even notice him. Pale with white-blond hair, Humphrey was bone thin. He didn't frequent a gym or work out. In fact, he reminded me of the old advertisements about ninety-pound-weaklings who had sand kicked in their faces. Oddly enough, we had become fast friends as adults.

When he answered the phone, I said, "Hi, Humphrey! A couple years back, I think you helped us test some food that had been poisoned. Could I impose on you to do that again?"

"Who died?"

"No one."

"I worry about you, Sophie."

"It's not for me."

"How do you get mixed up in things like this?" asked Humphrey.

"I'm just doing a favor for a friend."

There was a short silence. "Bring a sample on ice to the underground dinner tonight, and I'll get my buddy to check it out. I'll need to know what he's supposed to look for."

"Okay." He couldn't test for every poison in the world. I understood that. "Thanks, Humphrey! I'll see you tonight."

When I returned to the kitchen, Hollis was saying good-bye to Francie and Nina. I saw him to the front door and whispered, "Bring food samples to the dinner tonight. They should be on ice. And I'll need a list of suspected poisons."

Hollis frowned at me. "How am I supposed to know that?"

"There isn't a universal test for poisons. They need to know what to look for. What do you have around the house? Rodent poison? Antifreeze? There are probably poisonous plants in your yard."

"Like what?" He frowned at me.

"Hollyhocks, yew, foxglove . . ."

Hollis drew a deep breath. "This isn't going to be as easy as I had hoped. See you tonight, Sophie."

When I returned to the kitchen, Nina and Francie were arguing about the weather. Nina and I were scheduled to leave for North Carolina early the next day for sun and fun at the beach, but a hurricane was tracking over open sea just off the east coast of Florida.

"It's going to swing farther out to sea," Nina insisted. "I grew up in North Carolina, it happened all the time."

"You're deceiving yourself, sugar." Francie waved her forefinger back and forth. "Geographically speaking, North Carolina juts out and that storm is headed right for it."

"Has there been an update on the tracking?" I asked.

"No," Nina growled. "The stupid thing is picking up speed, though."

Francie tsked. "Well, I hope you girls get to go to the beach, but I can tell you from experience that *I'll* be gathering my candles and making a run to the store for nonperishable foods." She scooted out of the banquette. "See you tonight." After checking for stray bees, Francie ambled out the kitchen door.

Nina groaned. "I will be so doggoned mad if Hurricane Dorian spoils our plans! We should have booked flights to Paris."

"With our luck, the hurricane would have delayed our flight. Maybe it will peter out. I'm going to pack anyway so we'll be ready to take off early tomorrow morning as planned."

Still grumbling, Nina left, and I set out for the library.

Cindy Haberman, Hollis's ex-wife, stood at the desk and greeted me warmly. "Sophie! I was just going to call you. The library book sale is on Saturday. I was hoping you might be willing to help us out?"

Willowy, with fair skin that was so unwrinkled it put the rest of us to shame, Cindy was best known for her mane of hair. Thick black tresses rippled from her part down her back. They didn't look like contrived beach waves to me. I suspected her hair would be very curly if she wore it in a short cut.

"I'd love to help out, but Nina and I are planning a trip to the beach. We won't be in town."

Cindy stared at me for a long moment. In a whisper, she said, "Honestly, I wish I could go with you. A vacation at the beach with girlfriends sounds perfect to me. Margaritas, toes in the sand—it would be heaven. After all I've been through . . ."

I assumed she meant the divorce. "Is Gavin okay?"

She massaged her temple. "He's fourteen and ready to rule the world without a clue. They tell me the teen years are hard so we won't miss them when they leave for college. If you ask me, it's nature's way of being cruel to parents."

Gavin had walked Daisy and mowed my yard from time to time when he was younger. "But Gavin's such a sweet kid!"

"Mmm. He's still adorable when he's sleeping."

Someone walked up beside me and asked a question, so I wandered to the mystery section and nabbed a few books to take to the beach.

I spent the rest of the afternoon getting the house ready for Mars. When we divorced, neither of us could bear to give up sweet Daisy, so we worked out a sharing arrangement. While I was at the beach, Mars would be staying at my house with Daisy and Mochie, my Ocicat.

We had inherited the house from Mars's aunt Faye, who loved to entertain. She had expanded the house with a grand dining room and living room that could accommodate her lavish parties in the 1960s. When Mars and I divorced, I bought out Mars fair and square. The mortgage was hefty, but I loved the old place, creaking floors and all.

A portrait of Aunt Faye hung in my kitchen. Mars's mother dropped by sometimes to *talk* with her deceased sister, an oddity that came close to landing her in a nursing home. She sat in one of the chairs next to the fireplace in the kitchen and had conversations with . . . no one. Not anyone that I could see or hear, anyway. I was a little skeptical about her ability to speak with the dead, but who was I to determine what other people might be able to do? At worst, she probably got some worries off her mind.

In the late afternoon, I showered and slid into a sleeveless dress—white with a sunflower pattern. We would be walking over to the dinner, which meant high heels were out of the question. My white FitFlops were ideal for the brick sidewalks.

Shortly before six in the afternoon, my current beau, Alex German, arrived to pick me up. Now a lawyer in Old Town, Alex had served in the military and still had that amazing straight-shouldered bearing. He was, without fail, the tidiest man I had ever met. Sometimes I ruffled his neatly trimmed dark brown hair a little bit, but it always fell back precisely into place.

"Think it's okay if I wear shorts to this thing? It's hot enough to melt a person."

He wore navy blue shorts with a button-down white shirt, the sleeves rolled back, and brown leather Top-Siders. The outfit was nearly an Old Town uniform for men's casual wear, with a golf shirt an acceptable alternative. "I'm sure you won't be the only one dressed that way."

Francie and Nina met us at the curb.

"Nina, I thought your husband was coming this time?" said Alex.

A forensic pathologist, Nina's husband spent more time out of town than at home.

"He's still in San Diego because the trial ran long. I gave his ticket to Jay Charles."

The four of us walked over to the Garrett house, with Nina still scolding me about having kept the location of the underground dinner a secret.

Months ago, when there was still snow on the ground, Nina had been contacted by Madison Jenkins, who was planning the underground dinner. She had everything lined up, but couldn't find a location. That wasn't surprising, even with Madison's influential friends. Old Town Alexandria, Virginia, was a coveted site for weddings and other festivities. The quaint brick sidewalks and Federal-style houses dating back to the days of George Washington were as popular with locals as they were with tourists. Even a year out was barely enough time to schedule the most desirable venues.

Nina had sent Madison to me. As an event planner, I often dealt with the lack of available venues. I had turned to private homes as a possibility. Million-dollar price tags on houses in Old Town weren't unusual, but I'd had a hunch that a historic home with a heftier than normal price tag might not move fast. The property dated back to the 1700s, although the existing structure was built in the mid-1800s. From the outside, the only clue to its significance was the oval plaque denoting it a historical building.

Red brick clad the first two floors. A third floor featured dormer windows in the roof. The modest black front door and matching shutters weren't noteworthy, but an observant eye might catch the original bubble glass in some of the windows. To the left was a generous parking pad paved with brick, where everyone now gathered to show their tickets to the underground dinner. A white gate led to the garden and guesthouse in back.

A teenager stood alone on the parking pad, out of his element. At $200 a plate, no one else had brought kids. He held a phone in one hand, a book in the other, and stared shamelessly at Kelsey Haberman.

Chapter 3

Dear Natasha,
I was invited to a pop-up dinner, which I under-
stand is similar to an underground dinner. Except I
was expected to bring a dish and my own chair! I
thought chefs were supposed to cook fabulous din-
ners at these things.
       Confused in Beer Bottle Crossing, Idaho

Dear Confused,
What you are describing has long been known as a
picnic. Read the details carefully next time to be
sure you understand what the pop-up includes.
       Natasha

I wasn't surprised. Kelsey Haberman had caught the attention of most of the men. Her dress in shades of blue
hugged her curves, and the neckline plunged so wide and
deep that I held my breath in anticipation of an imminent
wardrobe malfunction.

I'd never spoken to her, but I had seen her at events.

"There's always one," muttered Francie. "When I was

young, showing your knees was enough to mark you as a tramp. That skirt's so short she might as well have worn a bikini. Can you imagine having that woman as your stepmother?"

The word *stepmother* gave me pause. "Is that Gavin Haberman?" I whispered in reference to the teen. I took a closer look. He had grown like crazy since I'd seen him last.

Francie nodded. "Poor kid. His parents' divorce turned his life upside down. I see him at the library sometimes, waiting for his mom to get off work."

When Alex excused himself to speak to someone, Trula Dixon sidled up to me and elbowed me gently. "You've solved a lot of murders, Sophie. What's the best way to get rid of a strumpet without getting caught?"

I knew she was joking so I smiled, but that kind of talk was dangerous. "You don't mean that, Trula."

"Don't be so sure. Half the women in attendance would like to remove that little coquette from our circles." A chunky silver bracelet slid along her tanned arm when Trula patted her short bob. "Her hair isn't even frizzing in the heat. Of course, we'd all be cooler if we were showing as much flesh as she is." She tilted her head. "On the other hand, that dress must be one hundred percent spandex to hug her that tight. Oof. Cotton and silk are the only ways to go when it's this hot."

Trula's husband Parker, a thin bespeckled man, was among Kelsey's admirers. Parker hailed from money. I guessed he might have been a bit of a nerd when he was Gavin's age, but that had probably paid off. He was a founding partner in the law firm of Dixon, Haberman, and Jenkins. He was lean, but his golf shirt and gray shorts revealed an unathletic physique without well-defined muscles in his arms and legs. He sat on several boards, including that of the local library.

I didn't think Trula had anything to worry about, but then, Cindy Haberman probably hadn't been concerned when Kelsey entered the scene, either. I did note, though, that not a single woman was chatting with Kelsey. Not even those her age. "We'll be sitting down to eat soon," I said. "I guess the trick is to find a seat far away from her."

"If Kelsey keels over, I guarantee a wife will be the villain," muttered Trula.

We showed our tickets to a man at the gate. He gestured for us to enter.

The sheer size of the garden was amazing, especially for Old Town, where lots tended to the small size. The current occupant, one Gilmer Garrett, was a gardening aficionado. Well into his eighties, he still toiled in his beloved garden every day.

"Are those grilled dates wrapped in bacon? Do you think they're stuffed with something?" Trula hurried toward a waiter who served the delicacies from a tray.

Flat slate stones formed a rectangular walkway that had been lined with dining tables. The lawn in the middle had been mowed as perfectly as a golf course. Beyond the walkway, a tall fence peeked through conifers, bushes, and aged trees. Purple hollyhocks, pink foxglove, golden sunflowers, brilliant red cardinal flowers, and masses of zinnias in reds, pinks, and yellows lined the outer edge of the walkway.

Unlike the modest front, the rear of the house boasted modern glass walls that looked out on the stunning garden. Happily, the house also featured a chef's kitchen. Doors were open on the detached guesthouse. A discreet sign directed people to use the restroom there.

Gilmer had been thrilled with the idea of entertaining as long as someone else did all of the work. He didn't get much company anymore, which meant he had few opportunities to share his beautiful garden. His Realtor had been delighted by the opportunity to show off the house to the well-heeled locals who would no doubt be in attendance.

It had been a win-win situation. I had arranged for a backup location in case the house sold before the day of the dinner, but luck had been with us. My involvement had been limited to finding the site. For once I was a guest, just like the rest of my friends.

A pretty waitress in her twenties presented a tray of olives to Francie and me. A tiny bit of orange on one end of each black olive had been carefully crafted to look like a flower. Francie and I each eagerly plucked one off the tray to sample. Not knowing exactly what it was, I bit into it with the slightest hesitation. The olive had been stuffed with smoked salmon in a tangy cream. The flower peeking out at the end was thinly sliced smoked salmon. It was delicious.

Francie paused to catch up with a friend, and I walked over to Gavin.

"Gavin, you're so grown up that I didn't recognize you."

"Hi, Mrs. Winston. Mom says I'm finally getting a big growth spurt. How's Daisy?"

"She's doing great. She misses seeing you, though."

"I'd like to get a dog, but we're renting a place now and the lease doesn't permit dogs."

"You're welcome to come by and take Daisy for a walk anytime you like."

"Thanks." An odd expression came over his face. "Uh, excuse me. Nice talking to you." He hurried off.

Just then, Hollis ambled up to me and handed me a small white cooler. "It's all in here."

I let out a nervous breath at the sight of him, glad to see him still alive. "Do you feel sick?"

"Naw. I'm relieved I can eat dinner tonight without worrying about it. If I'm right, it's being done very slowly. Death by a thousand little drops."

"Hollis, you need to go to the police. This is nothing to joke about."

"I have my reasons, Sophie." He handed me the cooler. "Now remember, not a word to anyone. You know how quickly it would get around."

I had agreed to do this. Nevertheless, I scowled at him. "If anything turns up and you don't report it, then I'm going to do it myself."

Hollis grinned at me. "Fair enough."

I felt a little bit better about it. In a way, I did understand where he was coming from. Being married to someone twenty years his junior had to be somewhat stressful. I hoped the samples would turn up clean and ease his mind.

Hollis shook his head. "I don't know what's wrong with the women around here."

"What do you mean?"

"Look at Kelsey. Only men will talk to her."

I was slightly amused by his interpretation of Kelsey's admirers.

"She told me she feels like Rudolph."

"The reindeer or Valentino?" I asked.

"The reindeer. You know, he wasn't allowed to play reindeer games. She feels like she's not accepted by the wives of my friends."

"I'm sure they'll grow to like her as they get to know her better."

"If they ever give her a chance. Excuse me, Sophie."

I watched as Hollis headed toward Parker.

Humphrey and I spotted each other at the same time. We walked along the garden path to meet.

"Sophie! Feels like forever since I've seen you."

I leaned forward and kissed his cheek. "Same here." I handed him the cooler. "Thanks for doing this."

"No problem." He squinted at me. "Sophie, please tell me that you're not the one being"—he gazed around and whispered—"poisoned."

"Definitely not."

Humphrey opened the cooler. "Oh good, it's on ice. If you'll excuse me, I'll stash it in my car before we start to eat."

"Of course! Hurry back." I made my way to the bar, where three drink combinations were being served. Francie opted for red wine sangria with peaches and berries. I chose mango iced tea.

Our friend Bernie Frei, manager of the hottest restaurant in town, joined us and selected an Italian spritz. "We've started serving these at The Laughing Hound. Apparently, they're all the rage in cocktails."

Bernie's English accent made him sound like an authority no matter what he said. The best man at my wedding, Bernie had traveled the world and surprised us all when he settled in Old Town. His sandy hair always looked like he'd just rolled out of bed, and his nose had a kink in it from being punched, probably more than once. No one had expected him to turn a restaurant into a gold mine for the absentee owner, but it turned out he had a knack for the business.

As the three of us clinked our glasses in a toast, a door flew open in the back of the house. Someone shouted, "Out! Out, out, out!"

Two men wearing chef's jackets had grasped a woman by her arms and were propelling her out the door. Behind them, a third man in a chef's jacket waved a wicked-looking chef's knife in the air.

Chapter 4

Dear Sophie,
My husband is a self-confessed salt addict. He's al-
ways coming into the kitchen and salting dishes
while they're cooking. I find them inedible then.
He'll listen to you. When does one salt dishes? At
the beginning or at the end of the cooking?
   Hold the Salt, Please in Salt Lake City, Utah

Dear Hold the Salt, Please,
It's generally best to layer salt, but sparingly. Tell
hubby that soups and sauces often reduce to inten-
sify the flavor. It's best to salt them at the end.
   Sophie

The woman who was being unceremoniously removed had perfectly coiffed, shoulder-length hair so dark that it verged on black. Her dress draped on her bony figure as perfectly as it would on a mannequin. The black sheath she wore had a round neckline, but a trapezoid was cut out at the top, revealing a touch of cleavage.

It was actually quite elegant and caused me to feel inadequate in my simple summer dress, which was usually the case with our friend Natasha.

"I should have known," said Francie.

"One of us should help her." I had a bad feeling I knew who that would be.

"Not me." Bernie calmly sipped his spritz. "I refuse to rescue her from the situations she creates."

Bernie and Natasha had never cared for each other. Bernie didn't kiss up to Natasha, and she resented that he didn't jump at her command.

I handed Bernie my drink and joined Madison in trying to make amends.

"Chef Wurst! I am so sorry!" Madison apologized while reaching for the knife he wielded.

"What did *you* do?" I hissed to Natasha.

"He's marvelous," she said. "He cooks just like I do!"

I certainly hoped not. Natasha was well-known for cooking with unlikely ingredients like hot peppers in chocolate chip cookies and squid ink in mashed potatoes.

Natasha whispered, "Did you see Trula's purse? I have to have it. It's the perfect size for events like this with a little gold chain to hang it from your shoulder so you can carry a drink around and still have a hand free."

"Really, Natasha? You upset the chef and all you're concerned about is Trula's purse?"

"It's probably Chanel or Gucci. She must have paid a fortune for it."

Madison beckoned to me and followed the chef inside.

I held my tongue and said simply, "Natasha, go join Bernie and Francie and get a drink, okay?"

I trailed after Madison. In the kitchen, Chef Wurst ranted, "She was salting my dishes! The nerve! They're ruined. *Ruined*, I tell you!"

Madison spoke in a soothing tone. "She's a local celebrity. A domestic diva who is well-known for her TV show and her fabulous dishes."

That was a little bit over the top. Natasha, who didn't use a last name in her quest to be the Martha of the South, grew up with me in a small town in Virginia. I happened to know that her real name was Natasha Smith. Her father had abandoned her and her mother when she was just a child. My mother was certain that was the event that drove Natasha to seek perfection and set lofty goals for herself.

As children, we had competed at everything except the beauty pageants she had loved. Natasha saw our domestic diva advice columns as more competition. I wasn't really the competitive type, so half the time she just annoyed me. For several years she had lived with my ex-husband, Mars, which was even more cause for annoyance. They had separated, much to her chagrin and his delight.

Nevertheless, I had to admit that she had doting fans who loved her show and followed her ideas for the perfect domestic life.

"Everything smells wonderful," I said, hoping to calm the irate chef. His jacket buttons threatened to fly off at any moment, and his tomato-red face worried me.

He eyed me. "She may eat. But she will not enter my kitchen again."

Madison hastily agreed. She grabbed my arm and hurried me into a hallway. "You would think someone like Natasha would know better than to mess with someone else's dishes. Especially a chef's. Do you *know* how hard it was to get Chef Wurst?"

"Natasha thinks she knows best. Always."

"I think the easiest thing is to assign someone to keep her out of the kitchen. Mars, maybe."

I shook my head. "Better pick someone else. Mars would not appreciate being Natasha's babysitter."

Madison gasped. "She said they were getting back to-gether."

It was my turn to be surprised. "Not that I've heard."

Madison's mouth shifted from side to side. "I'll ask Dr. Jay Charles. He's too polite to turn me down."

Voices in an adjoining room rose. There was no way we could avoid overhearing the conversation.

"He's fourteen, for heaven's sake. He doesn't want to be with you *or* with me. Don't you get that? Parents are not cool."

"He wouldn't think that if you didn't put the idea into his head. You've made me out to be an ogre. He's been dodging me all night."

She gasped. "Don't you twist this around and try to place the blame on me. I am not the one who brought an-other woman into our lives."

There was a long moment of silence.

In a tired voice, Hollis said softly, "Cindy, the divorce is final. Surely you don't want to re-litigate and expose the sordid details here, at a public event."

"Maybe we should. You would be too ashamed to admit that you're not paying for Gavin's education. What would your friends think of you then?"

"Do you really want to open *that* can of worms?" he asked calmly. "I think I've been clear about this. I'll pay, but only if you finally tell Gavin the truth."

"In the old days, men had honor, Hollis. It's a pity you're not more like Jay Charles."

"In the old days when wives became cumbersome, kings dispatched them and took new wives. I'm beginning to see the beauty of that."

"Is that a threat? You would rob Gavin of his mother? I've got news for you, Hollis. You may perceive yourself as a king in your own little world, but you cannot shut me in a tower to await my demise. Maybe you're the one who should be watching your step."

A door slammed, and we were caught. Madison gasped at the sight of Cindy rushing toward us, her nose and ears so red that they almost glowed against her pale skin. She had worn her hair pulled back in an effort to tame it, but soft tendrils escaped along the sides of her face, giving her a romantic look.

"Cindy! It's been so long." Madison held out her arms for a hug. When she let go of Cindy, Madison spoke confidentially. "Are you touring the house, too? Parker and Trula are thinking about making an offer." She placed her fingers against her chest. "Seems kind of pricy, even for them, don't you think? Did you know that John Dixon was one of Parker's ancestors? His house was said to be the largest in Old Town at the time. They tell me it passed out of family hands and burned to the ground. Sounds a little fishy to me."

The longer Madison rambled, the more Cindy seemed at ease. Apparently Madison's effort to explain our presence had its desired effect.

"It's a very special house," said Cindy. "Anyone would be lucky to live here. Are those dragonfly earrings?"

Madison reached up to her right ear and touched her earring, a dragonfly with a gold body and iridescent purple, blue, and green enameled wings.

"They were a gift from Gage about a month before he died. I wore them tonight so I would feel like he was here with me, giving me the strength to pull off this dinner."

Cindy reached out and touched Madison's arm as if she meant to prevent her from babbling again. "I miss Gage, too. If you'll excuse me, I need to find Gavin to check on him." Cindy hurried outside.

Madison turned toward me, her eyes huge. "I had no idea they were still squabbling. It breaks my heart. We were good friends once. I always thought they were such a happy couple. Of course, I never see them anymore now." She sucked in a deep breath. "Divorce and death—the two instant killers of a social life."

Madison's husband, Gage, had died less than a year before. I sought something reassuring to say, but she continued speaking, almost like she had to get it out of her system.

"In the beginning, everyone is so thoughtful and kind. There were days when I was surrounded by so many people that I couldn't hear myself think. They just buzz all around you, asking what you need, asking questions about caskets and hymns, and pushing casseroles in your face. And then one day they're gone. And all you can do is cry. As the months go on you realize that you're not being invited to the things you did as a couple. And then your married women friends begin to forget about you when they plan parties and luncheons and bridge. And one day, you realize that the phone hasn't rung in a week, that no one is texting you except your kids who need money, and that you haven't showered or left the house in three days." Madison gazed at me with sad brown eyes. "It's almost like I died when Gage did."

I wrapped my arm around her. "Is that why you planned this dinner?"

"I nearly quit! I was in the beginning stages of planning the underground dinner when Gage died. For a while my life was pure craziness, trying to take care of the kids and figuring out the finances. On the rare occasions when people talked to me, they asked me about the dinner. Maybe it was just to talk about something other than Gage's death, but I decided it would give me a goal and something to focus on while I got used to my new normal. I hate that phrase, *new normal*. When your husband passes away, nothing will ever be normal again."

"How are your kids holding up?"

"It was devastating for them. And embarrassing. I over-heard one of them telling friends that Gage had been racing a speedboat that overturned."

I winced. The truth was that Gage had far too much to drink at a local bar. He tried to walk home in his inebriated state, fell into the Potomac River, and drowned. "I'm so sorry."

"You know, Sophie, in a way, I envy my children. They have college to keep them busy. Between classes and Greek life and football games, they don't have time to dwell on it. I'm the one who goes home to an empty house, where Gage's absence smacks me in the face around every corner. I've thought about putting the house on the market. The kids don't want me to because we have so many memories there, which is the exact reason I want to sell."

"I have always heard it's best to wait a year after losing a spouse before making big changes," I said.

"Poor Cindy didn't have that luxury." Madison paused and gasped.

"What's wrong?"

"Here I am moaning about my troubles when she's been going through the same thing. Hollis didn't die, but once Kelsey was on the scene, Cindy was excluded from all of the law firm socializing. I hated seeing Kelsey at those events. I have to apologize to Cindy. Excuse me, Sophie."

Madison raised her chin defiantly, shook her hair and fluffed it, and marched out into the crowd.

I hadn't realized how lucky I was to keep my group of friends after my divorce from Mars. I wasn't as involved with Mars's political socializing anymore, but I hadn't missed that. Besides, he had asked me to arrange a few events for him, so I hadn't been totally out of the loop.

I had turned to leave when a door banged open. Kelsey was looking back over her shoulder. In her rush, she plowed into me sideways.

It happened in a split second.

"Oh no! I didn't see you there." Kelsey reached a hand down to me. I suspected she couldn't bend over. Her skintight dress barely contained her generous cleavage. One wrong move and her assets would be exposed.

I scrambled to my feet, taking in the scent of an abundance of Chanel No 5. Her blond hair tumbled over her shoulders. Her dress was way too daring for me, and positively gutsy for most women.

"I hope you're not hurt." She waved her hands near her face. "I just . . . just *had* to get away for a breath of air. It's so crowded out there."

I was a little confused by her explanation, but I assured her, "I'm fine, thanks."

She went on her way, walking hesitantly, as though she wasn't sure where she wanted to be.

I returned to the lawn and spied Nina, Francie, and Bernie waving me over to a table. But before I could get there, a gaunt woman in her seventies nabbed me and hissed, "Leave my son alone."

Chapter 5

Dear Sophie,
I confess that I am a picky eater. There are lots of things I just don't like. How do I politely say no at a dinner party when offered something revolting?
    Cheese Lover in Cheddar, South Carolina

Dear Cheddar Lover,
Unless you have an allergy or a religious or other dietary conviction (like a non-gluten or vegetarian diet, not one made up on the spot), it has long been the polite thing to try a little bit of every dish served. If you loathe it, scoot it around on your plate a bit so it looks like you ate it.
    Sophie

She looked vaguely familiar with high cheekbones and a long, thin nose. Her white hair was teased and swept back into an elegant chignon. She couldn't be the mother of my current boyfriend, Alex, could she? She must have mistaken me for someone else. "I beg your pardon?"

Steely blue eyes regarded me with contempt. "You *are* Sophie Bauer?"

No one had called me by my maiden name in a long time. After my marriage, I used the surname Winston. I stared at her, trying to smile in spite of her apparent disdain. The outer lids on her eyes had fallen, making her eyes almost triangular in shape. Her lips pulled tight. She was attractive, but cold in a slightly creepy way, like an old woman who resented the hired help.

But as I gazed at this stranger, her pasty complexion clued me in. My mother had always said Mrs. Brown had flawless, unwrinkled skin because she stayed out of the sun. She was Humphrey's mother! "Mrs. Brown? Forgive me for not recognizing you. It's been what? Twenty years or more?"

Despite my friendliness, she maintained her chilliness. "I understand you're a *divorcée* now."

She said it as though it were a mark of shame. Probably half the people present had been divorced. I bit my tongue. Whatever I said would be broadcast to everyone back in my hometown of Berryville, Virginia, not to mention that my parents would hear about it. Desperate for a lifeline, my gaze fell on Natasha. "Mrs. Brown, there's someone here you'll be thrilled to see."

I coaxed her to follow me. "Natasha! Guess who's here! You remember Mrs. Brown, Humphrey's mom."

Mrs. Brown's expression changed to one of curiosity. Who knew she liked Natasha? And why wouldn't she like me?

"I hear you're some kind of television star now," she murmured.

Natasha beamed. "Who'd have thought a little girl from Berryville would grow up to be a celebrity?"

While Natasha blathered, I realized that Mrs. Brown was looking past Natasha. She wasn't paying attention to

Natasha at all. I stepped aside to see what she was looking at. Apparently, Dr. Jay Charles had caught her eye.

I interrupted Natasha. "Mrs. Brown, it was lovely seeing you," I lied. "I need to get to my seat, but maybe Natasha can introduce you to Dr. Charles."

It was as though one word clicked through and caught her attention. "Doctor?" she asked, arching one eyebrow.

Dr. Charles went by the name "Jay," though I had heard that his real name might be John. Unfailingly polite, Jay Charles was the epitome of a Southern gentleman. In spite of the heat, he wore a bright red bow tie with a navy blue suit. Medium height, he was slender, possibly a runner. He smiled graciously and spoke softly with a distinct Southern accent.

Jay's wife had passed away five years ago, making him a popular target of single women in Old Town. He tolerated and might have even enjoyed the attention, but hadn't dated as far as anyone knew. A professor of pathology at a local medical school, Jay led a quiet life in the massive house next door to Hollis Haberman.

I tried not to appear to be running away from them, but I hurried to my seat at a table with Nina, Francie, and Bernie.

My ex-husband, Mars, had shown up and joined them at the table. A political consultant, Mars was as attractive as most of his clients. He'd been blessed with boyish looks and laughing eyes that made people immediately comfortable with him. In spite of our divorce, we remained good friends.

The first time I had dinner with my beau, Alex, and my ex-husband, Mars, I admit I was a bit uncomfortable. But we had shared meals often enough that it was no longer an issue.

Hollis and Kelsey sat at the table to our right, while Cindy and Gavin were at the table to our left. Somehow we had become the bumper between the warring Habermans.

A delicate white cloth with a green and pink leaf and flower motif covered the table on an angle. A bottle of wine rested in a champagne bucket, and red hurricane glasses held flowers from the garden. Blue plates matched the seat cushions on the chairs, and the wineglasses were a sky-blue hue. They looked to be sturdy blown glass with some bubbles in them, probably handblown in Mexico.

"Where have you been?" asked Nina. "We saved you a seat."

I scooted into my chair just in time.

Madison clinked a fork against her glass to get everyone's attention. "Welcome to Old Town's first fabulous underground dinner. One of the nice things about these dinners is seeing old friends unexpectedly and making new friends as well. We all share a love of food, and there's nothing more wonderful in life than great food in the company of friends. I know you're anxious to eat, so I'll let Chef Wurst tell you about your dinner."

The portly chef stepped up beside her. "I was most pleased to be chosen for this occasion. Chefs are often restricted by restaurant menus. It's a delight for us to be asked to create a special dinner for discerning diners like yourselves who are willing to try a surprise menu. For your dining pleasure this evening, I have drawn from the local markets and cooked with the freshest ingredients available. We will begin with red beet and goat cheese tartlets, followed by oxtail soup with chicken liver dumplings and green onions. Our fish course tonight will be pinecone smoked trout with a peach gastrique, which is so representative of the flavors of Virginia. Tonight's entrée will be roast rack of lamb with French lentil salad, roasted asparagus, and puréed eggplant. I'm told the dessert should remain a surprise. Enjoy your dinner."

He nodded his head and was off to the kitchen.

Nina stuck out her tongue. "Who wants my soup? I'm never going to eat liver dumplings. I can't think of anything more disgusting."

"My grandmother used to make them and add them to a chicken broth," I said. "They're not bad at all."

"Bleah." Nina turned the corners of her mouth down. "The lamb sounds good, though."

Francie elbowed me and nodded toward Gavin.

I turned to look at him. Seated next to his mother, Cindy, he held a book and read instead of joining the conversation at their table. But he raised his eyes every few seconds to gaze past us, probably watching his father and Kelsey. The fact that he wasn't engaged with the other diners didn't surprise me one bit. What I found interesting was that he tried to concentrate on a book instead of a phone or tablet.

The appetizer arrived quickly. I couldn't recall having eaten beets and cheese together, but they were an interesting combination of sweet and salty. At our table we ate every last morsel.

The mood was light and cheery as a gentle breeze kicked up and the air finally began to cool. Bernie remarked on the number of empty dishes the waiters returned to the kitchen. The food was a success, even the liver dumplings, which we had fought over.

Before dessert, I excused myself and headed for the ladies' room in the guesthouse, where I met Kelsey Haberman a second time.

She stood alone in the kitchen with her back to me.

The voices of two women drifted to us from the next room. "I can't imagine what she's thinking. Can you say tacky?" I knew the woman who was speaking. She wasn't exactly a fashionista herself.

"I know what every *man* in the room is thinking," the

other woman prattled. As she spoke, I recognized the voice as belonging to Trula. "Why would she wear a dress that practically dips down to her navel? And that big hair! Hellooo? The eighties are calling."

Kelsey and I both knew whom they were talking about. I was willing to bet it wasn't the first time she had heard that sort of thing. It was the grown-up equivalent of mean girls in high school.

Kelsey swallowed hard. She turned and saw me in the doorway, where I had stopped. The only way to the bathroom was through the room where Trula and the other woman were talking.

With her back to me again, Kelsey sucked in a deep breath and positioned her head high, as though bracing herself for hostility. She had to walk by them.

She flashed a desperate glance my way and my heart went out to her. It was like fourth grade all over again. I winked at her and said in a loud voice, "Oh my gosh! Is that a rat?"

The place cleared out immediately. Kelsey bestowed a smile on me. Her eyes glistened, though I wasn't sure if they were tears of sadness or joy.

For the second time, she held out her hand. "Kelsey Haberman."

I shook her extended hand. "Sophie Winston."

"I owe you one, Sophie. That was really nice of you."

"They deserved it."

Worry lines in her forehead, she asked, "Do you think this dress is too risky?"

Oh no! I searched for something to say that wouldn't offend her. "It's a nice dress."

"Then what's their problem?"

Oh great. I pondered for a moment and decided I could save her a lot trouble if I told her the truth. "Old Town has always been somewhat conservative."

"You mean politically?"

"No, I mean in the way people dress."

She examined my dress. "Like what you're wearing. A flower print." Kelsey said it dully. As though she was disappointed.

"It doesn't have to be floral."

She nodded. "I'm not sophisticated like the women around here. I'm just a country girl, and they treat me like roadkill. I wish I could be more like Natasha. I watch her show every day."

I laughed aloud. "Most of them weren't born here. Natasha and I are from a little town in Virginia. And I happen to know that one of the women who was being catty grew up on a farm in a forgotten corner of Alabama. Just cover up a little more."

She blinked hard like she was having trouble comprehending what I meant. "Thanks for rescuing me."

"Who were you running from earlier?"

"Just a guy I wanted to avoid. Thanks for the advice, Sophie."

When I left the guesthouse, Jay Charles approached me. "Are you enjoying the dinner?"

"I am. Wasn't the lamb fabulous?"

"Perfectly cooked. So juicy and tender." Jay gazed down at the ground for a second as though he was uncomfortable. "Mars tells me you have a ghost in your house?"

"Mars's mother thinks so."

"You don't believe in ghosts?"

Memories of a Halloween that challenged my beliefs raced through my head. I chose my words carefully. "Unlike Mars's mother, I have never spoken to a ghost. But I have experienced some unusual things."

He perked up. "Do you hear whispering?"

"No, I can't say that I do. But the portrait of Mars's

aunt Faye tilts a little bit almost every time Natasha enters my kitchen and criticizes it. I have always tried to attribute that to a draft from the ancient fireplace. And frankly, I think most of the things that move are helped by my cat Mochie. But there are a lot of ghost stories in Old Town."

Jay motioned for me to follow him to a distant spot in the garden. He leaned toward me and spoke in a low voice. "I am a man of science. I do not fall for every new trend or half-baked theory. The trouble is that I hear voices. They're not in my head. When I cover my ears I can't hear them. But I can't account for them, either. I don't recall hearing them before. Now I fear I'm losing my grasp on reality."

"I don't think you're alone. A lot of Old Town residences have a ghost."

"But you have never *heard* your ghost?" he asked.

"No, but I don't think you need to worry about your sanity. Inexplicable things do happen. There was a house in Old Town with a corpse hidden in the cellar. The house shared a wall with the next house, and those residents had long complained about an eerily cold area in their house. Once the corpse was removed and buried, it went away. That makes no logical sense, but that's what they experienced."

He lifted his forefinger. "That's exactly the problem. There is no scientific basis for this. That's why I am troubled. I've been researching my house to learn more about the previous inhabitants, but I haven't turned up anything unusual so far." He grasped my hand between his two hands. "Thank you for listening to my silly problem. I'm quite embarrassed by it."

"Nonsense. You're certainly not the first person to have this problem. Looks like dessert is being served. Do you have a sweet tooth?"

"You bet!"

We walked back together on the pavers, and I couldn't help noticing how many women seemed intrigued by our little meeting. Poor Jay.

As I slid into my seat Alex asked, "What was that about?"

Everyone at my table looked at me expectantly except for Mars, who made a production of examining his Chocolate Mousse.

I sidestepped the truth a little to save Jay from embarrassment since he had clearly drawn me aside to discuss ghosts in Old Town privately. "He's doing some research on his house."

"It's gorgeous," gushed Francie. "His wife understood how to retain the beauty of a historic house while making it comfortable for the current residents." She glanced over at Natasha. "Too many people are eager to throw out the amazing handwork of the ages, losing it forever."

We savored the rich chocolate mousse with coffee and after-dinner cordials of Grand Marnier. During the dessert, the crowd broke into applause for the chef and Madison.

I excused myself, intending to thank Madison. But when I walked into the house, I inadvertently barged in on the pretty waitress speaking with Parker.

"Is that your wife?" she asked him.

"Leave Trula out of this."

"In that case, *sir*, I believe we can call it even."

She smiled as she walked by me on her way out.

"I'm sorry, Parker. I was looking for Madison to thank her."

"Indeed. It was a most enjoyable meal. I'll come along with you."

We located Madison in the kitchen, where Hollis sat on the hardwood floor wheezing.

My first thought was that his food had been poisoned. "Hollis!" I fell to my knees and looked into his face.

"I want to call 911, but Hollis won't let me," said Madison.

Parker bent to his law partner. "Holl? Did you ever go to the doctor about this?"

"It's happened before?" I asked.

Hollis held up his palms as though he wanted us all to go away. "I'm fine," he wheezed. "Just a little short of breath. Don't go making a fuss."

Parker stood up straight. "Stubborn mule. Hollis, you can't keep ignoring this. It'll be the death of you."

"Asthma," Madison opined.

Hollis struggled to suck in air. "There's nothing wrong with me."

A line of people was forming, all eager to thank Madison.

"Get me out of here, Parker," Hollis growled.

Parker leaned over and helped Hollis to his feet.

Despite his condition, Hollis paused. "It was a splendid evening, Madison. Well done! I hope you'll arrange more of these dinners."

"I hope you'll do this again too, Madison," I said.

Parker bestowed a kiss on her cheek. "It was wonderful to see you. You must have dinner with Trula and me sometime soon."

Parker steered Hollis toward the door, and I followed.

As I was leaving the house, Natasha pulled me aside. "Sophie, you're my very dearest friend in the world. I hope you won't mind if I ask you a question that's quite personal."

I braced myself.

She waved at Jay as he walked out. "First, what do you know about Dr. Charles?"

"Jay? Not much. He seems to be a very nice man. He lives on our street, you know, just one block down."

"No! I had no idea. Which house is his?"

"It's next door to the Habermans. The one with the gray door."

"Oh, that one." Her tone conveyed her disappointment. "Pity. It's so old. Please tell me he's not married."

"He's widowed. He lost his wife a few years ago."

"Reaaally? Hmm. He's so delightfully perfect. I've never met a man with better manners. He was even lovely to Humphrey's mother, whom I now recall very well as a snobby witch."

"That's a shame. Humphrey is so sweet."

"She's a dreadful woman. Wicked to the core."

I would have to ask my mother about that. I didn't remember anyone saying things like that about Mrs. Brown.

"So here's the other thing," said Natasha. "Mars tells me that when you separated, you paid him for his share of your house. I can't imagine you were *that* stupid."

"I have never thought of it as stupidity. Yes, I paid him for his share." Thankfully, the question wasn't quite as personal as it could have been.

"You didn't!"

"The house belonged to his aunt until she died and left it to us. I would have understood completely if he had wanted to keep it in his family. It was only fair to buy him out. Why these questions?"

"Mars says since we're separated—"

I interrupted her. "You were never married."

"Really, Sophie. Must you rub that in? You know my dearest dream has been to marry. In any event, Mars thinks we should sell the house or I should buy him out. I think he should give it to me."

I laughed so hard I could barely breathe.

"I don't see what's so funny."

"In that case, why don't you give Mars your half of the house?"

"Do you know what it's worth and how much money I've put into that place?"

She didn't make the connection via my sarcasm. "Well, good luck with that."

She glared at me. "So what did you do? Make monthly payments to him?"

"I took a mortgage so I could pay Mars, and now I send a check to the mortgage company every month."

"So that's why you work at that sad little job you have."

I ran my own event planning business. There was nothing sad about my job! In fact, I thoroughly enjoyed it. But it wasn't worth snapping back at her. Besides, Francie, Nina, Mars, and Alex were waiting to walk home. "Sorry I can't be of more help, Natasha. Excuse me, Alex is waiting."

I walked away and joined my friends, glad that I didn't have to negotiate with Natasha. Mars was reasonable, but no fool. He would hold firm.

While we strolled the beautiful streets of Old Town, admiring houses, Alex took my hand and whispered, "Jay thought you might know something about his house?"

"Why Alex!" I took on a Scarlett O'Hara accent. "Are you suggesting it was somethin' else? I do believe you're jealous!"

"You're lucky you're cute. You make a terrible Southern belle. Still leaving tomorrow?"

"That's the plan." I looked up at the night sky.

The walk home from the underground dinner was delightful. The air had finally cooled and the humidity had abated. It seemed like all of Old Town felt the same way. People walked along King Street licking ice-cream cones. Everyone smiled, no doubt happy to have a few hours of relief from the heat.

We stopped in front of my house and shared a kiss.

"I'll miss you, Sophie."

"Hah! I'll be back before you realize that I'm gone."

Mochie, my Ocicat whose fur had swirls instead of dots, met me at the front door with Daisy, who whined greetings to me. Mochie wound around my ankles, and Daisy's tail wagged nonstop.

"Ready for a walk, Daisy?" I asked.

Her front paws bounced in little jumps and she twirled with joy.

Daisy stayed by my side while I fed Mochie. But as soon as he started to eat, she ran to the drawer where I kept her halter and leash.

I fastened them on her and we stepped out into the night. I took care to lock the front door behind us. It was closing on midnight as we strolled down to the Potomac River.

Bar hoppers and couples on dates kept that end of town lively. We walked along the waterfront, admiring lights on boats. In spite of the late hour, a few families strolled much as we did.

The next morning, my alarm clock went off at four o'clock. From the annoyed looks on their faces, I was pretty sure Mochie and Daisy thought it was a mistake. I wished it was. Every bone in my body wanted to roll over and go back to sleep. But I dragged myself out of bed to walk Daisy before leaving her and Mochie in Mars's care.

Mars would be staying at my house with them. I didn't know his schedule, though, and after ten in the morning it was too hot to walk for long, so I thought I'd better get in a walk for Daisy before Nina and I hit the road.

I pulled on a skort and a sleeveless cotton top. Daisy got the idea and raced downstairs ahead of me. She waited by the front door. I slid her harness over her head, slipped my cell phone into my pocket, and stepped into the blissfully cool morning. The sun hadn't risen yet. A few cars drove through Old Town, and a jogger darted across the street, but for the most part, the town still slept.

We strolled over to King Street and down to the river. I couldn't help thinking of Madison's husband, Gage. I didn't know where he had fallen into the river, but it would have been easy enough for someone who was stumbling or not thinking straight. What a shame that a night of drinking ended tragically when he had so much to live for.

Daisy and I turned back and headed home. As we neared Jay Charles's house, I made out someone staggering toward the sidewalk.

Daisy growled and backed up cautiously. To be on the safe side, Daisy and I crossed the empty street and walked on the other sidewalk.

When we drew closer, it appeared the person had come from Hollis's house. Not someone else stung by bees!

Arms outstretched, Hollis lurched into the street and collapsed.

Chapter 6

Dear Natasha,
Is it true that nighttime is the best time to knock
down a wasp nest?
*   Allergic in Bee, Nebraska*

Dear Allergic,
Bees and wasps are less likely to sting at night be-
cause they are less active. However, some bees are
always guarding the nest and will sting if they feel
threatened. Even worse, they release a pheromone
that summons other bees to come and help!
*   Natasha*

Daisy and I ran toward Hollis. He was a visible lump under the streetlights, but I was afraid a car might come along and hit him.

He lay faceup on the pavement, taking rasping breaths as though he couldn't breathe.

No cars were coming. I bent over. "Can I help you stand up?" I asked.

Hollis gazed up at me, beads of sweat on his forehead.

He grabbed my hand, coughed, and seemed to have some kind of spasm.

Oh no! I hoped he hadn't been poisoned. With the handle of Daisy's leash looped over my other hand, I reached into my pocket and called 911.

I told them where we were. "It's Hollis Haberman. Please hurry. He's in the middle of the street."

They told me to stay on the line, but I hung up and called Mars. He was renting a room from Bernie, just a few houses away. Maybe they could move Hollis, or at least bring out flashlights so we could be seen in the road.

Mars was groggy when he answered the phone. He listened to me, then murmured, "What do you mean you're in the street?"

"Get Bernie and some flashlights. Hurry! We're just outside of the Haberman house."

I hung up and dropped the phone into my pocket. "Hollis? Hollis? Can you hear me?"

The lights of an approaching car grew brighter as it neared. I stood up straight and waved my hands, directing it around Hollis.

"Sophie? Where are you?" Mars yelled.

I hated to wake everyone on the block, but I shouted back, "Over here!"

Actually, I hoped I might wake Jay. We could use a doctor right now. I glanced at his house. His front drapes were closed. As close as our houses were to the sidewalk and the street, that wasn't terribly surprising.

Mars and Bernie sprinted toward Hollis and me.

"What happened?" asked Mars.

"I have no idea. He staggered out here and collapsed."

Bernie was on his knees. "Hollis! Hollis? We're going to try to move you. Can you hold on to us?"

"Let's see if he can sit up first," Mars suggested.

Mars knelt on Hollis's other side. Each of them took an

arm and tried to hoist him. It seemed to me that Hollis didn't have the strength to sit.

His head lolled back, which made breathing even more difficult for him.

"Guys, I think we'd better leave him on the road," I said. "The ambulance should be here soon."

They lowered him to the asphalt. "Hollis!" shouted Mars. "Can you speak? What happened?"

"Are you asthmatic?" asked Bernie. "Do you need an inhaler?"

"He had an attack like this last night," I said.

Mars shone a flashlight near Hollis's face so we could get a better look at him. None of us said a word. He was deathly pale with beads of perspiration clinging to his face. He hadn't looked that bad the evening before.

He blinked at us. "I feel nauseous," he wheezed.

My stomach lurched. Poison!

A police car slowed and stopped just short of us. Officer Wong stepped out and walked over. She shone her flashlight at us. "What's going on here?"

African-American, Wong credited her last name to having married the wrong-by-a-long-shot man, but she liked surprising those who expected her to be Asian. She wore her hair short, with a sassy curl falling onto her forehead. Her uniform was always a little too tight on her curves thanks to her fondness for cupcakes and other sweets.

I told her what had happened and in case it was somehow related, I told her about Angus and the beestings.

Her forehead wrinkled. "Was Angus sweating like this?"

"No, and it was already hot outside." I frowned. "Do bees fly around at night? Seems to me my dad always knocked down wasp nests early in the morning while they were sleeping."

Wong bent over. "Hollis, can you tell me what happened?"

His voice was weak. "Don't know. Went to bed and woke up feeling dizzy and sick."

"Dizzy!" I said. "Angus was dizzy."

"And you ran out in the street?" Wong asked.

Hollis wheezed, seemingly unable to breathe. "Needed . . . air."

Fortunately, the ambulance arrived and the professionals took over. Wong and I told them what little we knew.

And then I broke my promise to Hollis. Under the circumstances, I had no choice. "He was afraid someone might be poisoning his food."

All of the emergency medical technicians stared at me.

"He's having some food tested. I don't know anything more than that."

It wasn't until one of them asked if Hollis lived alone that I remembered Kelsey. "He's married, but I haven't seen his wife."

I started for the house, but an EMT stopped me. "Ma'am, wait out here, please. We'll check on his wife."

I stopped short. But I was worried about Kelsey. Why hadn't she appeared yet? I hoped she was okay.

The EMT had just reached the front door when it opened.

Kelsey stepped out in a flowing silk bathrobe and coughed. "What's going on out here? Did a car hit someone?"

"Are you Mrs. Haberman?" he asked.

I walked closer. "Kelsey, Hollis is ill."

She turned to gaze at me for a second, surprise and confusion mingling on her face as she took in the situation. She darted toward the street, crying, "Hollis! Hollis!"

Wong intercepted her. I couldn't hear what she was saying, but Kelsey tore away from her, covering her mouth with a fist as she coughed.

The EMTs were loading Hollis on a gurney. He had a

clear mask over his nose and mouth, no doubt to help him breathe.

Kelsey picked up Hollis's hand. "What's wrong with him? Is it a heart attack?"

"Doesn't look that way," said an EMT. "Ma'am, how do you feel? You seem to be coughing a lot."

"I'm fine. I don't know why I'm coughing."

"Maybe you should come along with us."

Terrified, Kelsey took a step back. "You mean I could have the same thing?"

Chapter 7

Dear Sophie,
I love fried eggs with soft yolks, but when I try to
make them, crunchy edges form on the whites. Is
there a secret I don't know?
    Softie in Two Egg, Florida

Dear Softie,
There is a little trick! Put a lid on the eggs and turn
the heat to medium low. When the whites have
cooked, remove the pan from the stove, but leave
the lid on for about one more minute. Don't forget
that you run the risk of salmonella poisoning from
eating soft yolks!
    Sophie

"We don't know what he has yet," said the EMT. "But if you were with him, that's certainly possible."

"I don't have my phone or my makeup. I'm not dressed."

The EMT must have heard that kind of argument often.

"Ma'am, your husband needs to go to the emergency room right away. You don't want him to get worse."

Just then Kelsey had a little coughing fit. "Okay," she choked out.

My phone buzzed as I watched them close the ambulance doors. It was Nina.

"Good morning," I said. "Ready to roll?"

"Obviously you haven't seen the news. You won't believe this. The hurricane swung out into the Atlantic and isn't a threat, but something knocked out power in the Outer Banks, and they're evacuating! They're showing pictures of the highway. They've closed all beach-bound lanes. And now they're saying a line of storms is approaching Old Town. It's like we're cursed."

I looked up at the predawn sky. No sign of inclement weather in Old Town—yet. I heaved a great sigh. Girls' week at the beach was biting the dust. I tried to be positive. "Maybe it will pass quickly and we can go in a couple of days."

"I'm so disappointed! I was looking forward to hush puppies, shrimp boils, and giant daiquiris."

"Me too. Well, since we're all up, why don't you come over for breakfast?"

"Who is we?"

"We'll tell you all about it over breakfast."

"Fried eggs with soft yolks?"

I couldn't help laughing. "If that's what you crave, sure. See you there." I hung up.

The ambulance had rolled away. The first strains of light showed in the sky, and morning traffic had already begun.

"Breakfast, Wong?" I asked.

"Thanks, but I'd better take a rain check. I need to secure the house and write up my report."

Bernie, Mars, Daisy, and I strolled back to my house.

"Is your trip off?" asked Bernie.

"Looks like it."

Mars reached for Daisy's leash. "That was one of the weirdest things I've seen. I hope it wasn't something Hollis ate last night at the underground dinner. Do either of you feel sick?"

Bernie and I glanced at each other and shook our heads.

"Me either," said Mars.

"Parker said this had happened to Hollis before," I said.

Bernie's eyebrows lifted. "Odd that Kelsey appears to have it, too."

I unlocked the door, and we piled into the foyer. Mochie mewed a welcome and greeted us by winding around our legs.

In the kitchen, I ground Jamaican Blue Mountain coffee beans and spooned them into my French press. After preheating the oven, I pulled out two large frying pans for the eggs.

Mars went straight for his old favorite, the oversized Fiestaware coffee cups. I was amused when he selected four different colors. The jumbo cups in tangerine, turquoise, poppy red, and bright sunflower yellow would make for a happy breakfast table.

In preparation for his stay at my house, I had thrown a French print tablecloth of blues and yellows on the kitchen table the night before.

Mars opened a can of kitty tuna for Mochie and fed Daisy one of her favorite dog cookies.

Bernie opened the kitchen door for Nina, who carried a box from Big Daddy's Bakery. "I thought we'd munch on these during the drive. They'll be stale tomorrow, so we might as well enjoy them now."

She opened the box and arranged the contents on a

poppy-colored platter. Chocolate croissants, ham croissants, cherry Danish, cinnamon rolls with vanilla icing, and bear claws threatened to tumble off the platter.

"I thought it was just the two of you going to the beach," said Mars, biting into a ham croissant.

"It was." Nina selected a bear claw.

I sprinkled medium grind pepper over bacon and slid it into a hot oven.

"Are you kidding? You thought the two of you would eat all of these?" teased Bernie.

"It's a long drive. There are a lot of Kristy Kremes in North Carolina, but when you whip by one on the highway it can be hard to turn around and find the side road that leads to it."

"You don't really care about the beach, do you?" Mars bantered. "It was a foodie road trip in disguise."

Nina, who lived catty-corner across the street from me, loved to eat but never cooked. Her idea of the perfect kitchen utensil was the telephone for takeout. One memorable holiday she had food delivered to my house, where she transferred it to pots and pans so her mother-in-law wouldn't know she hadn't cooked it. She even lit candles scented like turkey and stuffing, pumpkin pie, and roasted sweet potatoes to complete her little cover-up. Nina insisted no one was the wiser, though I found that hard to believe.

I took the bacon out of the oven and placed it on a platter covered with paper towels. Mars whisked it to the table, where the three of them chowed down like they were famished.

I cracked the eggs into the frying pans, then salted and peppered them. With the lids on the pans, I lowered the heat.

Over coffee and bacon, Mars and Bernie told Nina about Hollis and Kelsey.

I kept an eye on the eggs, waiting for the whites to cook. If my attention drifted for even a minute, the yolks would be cooked through.

Nina was horrified. "What's going on at that house? First the attack of the killer bees, and now some mysterious illness?"

I pulled the eggs off the stove but left the covers on for them to finish cooking. "I wondered about that, too. But Hollis's symptoms seemed different from Angus's."

I slid the eggs onto plates and handed them to Bernie, who set them on the table. "Mmm. I love a good runny yolk."

When I joined them, Nina said, "Now that we're not beach bound, maybe we should visit Hollis in the hospital to get a handle on what he has. It's a little unsettling that their house is so close to ours."

Mars sipped his coffee. "What with Hollis taken ill, maybe we should check on those bees. I'd feel better if we knew they had been relocated. We wouldn't want some kid stumbling into them."

Bernie turned to me. "And I thought you were the snoopy one."

"I am not!" I raised my hands, palms out, like he was holding a gun at me. "I haven't been involved in any murder investigations in over a year."

"Shh. Don't say that out loud. It's like you're inviting the fates," Mars joked.

"Count me out." Nina reached for a chocolate croissant. "The closest I'm going to any bees is their honey in the grocery store. There's no way I'm spending my vacation in the emergency room. Not taking any chances that one of them will sting me. For all you know they're killer bees."

"Killer bees don't come this far north," said Mars.

Bernie's expression told me he disagreed. He probably felt like I did—there was no point in scaring Nina.

"You don't know that," protested Nina. "What if they stowed away in some shipment? I'm always reading about tropical snakes that hid in a shipment to a big box store."

"Unlikely," said Mars.

"There's always a first time." Nina licked her fingers. "You couldn't pay me to go over there." She pulled out her iPhone, looked at it, and moaned.

Bernie gazed at it over her shoulder. He spoke calmly. "We'd better batten down the hatches. A line of severe storms is on the way."

Mars switched on the TV, where a local station was issuing warnings to stock up on batteries and water in case of power outages. Our peaceful breakfast ended rather hastily after that. I thought we had plenty of time to prepare, but it wasn't the way I had hoped to spend my vacation.

Mars took Daisy with him, which always left the house feeling empty. After cleaning up the kitchen, I found Mochie in the sunroom washing his fur.

Promising to be back soon, I walked to King Street and hit the stores for supplies.

I stocked up on water and wine, uncertain which would be in more demand, then perused the offerings of my favorite butcher. Inspired by the dinner the previous night, I was eager to try a few different flavor combinations. But I thought I'd better keep some things simple in case we lost power.

Bread, tuna, and peanut butter had already disappeared, leaving those shelves bare.

I had plenty of veggies growing in my backyard garden, but I bought chicken, red and green cabbage, a couple of crisp apples, farm-fresh eggs, strawberries, blackberries, and blueberries.

The store was offering a new delivery service, which delighted me. No lugging heavy water and wine bottles anymore. I stopped by the hardware store to stock up on batteries, certain that the mere act of buying them would mean I wouldn't need them.

On the walk home, I passed the Habermans' house. It was quiet and peaceful. No one would ever suspect that something terrible had happened there only hours ago.

The groceries were delivered after lunch. I had just finished putting them away when someone banged the door knocker on my front door.

It took my breath away a little bit to see Wolf Fleischman, a criminal investigator in the Alexandria police department, on my doorstep. I hadn't seen him in ages. My first instinct was to hug him, but I knew I shouldn't and resisted the impulse.

Wolf and I had dated for a few years. A strange twist of life had interfered and our relationship had ended somewhat abruptly. Nevertheless, I still considered him a dear friend. He carried a sport coat hitched on his thumb over his shoulder, and I could tell he had lost a little weight. Wolf liked to eat, and like me, he often fought creeping pounds. The silver hair at his temples gleamed in the sun, and I thought there might a little more silver than the last time I saw him.

"Hi, Sophie." Wolf bent immediately to pick up Mochie, who didn't feel any awkwardness about seeing him and was simply joyful about his presence. I had met Wolf on the same day that I rescued Mochie, and Wolf had even been present when Mochie was named.

"I didn't expect to see *you*. Could I offer you a cold drink?"

"That would be great." He followed me into the kitchen, still carrying Mochie, whose purrs were loud enough for me to hear.

I poured both of us iced tea. "It's been a while," I said.

Wolf tossed his jacket over a chair and studied me. "Feels like it was just yesterday that I was here in your kitchen." He gulped the iced tea like he was parched. "You can imagine my surprise when they told me that one Sophie Winston reported that Hollis Haberman thought he was being poisoned."

We migrated to the kitchen table and sat down. My smile faded as I realized what Wolf's presence meant. He wouldn't have come around if he wasn't investigating. And he wouldn't be investigating unless they had called him in on a case. My spirits plummeted. "Hollis didn't make it?"

"I'm sorry, Sophie. Was he a friend of yours?"

The news knocked the stuffing out of me. I hadn't thought Hollis would die. A long stay in the hospital maybe, but not this. "Not really. He was a neighbor, but we weren't particularly close."

Wolf raised his eyebrows. "Yet he confided in you that he was worried about being poisoned?"

I nodded. "He thought I might know how to test food for poison."

"That didn't worry you?"

"Well, of course it did! I told him he should go to the police. Told him that at least twice, maybe three times as a matter of fact. He didn't want to. Hollis said he had his reasons. Now I wish I hadn't agreed to his request. If he had contacted the police he might be alive today." I winced and took a moment to collect myself. Why had I done that? Why had I agreed to keep his concerns quiet? I should have taken him by the arm and dragged him to see Wolf, or at least Wong.

I looked up at Wolf, who calmly poured himself another glass of tea. "I assumed he didn't want to throw a wrench in his marriage to Kelsey. Can you imagine if he had gone to the police and said he thought she was poisoning him? That would have been a fast track to divorce."

Wolf leaned back in his chair. "It might have been at that. But it begs the question why he would want to remain *in* the marriage if he suspected his wife of poisoning him."

Chapter 8

Dear Sophie,
At the last funeral I attended, a woman's cell phone
rang, and she had the nerve to answer it! We're still
talking about this. Do we have to put up a sign
that says "Cell Phone Free Zone"? Is that what we
have come to?
   Appalled in Transylvania County, North
   Carolina

Dear Appalled,
Alas, such signs have become commonplace at
weddings and parties. There is simply no excuse
for taking a phone call at a funeral. Leave the
phone in the car.
   Sophie

Wolf had a very good point. "It does suggest that the marriage might have been on a downward trajectory," I said. "I can't imagine suspecting my spouse of wanting to harm me. It must be terrible to live that way. I guess he wanted to be sure. He could have just separated from her."

"Did he have any food tested?" asked Wolf.

"I gave the food to Humphrey. He has a pal who is testing it."

Wolf nodded. "Thanks. I'll check with him."

"He definitely died from poisoning? It seemed like he had a respiratory problem." It certainly sounded that way, but I had to ask. I felt as though I'd had a hand in it by keeping Hollis's secret for him.

"He was poisoned but it was from something he inhaled, not something he ingested. I doubt that they'll turn up anything in the food, but I'm obligated to check it out."

I felt a little bit better. "So it could have been accidental."

"We'll know more after the autopsy. What's the scuttlebutt on Haberman's wives? Any gossip I should know about?"

"It was an ugly divorce—"

"Aren't they all?"

"Mine wasn't. Mars and I were very civilized."

"An exception, I'm sure."

"Unfortunately, I overheard Hollis arguing with his ex-wife at the dinner last night. Seems he didn't want to pay for their son's education."

Wolf's eyes narrowed. "Any threats?"

"On both sides."

"How about the new wife? The one he thought was poisoning him?"

"I don't know her well. But I spoke with her a couple of times at the dinner last night. She's young and insecure, but in a way she was very sweet. I wouldn't have thought her capable of poisoning anyone, much less her husband."

Wolf grinned. "Aw, come on, Soph. You know better than that. Murderers come in every shape and size."

He was right, of course. Still, some little part of me wanted to believe that Kelsey hadn't meant to kill Hollis.

Wolf gazed around my kitchen. "I miss coming here. You ready for the big storm?"

I tried to toss it off lightly, as though I wasn't concerned. "Oh, sure. It ruined my beach plans, but this house has been around since the 1800s. I don't think a few storms are going to blow it away."

Wolf stood up. "I'm sorry to have been the bearer of bad news."

"Wolf? Is there any possibility that Hollis's death could have been related to a beesting?"

He shrugged. "I think they're concentrating on his respiratory system. I guess that could be the case with a beesting, but it seems unlikely unless it was an anaphylactic reaction."

Wolf gazed at me like he could see right into my thoughts. "Don't kick yourself about this, Sophie. You were doing what you thought was right."

"But I was dead wrong."

He laid a reassuring hand on my shoulder. "None of us have crystal balls. You can't begin to imagine how many times I wish I had handled something differently. Besides, chances are very good that he didn't die of poisoned food."

I appreciated his kind words, but I still felt enormously guilty. I walked him to the front door and opened it.

Wolf stepped outside. "The wind has kicked up."

The two of us watched tree leaves twist in the air. The sky was still blue, but a band of clouds was filtering in, like cream mixing in a sauce.

"Will Mars or Alex be here with you?" asked Wolf.

"I have no idea. I'll be fine."

He nodded. "Call me if you need help."

It was a generous offer. I watched him walk away, knowing full well that I would never take him up on it. *Never say never, Sophie*, I reminded myself. But deep in my heart, I knew I would have to be desperate to make that call to Wolf.

I closed the door and was thinking about the fact that Nina and Francie would probably rely on me for meals if the power went out. The phone rang, interrupting my thoughts.

I answered it and Humphrey said, "Please tell me that my friend isn't testing food for a Mr. Hollis Haberman."

"I'm afraid so."

"In that case, I think we should turn the samples of food over to the cops. Are you okay with that?"

"Absolutely. You may get a visit from Wolf. He was just here asking me about Hollis. You . . . you don't have any results yet, do you?" I held my breath.

"No, I was just over at the morgue and everyone is talking about Haberman. There's a lot of speculation about what happened to him."

"Oh?" I said, afraid to hear what they might suspect.

"Conflicting symptoms. It will be interesting to hear what caused his death. One thing's for sure—no one expects it to be natural causes."

"Keep me posted, okay?"

"Sure."

I hung up, feeling miserable and wondering what I should have done that could have prevented Hollis's death. Still thinking about him, I pulled out tapioca, lemon, sugar, and fresh blueberries to make a blueberry pie.

The sky grew dark early in the evening. When Mars, Daisy, Nina, Francie, and Duke, Francie's golden retriever, gathered in my kitchen, the sky unleashed a downpour. We had just sat down to a dinner of roast chicken and rice when Mars calmly said, "Sophie, someone is lurking outside in the rain."

We all rushed to the bay window in the kitchen. Not the smartest thing to do since we were backlighted. The person outside could probably see us far better than we could see him.

He stood there without as much as an umbrella. The rain poured down so hard that it pelted the window and left streaks on the glass.

The lurker covered his face with his hands, and there was something about that movement that caused me to think I knew who was out there.

I flung open the front door and dashed out into the rain but hadn't expected the sheer strength of the wind. I had to bend forward against its force to make any headway. The rain had seemed different inside the house. Outside, the wind drove it at me in sheets.

My steps were painfully slow, like an ancient person who could barely move one foot ahead of the other. The elements plastered my clothes against me. I pitied anyone caught outside in this weather.

The lurker staggered backward into the street, her arms stretched out wide.

Still bent forward, I forced my hands straight ahead, but it was slow going. I finally reached Kelsey Haberman and managed to grasp her wrists.

Chapter 9

Dear Sophie,
I have spent so much money on cutting boards, but after a while they look terrible and I end up throwing them out. What am I doing wrong?
Not Making the Cut in Oak Brook, Illinois

Dear Not Making the Cut,
Wood does not like water. Never put them in the dishwasher. Wash them by hand and be sure to dry them thoroughly. You should also oil your wood cutting boards. Food-safe mineral oil is favored, but a refined coconut oil made specially for cutting boards is also popular. Rub the oil on the wood and allow it to be absorbed.
Sophie

I hooked my arm into Kelsey's and held tight. Together we ducked and leaned forward to combat the forces that threatened to slam us into the house.

We finally approached the front door, where Mars and

Nina reached out to us. We blew right past them into the foyer. The door slammed behind us, as if some unknown force had shut it against the evil waging war outdoors.

Kelsey Haberman was a far cry from the flirting bombshell she'd been only the day before. Her beautiful blond tresses were matted to her head. The wind and rain had driven her dark eye makeup into bizarre streaks. Her eyes would have faded into her pale face had it not been for the red rims from crying. Her summer dress was drenched and glued to her body. She had lost her shoes somewhere along the way and stood in my foyer barefoot and dripping wet.

I was certain that I looked equally pathetic.

Nina handed each of us a towel.

Daisy wagged her tail and sniffed Kelsey curiously. Kelsey fell to her knees and buried her face in Daisy's fur. Kelsey's body wracked as she sobbed.

Daisy stood very still and let her cry as if she understood that something was wrong with this stranger.

Kelsey raised her head and whispered, "Hollis is dead."

"We heard, Kelsey. I'm so sorry."

Francie shuffled toward her. "Child, we'd better get some dry clothes on you. I'm sure Sophie has something you can wear."

"Of course I do."

Francie, Nina, and I escorted Kelsey upstairs.

Nina pawed through my closet. "Honestly, Sophie, why are you so short?"

At best, she was an entire three inches taller than me. "Hah! You say that as though you're a towering willow."

In spite of that, she dug up a jean skirt from my thinner days. I hadn't worn it in years. Armed with clothes, she led Kelsey to the bathroom to change.

I dried off, pulled my wet hair back into a ponytail, and dressed in a short skirt and a cotton V-neck tee. I hurried downstairs to dry the hardwood floor in the foyer.

Looking very young and vulnerable, Kelsey walked down the stairs with Francie and Nina.

I wrapped an arm around Kelsey and guided her into the kitchen. She buried her face in my shoulder and bawled. There was nothing I could do except pat her back.

When she let go of me and wiped tears off her face with the backs of her hands, I asked, "Have you eaten anything today?"

She sniffled. "No, I was at the hospital most of the day. And then the police questioned me."

"Hot tea or iced?" I asked.

"Hot, I think. I feel like I'll never be warm again."

Nina had given her a fluffy sweater to wear. Kelsey held her arms crossed against her chest as though she was freezing.

I put the kettle on while Duke and Daisy vied for Kelsey's attention. I watched her from the stove, wondering why she had come to my house. It wasn't as though I was close with her or Hollis. His death saddened me greatly, but I wasn't a confidant of theirs.

"How are you feeling?" Mars asked. "Physically, I mean. You don't seem to be coughing anymore."

"Crying hasn't been helping. It gets me all congested and then I end up coughing again."

"They released you from the hospital, so that must be a good sign," said Nina.

I poured boiling water over black tea, which helps calm the nerves. I set her mug on the table with sugar and a little pitcher of milk.

"Thank you for being so kind to me. I'm really a stranger to you all, but you're being so nice. I . . . I didn't know where to go. I just knew I couldn't be alone right now." She sat on the banquette and rested her elbows on the table. Her fingers gently massaged her temples. Staring at the teacup, she picked it up and held it in both palms. Ripples in the tea gave away a slight tremor in her hands.

"All of you saw Hollis at the dinner last night. Right? Did he look sick to any of you?"

"No, he did *not*." Trust Francie to get right to the point.

"How can a person go from being perfectly fine to being dead in only a few hours?" asked Kelsey.

"Did they tell you what they thought was wrong with him?" asked Mars.

Kelsey sipped her tea. Wincing, she said, "They're not sure. They're going to do an autopsy." Tears welled in her eyes and spilled over onto her cheeks. She coughed, her body jerking as she hacked.

We all stared at her in concern.

"What did the doctors say about your coughing?" demanded Francie in a no-nonsense, grandmotherly way.

"They said we must have inhaled something. I just got less of whatever it was."

I handed her a box of tissues. Trying very hard to change the subject, I said, "Your timing is perfect. We were just going to eat dinner." I rose and gathered a plate, napkin, and silverware for her. "What did you think of the food at the underground dinner last night?" I placed everything before her on the table.

She blew her nose and turned surprised eyes toward me. "I liked everything except the liver soup."

"My feelings exactly." Nina high-fived with her.

"Hollis ate mine and his." Kelsey gasped. "The soup! Maybe someone poisoned the liver soup. I only tried a spoonful, but Hollis ate it all."

We were silent for a moment as we processed her idea.

Mars was the first to speak. In a gentle and kind tone, he said, "Kelsey, I can understand why you might think that. But we ate the soup, too. Sophie, Francie, and I all ate it, and we're fine."

"It was a good idea, though," said Nina. "Must be easy

to hide disgusting poisons in something that's as gross as liver."

Kelsey appeared to be thinking about it. "Maybe they only poisoned *his* soup."

Francie patted her hand. "I don't think so, dear. Didn't you say it was inhaled?"

I stopped in the middle of passing a platter of sliced and salted pink Brandywine heirloom tomatoes from my garden. I wanted to like Kelsey, especially the Kelsey seated at my table. The one without cleavage showing. The one looking so helpless and weary. Consequently, I was more than a little ashamed when the thought that she might be playing us drifted through my head.

I'd had a murderer as a guest at my dinner table before. Of course, I didn't know which guest it was at the time. But this was a new twist for me. I couldn't recall being in a situation where I was trying to comfort the very person whom the victim suspected of poisoning him.

If Kelsey had intentionally poisoned Hollis, then she had a lot of moxie to come to my house seeking comfort. If that was the case, she was putting on a very good act as the bereaved.

I hoped I was wrong and that Kelsey was the clueless and distressed young widow she appeared to be.

"Kelsey," said Francie, "where are you from?"

"Mostly the South."

"You moved around a lot?" asked Mars.

She nodded.

"So where's your hometown?" asked Nina.

"I don't believe I've ever had one."

"Your parents were in the military?" guessed Francie.

"I wish!" Kelsey heaved a big sigh and helped herself to chicken. "My parents were real young when they had me in South Carolina—still in high school, actually. When I was a toddler, they died in a car accident."

"Oh no! Were you in the car?" asked Nina.

"My baby sister and I were at the sitter's house. No-body wanted us, I guess, so my father's great aunt in West Virginia took us in. She was a sweet woman. Chubby and smiling and warm. When she wasn't knitting, she was gar-dening or canning."

Nina clapped a hand against her chest. "I'm so glad you landed in a good home."

"She died when I was six."

"Why you poor thing!" Francie gasped.

"They sent us to live with my mother's sister, Delilah Jean, in Tennessee. She had a bad marriage and a bunch of kids. When I was eleven, her ex-husband came to the back door and shot her dead while she was calling the police."

I stopped eating and stared at her. How could one child have so much bad luck?

"What did you do then?" asked Mars.

"They split up the kids. My sister and I were sent to a distant cousin of my father's in North Carolina." She smiled at Duke and Daisy. "She had a lot of dogs."

"So you finally found a good home?" asked Nina.

"Not so much. Sassy wasn't the type to teach us to sew a skirt or bake cookies. Sassy liked three things—bourbon, men, and dogs, not necessarily in that order depending on the day, though bourbon usually took first place. She didn't have much time for little girls. Unfortunately, she changed boyfriends like most people change pillowcases. The older I got, the more interested they were in me. When I was six-teen, a guy named Wayne Khropinki moved in with her. Sassy didn't believe me when I told her I had to fight him off." Kelsey sighed. "For a long time, I blamed her for that. The pathetic truth was that Sassy was too drunk to under-stand or care. One night I walked in on him trying to have his way with my little sister. I slammed him over the head with a bottle of Sassy's bourbon, grabbed my sister, and fled in Sassy's car. It took the authorities an entire year to find us. I put on a lot of makeup, lied about my age, and served drinks in a scuzzy joint where I figured no one would care enough to ask questions about the new girl. It worked out pretty well. Living with Sassy had taught me how to deal with drunks. One afternoon, I came back from the grocery store. There was a cop car in front of our apartment, and I saw them placing my sister in it. I kept driving. I knew I couldn't help her if I was in custody, too. They took her straight back to Sassy's." She gazed at us, one at a time, as though she was assessing our reaction.

"Wayne murdered her that night. She never had a chance. Sassy drank herself into a grave the next year. I never went back, but I saw her obituary online."

"Good heavens, child!" Francie shook her head. "It's a wonder you can walk and talk. I've never heard of such a terrible childhood."

"It's like I'm cursed. I overheard some relatives talking about me when I was little. They didn't want me living with them because they thought I brought bad luck. And now my husband is dead."

Silence fell over us.

Francie was the first to speak. "That's utter nonsense. You had a terrible start in life, but none of that was your fault. You didn't make Sassy drink. You didn't shoot your mother's sister. Those things were completely out of your control. My goodness. You were just a child. I'm sorry I didn't know you. I would have taken you in."

"How did you meet Hollis?" asked Nina.

"I had a car accident and met him at his law firm."

That one sentence quickly reminded us that Cindy Haberman accused Kelsey of ruining her marriage. I hurried to change the subject. "What did you think of the chocolate mousse last night?"

Kelsey put down her fork. "I'm so sorry. I didn't mean to barge in on your dinner."

"You're not barging in at all. You're a neighbor. Now eat something, young lady." Francie pointed at her. "I'd like to hear more about your interesting life."

Rain pounded at the windows while we ate. I found it interesting that Kelsey passed on the wine. Maybe Sassy's drinking put her off alcohol.

We were clearing the dishes from the table to make room for dessert when the lights went out.

Chapter 10

Dear Natasha,
I'm putting together power outage kits for each
member of my family. Other than the obvious
flashlight, batteries, and first aid kit, what should
they contain?
    Worried Mom in Rough and Ready, California

Dear Worried Mom,
Cash. Banks won't be open and in a power outage,
the ATMs won't function, either.
    Natasha

Mars jumped up and peered out the bay window.
"Everybody's out. Even the streetlights."

I had placed candles and matches on the countertop,
ready for use if necessary. It took me a few minutes to feel
my way across the kitchen and light them.

I set candles on the windowsill over the sink, while
Mars placed some in the bay window and on the fireplace
mantel.

"Wow. I don't remember seeing the streetlights out,"

said Nina. "This must be how the street looked at night before electricity."

"Wouldn't they have had gas lamps back then?" asked Francie.

"Forgot about those. It's a little creepy out there. Everything is so dark."

I fetched some battery-operated lanterns, which brightened the kitchen considerably.

"I call dibs on Sophie's second-floor guest room," Nina announced. "I'm not sleeping alone without lights."

I grinned. So like Nina. I didn't tease her, though, because I welcomed the company. There *was* something a little spooky about being home alone in pitch-black darkness.

Francie snorted. "What's to be scared of? Good thing you didn't live one hundred years ago, Nina."

"Thank heaven," said Nina. "I like my creature comforts. What's for dessert?"

I set the blueberry pie on the table. "It's times like this when I'm very glad I have a gas stove. Would anyone like coffee or hot tea?"

Everyone except Kelsey and I voted for an after-dinner drink. Carrying candles, Nina and I retrieved cordial glasses from the dining room, along with a bottle of raspberry liqueur.

In the shadowy light, I observed Kelsey and wondered how she felt about being alone in the dark. If, heaven forbid, it had been Mars who died, I would have wanted to be alone with my sorrow. I wouldn't have cared about the driving rain and darkness around me. I might have even felt they reflected my mood. But I suspected that not everyone would react that way.

"Kelsey, will you be okay by yourself tonight?" I asked.

She looked up from her pie. "I think so."

Nina pulled out her cell phone and poked around on it.

"Maybe the power won't be out for long. I'll see if I can pull up any information."

Francie sipped her liqueur. "Have you notified Hollis's relatives yet?"

Kelsey released a faint gasp. "Cindy!" she hissed. "She hates me! I guess it would be impolite to text her, but their son needs to know about his dad."

I could just imagine what a nightmare that call would be. "Did Hollis have any siblings?"

"They came to the wedding and were very nice to me." She covered her eyes with her fingers for a few seconds. "I was so self-absorbed and in shock, I guess, that I didn't even think about anyone else. His parents are deceased. I'll have to call Parker at the law firm, too, to let them know. I don't know what to do first."

I jotted down Humphrey's name and the name of the funeral home where he worked. "You should probably contact Humphrey as soon as possible. That way when the autopsy is over, you'll be ready."

Even in the dim light of the candles I saw her blanch. Given the way news traveled in Old Town, I had a feeling Parker and Cindy already knew. But maybe the storm had distracted people and slowed the news of Hollis's demise.

"I can walk you home," offered Mars. "Maybe Sophie will lend us some umbrellas."

Nina looked up from her phone. "I'm trying to get the electric company website, but nothing's happening. I can't even get Google. It's like we've been cut off from the world!"

Francie guffawed. "I concede that I do appreciate electricity, but there's something very peaceful about reading a book by lantern. It's so quiet. It's as though the rest of the world vanishes and one merges into the story."

"You can do the same with an electric light," Nina pointed out, sounding a bit testy.

Francie insisted on going to her own home next door and acted offended when I offered to walk with her. I insisted she call me as soon as she was in her house. What she didn't know was that I grabbed an umbrella and stood outside in the driving rain until I saw her safely step inside her own home.

Kelsey agreed to Mars seeing her home. The two of them borrowed umbrellas and set out into the night.

I lent Nina an oversized T-shirt to sleep in and gave her a fresh toothbrush. Except for one more after-dinner drink, that was all she needed.

In the morning, we woke to a mess. Tree limbs littered the streets. Chain saws screamed in the distance. The sun shone brightly in a blue sky, as though nothing had happened. The only difference was slightly cooler air. Our block appeared to have fared well, but no one had electricity.

Neighbors gathered in the street, checking for damage and telling tales about their night. I hustled back inside and made two pots of strong coffee, while Nina loaded trays with cream and sugar.

Mars and Bernie showed up and carried lawn chairs out into the street. No cars could pass for the time being because of the branches, and what could have been a horrible morning quickly changed into a block party breakfast.

I made bowl after bowl of pancake batter, and Bernie acted like a short-order cook, flipping pancakes as fast as he could. Mars carried them outside, where neighbors had donated maple, blueberry, and blackberry syrups. Someone emptied her refrigerator of yogurt, another brought pints of fresh blueberries, and Nina offered the pastries we hadn't consumed the day before. Even slightly stale, they were a welcome addition.

Alex came by to see how we had fared. "Good grief, Sophie. You turn everything into a party." He kissed me lightly.

"Please. It's not as though I planned this. Not everyone has gas to cook with. I know I'm a bear if I don't have my morning coffee or tea."

In spite of his teasing, I noted that he poured himself a mug of coffee immediately and didn't hesitate to join us for breakfast.

The news of Hollis's death spread like wildfire, putting a damper on spirits as people learned what had happened to him.

I called Kelsey to see if she wanted to join us, but no one answered. I was worried enough to slip away for a moment on the pretense of walking Daisy. We ventured down the street to the Haberman residence. Someone, Cindy, I guessed, had painted the shutters and front door peacock blue, which accented the red brick nicely. We stepped up to the front door with a traditional glass fan over the top of it, and I banged a door knocker in the shape of a fox's head.

We could hear someone inside hurrying toward the door. Kelsey opened it. Dark circles under her eyes suggested she hadn't slept a wink. They were still red-rimmed from crying.

"How are you feeling?" I asked.

"Ugh. I have a headache that feels like a drummer is in my head." She motioned us in.

Daisy and I stepped into an exquisitely appointed foyer. A large gilt mirror above a marble-topped demilune table gave it depth even though it wasn't wide. The parlor beyond featured a wall of fine woodwork. A painting of horses and hounds hung above the fireplace. Bookcases overflowing with books flanked it and filled the wall. But an acrid odor hung in the air. Faint, but enough to make me wonder what smelled funky. "Why don't you come and have some breakfast? A cup of coffee might help clear your head."

She took a deep breath. "I'm not dressed." She gestured toward her T-shirt and old jeans.

"You're just fine. No one else looks any better."

"Okay." She grabbed keys from the table and locked the door behind her.

"I called, but no one answered."

"I unplugged the landline phones. They just kept ringing and ringing. As people heard what happened they couldn't believe it and tried to call Hollis. After the first couple of calls I couldn't handle it. Is that awful of me? They were his friends, people who cared about him. But I couldn't talk about it. I just sobbed and could hardly speak. I think I needed time to process it, you know? It was like the day my aunt was shot. In one second she was gone and everything changed. The repercussions of a sudden death are so far-reaching. My mind is completely scattered. I can't focus because it's so overwhelming."

She stopped walking. "Why are all these people in the street?"

"We're having breakfast."

"Oh. Okay."

Natasha, who was the only person on the street in full makeup and high heels, propelled toward Kelsey with her arms wide. "I was crushed to hear about Hollis." She pulled Kelsey into a hug but released her quickly. "He was such a lovely man. I'm simply heartbroken." Natasha linked her arm through Kelsey's and steered her away from me, but turned back long enough to hiss at me, "Dibs on Coca-Cola cake." As she walked with Kelsey, she asked, "Have you made the arrangements yet? I would be happy to help you."

Nina scooted up beside me. "Oh no! How could you let Kelsey fall into her clutches?"

"This is one time when it might work out. Kelsey could use some guidance, and it would keep Natasha busy."

Francie ambled over. "I really put my foot in it this time. You will not believe what happened. I was supposed to work as a volunteer at the library sale today. Early this morning I called Cindy to see if it was still on. I thought they would cancel because there's no electricity and Cindy's ex-husband had died. She didn't know! I was the one who broke the news to her about Hollis's death!"

I felt for Francie. "How awkward for both of you. How did she take it?"

"You know Cindy. There was stunned silence at first, which was when I began to realize what I had done. Of course, she asked how he died and started to cry. Apparently she had been over at the hospital yesterday morning but hadn't heard that he didn't make it."

"I cannot believe you!" Nina frowned at Francie. "So the library sale is off, I guess."

"Absolutely not. Cindy said she couldn't let everyone down. They had advertised it and prepared everything. There was no way to call it off now."

"I doubt that," I said. "The lack of electricity alone would have been a good excuse."

"She insisted that it made no difference because it's being held outside on the sidewalk and they have a generator to protect the historical documents from extreme temperatures." Francie shrugged.

"It doesn't surprise me one bit," said Nina. "Cindy looks so delicate, like a flower that could wilt in too much heat or rain. But she's actually one determined cookie."

Nina was right. Cindy had a lot more grit than most people thought.

I returned to my kitchen, expecting to find a mess, but Bernie and Mars were washing and drying dishes.

"I must be dreaming," I said.

"The water is cold, but we heated some in the kettle for washing." Mars turned to Bernie and high-fived him. "Pioneer men! We also wrestle bears."

I couldn't help giggling. "You're very cheerful in spite of the lack of electricity."

"Almost everything is closed," said Mars. "They're asking people not to drive because traffic will slow down the clean-up crews."

Bernie handed him a coffee mug to dry. "The Laughing Hound is closed until further notice. We have gas for cooking, but without lights we can't bring the public inside."

"Mind if I take Daisy since I have a day off?" asked Mars. "I was supposed to have her this week anyway."

"Sure. Go ahead."

After they left, I wandered into my sunroom. It would be too hot in there soon without any air-conditioning. Through the windows, I had a perfect view of the mess in my backyard. I ought to pick up the branches from the storm before the heat returned. But before I got started, the phone rang.

Francie was calling from the library book sale. "We need extra hands down here. What with the stores and restaurants closed, they have a crazy crowd. Think you and Nina could come help us out?"

"Of course. We'll be there soon."

I phoned Nina, who was game to help out. After all, we had planned to be away and didn't have anything scheduled. Wearing a white sleeveless cotton top, a sky-blue skort, white sandals, and a sun hat, I walked over to Nina's house.

The two of us strolled down to the library.

Cindy Haberman rushed us the minute we arrived. "Thank you for coming," she said in her gentle voice. Although she had pinned up her long locks, a few tendrils had worked their way loose around her face, giving her an angelic appearance. "Sophie, can you replenish books as they're sold? And, Nina, maybe you could assist Francie under the tent where people pay. I think the crowd is a little overwhelming for her."

I placed my hand on her slender arm, which was surprisingly cool. "I'm so sorry about Hollis."

"Me too," said Nina. "He was far too young to die."

Cindy spoke softly. "Thank you. I'm in shock, of course. I was terribly ugly to him at the underground dinner. I'll always regret that we fought to the bitter end."

"Don't beat yourself up about it," said Nina. "I'm sure we would all act differently if we knew what fate had in store for us."

Cindy gazed away, and I realized that she was looking at Gavin. "I'm putting all my energy into this sale. Work is the best therapy, don't you think?"

I agreed but wondered why she hadn't put Gavin to work. He had settled away from the sale, his back to the brick building, his knees drawn up, looking very much the petulant teenager.

A bearded gentleman interrupted to haggle about the price of a one-dollar book. Nina and I hustled to our assigned jobs. The tables were labeled according to the type of book, so it wasn't difficult to pick up a stack and fill empty spots on the tables.

Browsers whisked them away with amazing speed. Cindy was kept busy overseeing everything, but I felt awful for Gavin. After an hour, I grabbed two drinks from a cooler and walked over to him.

I sat down on the ground next to him, glad I'd worn a skort, and handed him a drink.

"Thanks."

"I'm sorry about your dad."

He fidgeted with the bottle in his hands. "It's okay. I never saw him anyway. It's not like it will be any different."

"I guess both of you were busy."

"Yeah, I feel kind of bad about that now."

I listened, waiting for him to say more.

"I never wanted to do stuff with him. Especially not if *she* was there. And now I'll never have a chance to make up for that."

"It's rough. I'm sure Hollis understood."

"If he understood, he never would have ditched my mom and me in the first place."

Ouch! I didn't know enough about their situation to refute anything he was saying, but I tried. "He divorced your mom, not you."

"It doesn't matter." He flicked a blade of grass away. "It was like he died when he left us. Nothing would have changed if he had lived longer."

Gavin was breaking my heart. Unfortunately, he was probably right. The divorce had cut deep in Gavin's soul.

"Mrs. Winston? Do you think she killed him?"

Chapter 11

Dear Natasha,
My uncle died yesterday. I just came from my aunt's home, where the bereaved family and friends are gathering. I dutifully brought a funeral casserole that I had baked for the occasion. I was horrified to see people bringing store-bought foods! Is it just me? I thought if it wasn't homemade, it didn't count!
Raised Right in Tombstone, Arizona

Dear Raised Right,
The mourners probably claimed they were too upset to prepare a proper dish. You were indeed raised right. One can only hope that fast food will be served at the funerals of the mourners who brought store-bought foods.
Natasha

"Gavin! Why would you ask that?" I stared at him, trying to read his expression.
"Why else would she have married him?"

I wondered if he was repeating something Cindy had said, or if he had come up with that conclusion on his own. It probably wasn't the best time to talk about the possibility that Kelsey had loved Hollis.

I chose my words carefully. "Do you have any evidence of that?"

"That's what I would need, isn't it? I'll come up with something."

"Gavin!" I playfully pushed his thin upper arm. "Don't do anything stupid."

He laughed at me. A truly lovely genuine laugh, like the one I'd heard often when he was a kid. "I'm a teenager, Mrs. Winston. I do stupid stuff all the time."

Cindy was watching us with a frown on her face. I scrambled to my feet. "I'd better get back to work. Promise me you won't go snooping around for evidence."

"Not a chance."

I wasn't sure whether he meant not a chance that he would make such a promise or not a chance that he would snoop. "Behave yourself," I warned as I walked away.

Cindy caught up to me. "Thanks for taking the time to talk to Gavin. He's been in an awful funk. They tell me all teenagers are like this, but he was such a sweet little boy that I have trouble accepting his moodiness."

Was she kidding? "He just lost his father. I think I'd be melancholy, too."

"Oh, that's not what's making him crabby. He's grounded. He's not speaking to me at the moment to convey how terribly unfair I am. But I don't dare give in. It hurts me to see him this way, but I have to be firm."

I drew in a sharp breath and tried not to appear shocked. Was she really trying to pass off his father's death as inconsequential? Gavin could put on a brave face and pretend that nothing had changed now that his father was dead, but Cindy knew better than that. Teens were an enigma to me, but a parent's death was life-changing and crushing, no matter what age a person was.

A bit wimpishly I uttered, "He'll get over being grounded. We all did." He would never get over the way he had treated his dad after the divorce, though. Some wounds never healed. "What did he do to earn that punishment?"

"He has this friend named Chadwick, who is actually a great kid. Polite, good student, relatively sane for a teenager. But Chadwick now has a girlfriend, and unfortunately, he's in the habit of sneaking out at night to meet up with her. She brings a friend, and Chadwick drags Gavin along. I shouldn't say *drags*. Gavin goes all too willingly. He punches up pillows on his bed and covers them with a blanket. Seriously, Sophie, it's not even original! My brother did the same thing when we were kids. But I'm not going through another sleepless night, sitting in the living room and imagining all the awful things that could happen to him when he's running around in the dark. I had to put my foot down. No cell phone for a month. I think that hurts the most, but I can't have him texting with Chadwick. And one month of being grounded."

It was noon when Nina and I insisted Francie go home. The heat would still be intense, but she wouldn't be sitting in a tent out in the blazing sun. Streets were still blocked by work crews, and the sounds of hammering reverberated through the neighborhood.

Wolf flagged us down as we approached the Haberman house. "They've set up a cooling room for seniors at one of the government buildings with a generator, Francie. I hear they're setting up games."

I thought she might kick him in the shin.

Pulling back her shoulders and raising her chin, she said, "I'm no lily-livered pantywaist. Who do you think you're talking to?"

Wolf bit back a grin. "I wouldn't mind a break from this heat. Any damage to your houses?"

"Looks like we're all okay," said Nina.

"Good to hear that." Wolf sucked in a deep breath. "It's going to be in the papers tomorrow, and the way news travels around here, half of Old Town will probably know in a couple of hours, so I might as well tell you. Sophie, you'll be glad to know that Hollis did not die from anything he ate. The cause of death is acute respiratory illness. At this point, they're thinking it was related to pesticide use."

"The bees!" said Nina.

"It's a possibility. I'm waiting for Angus to show me where the bees are."

"So it's not a homicide." I breathed a little easier knowing that.

Wolf shot me an odd look. "I didn't say that. But it's possible that Hollis sprayed the bees and inhaled the poison, which triggered some underlying respiratory problem."

That made sense. It explained the previous episodes of breathing issues.

Angus strolled up, yawning as if he'd just gotten out of bed. "You ready to see the bees?"

"Not me!" Nina took Francie's arm. "I'd better get Francie home and out of this heat."

The two of them strode away with Francie protesting, "Stop treating me like a melting Popsicle."

"Are you coming with us?" Wolf asked me.

I was torn. Part of me itched to see the bees, while another part of me did *not* want to be stung. "I'll hang back a little bit, but I admit that I'm curious about these bees."

Angus led the way along the side of the house to the back.

A lovely, but quite old white porch spanned the rear of the home. On the side of the house, a small tree house was almost hidden in foliage. A vestige of young Gavin's residence there.

Angus pointed up at an interior corner of the porch. "They're right up there."

None of us walked any closer. We didn't have to. Bees swarmed in a corner of the blue ceiling. I had never seen so many bees.

Wolf held out his arm to prevent me from nearing the bees. It was completely unnecessary. I was more likely to bolt and run away than to get any closer.

"Does it look to you like they've gotten inside the house?" I asked.

"Can that happen?" asked Angus.

"I don't know why not," said Wolf. "They wouldn't need much of a crack to enter and exit easily. Did you call someone about this?"

Angus ran a hand through his hair. "Not me. Hollis came to the hospital after I was stung and told me he was going to take care of the bees."

Wolf checked his watch. "Looks like Hollis took it upon himself to spray them, but *he* inhaled more than the bees. I'll talk to Kelsey about getting someone over here today. We don't want them attacking anyone else."

We walked around to the front of the house. Wolf knocked the fox door knocker.

Natasha opened the front door. She was dressed in a tight black dress that screamed Halloween costume, except without the peaked hat. She wore a flat-topped hat with a double black veil rimmed with a black satin ribbon. Kelsey was right behind her in a sleek black suit. I couldn't help wondering if Natasha had dressed her that way. In this heat? I had trouble imagining that Kelsey just happened to have a black pillbox hat with a net-style veil.

In a low voice, Natasha said, "How kind of you to come." She stepped aside so we could enter.

Natasha gasped. Her gaze swept over us. "Not a one of you brought food? Sophie Winston, I *know* you were brought up better than that."

"This isn't a social call, Natasha," I said.

Wolf did an excellent job at hiding what he thought of their attire. "I'd like to have a word with Kelsey, please."

Like a prim housekeeper, Natasha said, "Then you will have to return later. Mrs. Haberman is receiving at the moment."

I glanced into the living room. If she was receiving, no one had arrived. It was all I could do not to laugh. *She's receiving?* I felt for Kelsey and sympathized with her grief, but Natasha seemed to have drawn a page out of a 1920s movie.

Wolf wasn't laughing. In a dead serious tone he growled, "Mrs. Haberman, we need to talk."

Kelsey stepped past Natasha and gazed at him with big eyes.

"We've had a look at the bees. I think it would be advisable to get someone over here as soon as possible. Maybe even today."

"But we have to select Hollis's coffin this afternoon," protested Natasha.

"I'm sorry to intrude on your grief, *Mrs. Haberman*," Wolf emphasized her name as though he wanted to be sure Natasha understood she was not part of this equation. "The bees need immediate attention. I'm not certain that it's safe for you to sleep here."

"Oh no!" Kelsey appeared frightened.

Angus blurted, "What movie did you two get those costumes from?"

Kelsey shot Natasha an annoyed look. "I told you."

"Really? You take your etiquette cues from him? *He* doesn't understand what's expected of the bereaved," said Natasha. "He didn't even bring a covered dish with him."

"We'll put off the trip to the funeral home while I line up a bee person. Gosh, I don't even know what to look for. A beekeeper? An exterminator?" asked Kelsey.

She disappeared with Wolf and Angus, presumably to locate the appropriate person, leaving me alone in the foyer with Natasha.

"Well, don't just stand there. There's work to do." Natasha crooked her finger at me.

Not that I minded pitching in, but I followed her out of curiosity more than anything else. She walked into the elegant dining room, slid on gloves, and proceeded to polish silver in her witchy black getup. It was one of the funniest things I had ever seen.

"Can you imagine?" she asked. "The silver is tarnished. Hollis has been dead for an entire day and Kelsey hasn't even bothered to clean the silver."

"Oh, the horror of it! Her husband died. She herself was in the emergency room and then was questioned by police. How could she possibly have overlooked cleaning the silver?"

"Are you going to help me or not?"

I suspected *not* wasn't going to go over well.

"See if you can find the good china. We can't have people eating off paper plates. And if you run across cloth napkins, we'll need those, too. Honestly, Sophie, she hasn't done a thing. Oh, and when you're done with that, clean out the refrigerator. People will be bringing food by the tons."

I had nothing else to do. It took me all of two seconds to open the hutch in the dining room and find the good china. Ironically, it was Lenox's Opal Innocence, a tone on tone pattern of white and off-white dots and vines, accented by a platinum band. When Natasha wasn't paying attention, I swiped her black tablecloth and replaced it with a luxurious white damask tablecloth with vines reminiscent of the china. After stacking teacups, saucers, luncheon plates, and dessert plates on the table, I poked around in drawers of the sideboard in search of napkins. Kelsey probably received them as wedding gifts. I laid them out in a tight semicircle.

That taken care of, I wandered into the kitchen and peered in the fridge. Given Hollis's fear of being poisoned, I considered the contents with interest. Yogurt, difficult to poison, probably because it wouldn't hide a bitter taste. Sticks of butter, low-fat cheese, a package of chicken tenders, salmon, fresh peaches and blueberries, cottage cheese, eggs, bottles of water, salad and spinach, beets, carrots, and a whole host of unsalted nuts.

I glanced around the kitchen counters. They were spotless. Not a bag of bread, a doughnut, or anything sinful. Surely they had ice cream in the freezer. I peeked inside. Frozen green beans and corn, chicken legs, lima beans. The Habermans ate a very healthy diet. Odd, considering Hollis's rather beefy figure. Or had Kelsey thrown out all of Hollis's favorites after his death because they had been poisoned? As much as I liked her, I had to consider that possibility.

There really wasn't much to throw out. I moved a few things around to make room for the casseroles and cakes that would soon arrive.

Reluctantly, I returned to the dining room, where Natasha buffed fish forks, which were highly unlikely to be needed. I watched her, wondering how to politely suggest that her outfit might be over the top, when I heard Bernie's voice in the foyer.

"Sophie!"

I hurried out to him. Natasha followed me.

When Bernie caught sight of Natasha, he muttered a polite hello before turning his attention to me. "I've been calling you all morning."

"Cell phones aren't working," said Natasha. "Two towers were damaged in the storm."

"Is that the problem? No wonder everyone is complaining about their cell phones. But Sophie wasn't answering her landline, either. Soph, since I can't open the restaurant, I have a ton of food that needs to be used. The freezers will keep some of it good for a few days, but I have meat that has to be used or tossed tomorrow. How about a neighborhood party in your backyard tonight? Mars and I can get the grill going, and we can serve sort of a charcuterie."

"Great idea! I'm game."

"It's unseemly to celebrate when Hollis is dead." Natasha glared at Bernie.

"We still have to eat. Besides, Hollis would be the first to belly up to the grill," said Bernie.

"In that case, I shall bring my famous Chipotle Kale Cake for dessert," Natasha declared.

Oh joy.

Bernie shot me a look of desperation. "I thought we'd have an ice-cream board. It makes so much sense given the situation. There's a lot of ice cream that's going to melt if it's not eaten today."

"Maybe that's a better idea, Natasha. Besides, unless you have a generator, your mixer won't work," I pointed out.

"I keep forgetting that the electricity is out. Perhaps I'll bring appetizers."

"That's very nice of you." There was no telling what she would bring, but it was only polite to accept her contribution, whatever it might be. "Spread the word among our neighbors, okay?"

Kelsey, Wolf, and Angus returned. All three of them were smiling.

"Some guy who calls himself The Bee Man is coming in an hour. Natasha, I called the funeral home and cancelled the appointment. If you'll excuse me, I'd better change clothes." Kelsey hurried up the stairs.

"Well! She better take me with her when she selects Hollis's coffin. She didn't even know enough to wear black. God love her, the girl is clueless. Tell her to call me when she's ready to deal with reality. It won't be long before she realizes that she needs me." Natasha stalked out the door, clearly offended.

Bernie and I left, too. The bees had been interesting to see, but I didn't need to stick around for their removal.

I spent the next couple of hours gathering lights. In the attic, I located some battery-operated strings of white Christmas lights and ran them along the fence to the backyard to help people see as they entered and exited. In the garage, I dug up two dozen wrought-iron lanterns in a bird and pinecone pattern that I had used at several parties I had arranged. We didn't need them all, but as I set them around, I was glad I had so many.

Between my garage and my house was a covered porch. I'd had plenty of parties out there but had relied on electricity for lights. I pushed two long tables together and set to work laying short cream-colored runners across the tables. Each would serve as a placemat for two people sitting opposite each other. Then I unrolled long festive turquoise runners lengthwise along the middle of each table. That way, small areas of bare wood showed, bringing a more casual feel to the upscale setting.

When I was done, I stepped back and eyed it. I set the lanterns on the tables along the middle, leaving room for the boards with meat. Chunky and bronze, the lanterns had a weathered patina, which added to the rustic elegance of the tablescape.

I wandered the house, collecting an assortment of candles, which I added along the length of the table and on top of the mantel. I ran more battery-operated lights around the base of the porch so people could see to step on and off of it.

I carried out trays of glasses and set up a table for drinks, where people could help themselves. After hauling plates, cutlery, and paper napkins outside, I cut zinnias from my garden and popped them into vases that I placed around the porch.

Two hours later, I was in my kitchen, chopping cabbage for coleslaw for the dinner that night, when Wolf knocked on my kitchen door and let himself in.

"Did The Bee Man come?"

"He did. He really knew his stuff. It's called a swarm removal. Apparently it's not unusual for them to enter a wall, which is what they did at Hollis's house. They can get in a small space around a light fixture, or as in this case, a tiny space in the joint where the porch roof met the wall of the house. But here's the thing—the bees that were inside the house were dead."

Chapter 12

Dear Natasha,
My husband throws a hissy fit when I toss out food
after a power outage. Will you please settle our ar-
guments once and for all by telling us what is safe
to eat?
Hungry in Buzzards Bay, Massachusetts

Dear Hungry,
When in doubt, throw it out. The federal government
says most refrigerated food should be fine for four
hours. Highly perishable items, including meats,
cheeses, and dairy, may not survive that long. Con-
sult the charts at https://www.foodsafety.gov/keep/
charts/refridg_food.html for further information.
Natasha

"I'm not sure I understand. Half the bees were dead,
but not the other half?" I asked.

"Pretty much. The Bee Man is removing the dead bees
right now. He says it's most likely due to one of two things:

either a colony collapse disorder or someone sprayed them from the inside."

"The latter being consistent with your theory of Hollis's death."

"Seems that way. It's hard to imagine how or why he inhaled so much of the stuff, though."

I grabbed a couple of ice cubes that were beginning to look sad, plunked them into a tall glass, poured tea over them, and handed it to him. "Nor does it account for Kelsey's exposure unless she was there with him when he sprayed. Or maybe she left the room faster than he did?"

Wolf gulped the tea. "That's where it gets interesting. She was exposed, but not nearly as much as he was. I'm not sure how that could happen unless she was with him at some point when he sprayed the bees. But she insists that she didn't know he sprayed them last night."

Wolf stood up. "Here she comes. See what you can get out of her." He drained his glass. "I'll let myself out the back way." He hustled toward the sunroom, no doubt to cut through my office and sneak out the French doors in the living room.

Sure enough, the door knocker sounded on my front door. I opened it to find Kelsey looking disheveled and desperate.

She rushed inside. Her chest heaved as though she had run up the street. "They're going to arrest me. They think I murdered Hollis."

I was taken aback. So many thoughts went through my head I barely knew what to say to her. Mostly I had questions. Playing coy, I asked, "Then they've figured out what caused his death?"

She curled her upper lip inward and bit it. "They think he inhaled bee spray."

I coaxed her into the kitchen, where we sat down at the

kitchen table. "Kelsey, unless you held Hollis down and sprayed him with the bee spray, which I don't think would have been physically possible, I don't see how they could blame you for his death."

"The cops asked me if they can search the house. I think need a lawyer. I called Parker Dixon, you know him—one of Hollis's law partners. He said something about it being a conflict of interest and that I would need a lawyer outside the firm."

"And you heard that I date a lawyer."

"Could you put in a good word for me? I mean, I know I'm asking a lot, but I'm so scared. I don't have anyone else to go to."

I reached for a pad of paper and wrote down Alex's name and business phone number. I slid it across the table to her.

She watched me intently. "Hollis told me you solve murders."

I saw where this was going and rushed to set her straight. "I don't do it professionally. Call Alex. He might hire a private investigator. I just got lucky a couple of times."

Tears welled in her eyes. "I'm so scared. They're all going to gang up on me."

"Who? What are you talking about? Do you know who killed Hollis?"

"No! I have no idea. But I'm the outsider here. I was"—she made quotation marks with her fingers in the air—"the other woman. Everyone hates me. Do you think I don't hear what they say about me when I walk by? Cindy was," she corrected herself, "*is* an Old Town institution. Everyone knows her from little kids to old ladies. They all go to the library. She's like a local hotshot. And I'm the one who replaced her," she wailed.

Unfortunately, there was some truth in what she said. The people in town weren't cruel or closed to newcomers, but Cindy was one of them and had been for a long time. She had raised her son with their kids and read to their children at the library on Saturday mornings. She ran the annual book sale at the library and volunteered to help at local events.

"How people feel about Cindy shouldn't make any difference in your legal case." I said it with confidence that I didn't feel. "I'm sure the truth will come out and they'll realize that you didn't murder Hollis."

"They'll all think I killed him for his money. Please, Sophie. I don't have anyone to turn to. They're going to arrest me." She paced the floor. "I thought about leaving town. Just running like I did when I was young. Maybe I *should* do that. I'm not sure I could pull it off anymore. Times are different. There are cameras everywhere. They'd find me for sure."

Oh no. Hollis was right. Why, oh why, didn't he leave her? My breath caught in my throat. "Kelsey, did you kill Hollis?" I asked as gently as I could.

"Of course not. What is it about a twenty-year age difference that makes everyone suspect me? Or is it just me? Because I'm not a socialite? It's easier to blame me and be done with it all than to have to face the truth."

"What is the truth?"

"Sophie, with Hollis gone, there's no one in the world to look out for me. Please, Sophie! I need your help. No one will care about me. Don't you see? They're going to railroad me." Her breath was ragged and uneven. She watched me with frantic eyes.

"That's not going to happen," I said softly, hoping I was right.

Her chest heaved, and when she exhaled her breath shuttered out in ripples. She gasped for air and began to cough. She bent forward and sucked in great gasps of air.

I grabbed her arm and hustled her to the closest chair, one by the fireplace in my kitchen. She collapsed on it.

I searched the pantry for a small paper bag and handed it to her. She placed the opening over her nose and mouth. The bag reminded me of a third lung the way it inflated and deflated. With the bag still over her mouth, she said, "Sophie, something weird is happening."

I gave her some time to recover and returned to chopping cabbage. I tossed it all into a giant bowl and started to peel carrots.

After a short hacking fit, she seemed to be able to breathe more normally again.

"Would you like something to drink?"

"I'm sorry to bother you. A glass of water?"

I popped one of the sad ice cubes into a glass and added water. When I brought it to her, she held it to her cheek first.

Since the food processor wasn't available, I shredded carrots with the vegetable peeler, hoping that if I worked calmly, she would relax. I tossed the carrots into the bowl, then chopped two sweet onions and four crisp apples and added them to the bowl as well. I pulled out a four-cup measuring glass, added sugar, dark brown sugar, bright yellow mustard, delicious smoked paprika, celery seeds, apple-cider vinegar, and a hefty helping of creamy mayonnaise and whisked it all together.

Kelsey watched quietly as I poured it over the cabbage and turned it all several times. I stashed it in a cooler on ice cubes, then turned my attention to her.

I walked over and perched on the other fireside chair, my body positioned toward her. "Do you want to talk, or do you want me to call Alex and arrange for you to speak with him?"

"Both." Her voice was so faint I had a hard time hearing her.

"Okay. I'll call Alex first." I figured his office wasn't open, so I called his cell phone and explained the situation. He promised to come right over. I hung up the phone and smiled at Kelsey. "He's on his way."

I had mixed feelings about prying. While I was itching to know what was going on, I didn't relish the idea of being a spy for Wolf or having to testify against her.

I rose and put on water to make big batches of tea for dinner. I opened a cabinet and pulled out giant pitchers. "We're all having dinner here tonight. You'll come, won't you?" No sooner were the words out of my mouth than I wondered if I had invited a killer.

She nodded and gazed at me. "Can I do something to help you?"

"Thanks, but Bernie's bringing most of the food. I'm just getting iced tea ready. I hope he has ice!"

Alex rapped on the kitchen door as a formality as he opened it and walked inside.

I made quick introductions and was fascinated by the fact that Kelsey sat up straight and wiped her face with her fingers.

There was no doubt that Alex was good-looking, and since she had married Hollis, she clearly didn't have an issue with older men. Not that he was old, just older than Kelsey.

"Maybe we could go into the living room to speak privately?" asked Alex.

"That's not necessary," said Kelsey. "I would have told Sophie everything that happened anyway."

Alex frowned. "All right, but I may stop you if I think there's anything Sophie shouldn't hear."

Kelsey seemed surprised. "Okay." She told him about Angus and the bees and then about Hollis's death.

Alex focused on her intently.

"So when The Bee Man came today, he discovered that

most of the outside bees were alive, but the bees inside the house were dead."

Alex looked over at me and tilted his head.

He was very cute when he did that, like a confused dog. I couldn't help grinning at him. Mostly, though, I was impressed with Kelsey's amazingly logical explanation. There were no tears or coughing fits until she said, "And now they're going to arrest me."

"Either you have omitted something," said Alex, "or they don't have any cause to arrest you."

Of course, Alex didn't know about Hollis's fear that he was being poisoned . . . and since Kelsey hadn't mentioned it, I wondered if she knew about it.

Kelsey gazed at her hands and nervously intertwined her fingers. Sparkling flecks in her blue nail polish flashed as her fingers moved. "The cops asked if they can search the house. They said they can get a search warrant if I say no."

"Alex," I said, "the police think that Hollis must have sprayed the bees and somehow inhaled too much of the pesticide."

"Then I don't see the problem, Kelsey."

She leaned forward. "Then why is that Wolf guy hanging around?"

A furrow formed between Alex's eyes. "Wolf, huh? Maybe it's because he has a thing for Sophie." Alex winked at her.

I shot him a nasty look. "That's not true, Kelsey. Wolf is married, and he loves his wife very much. Honestly, Alex, you're going to get me into trouble spreading nonsense like that."

His eyes narrowed, but not because of me. "You're certain that you've told me everything, Kelsey? There isn't some tiny little thing you might have omitted? I'm not quite sure why Wolf would be interested in your bee problem."

Kelsey gulped. "That's what I thought. What if they're trying to frame me?"

"For Hollis's murder?" asked Alex.

Kelsey gulped and started hacking again.

I handed her the paper bag.

Alex raised his eyebrows in surprise.

When her respiration had returned to normal, Alex said, "Tell you what, come down to my office tomorrow morning. I'll sign you on as a client. And if big, bad Wolf comes knocking at your door again, you tell him he has to talk to me. That's all I want you to say. Nothing else. Just send him to me."

"Oh! You're wonderful!" Kelsey launched herself at Alex, who nearly toppled over from her exuberant hug.

"I'm glad to help." He gently untangled himself from her arms.

"Are you coming to Sophie's dinner tonight?" asked Kelsey.

"Dinner? I don't believe I have been invited."

"Bernie needs to use up some food from the restaurant. I hope you'll come," I said.

"Are you sure there's enough?" Alex asked. "I don't want to butt in."

"There's always enough for you."

"Do we have hot water?" asked Kelsey. "I think I could use a nice, long bath."

"Only if you have a gas hot water heater," said Alex.

She winced. "Everywhere I turn, everything I do, there's something Hollis would have known about. I have no idea what kind of water heater we have. Or if we even have one!"

"It's probably in your basement. But that doesn't matter. Just turn on the hot water in the sink. If it gets warm, you're in luck."

Kelsey toddled over and embraced me. "Thank you, Sophie. You're a lifesaver. I came in here a mess and now I have a lawyer, and I might even get a bath."

She left through the kitchen door, and I couldn't help thinking how different she was from the time she had arrived.

Alex was leaning against the kitchen island. He held out his hand to me. When I took it, he pulled me to him for a very romantic kiss. His arms still around me, he asked, "So why is Wolf suspicious of young Mrs. Haberman?"

"Because Hollis came to me less than twenty-four hours before he died and asked how he could find out if someone was poisoning his food."

Chapter 13

Dear Sophie,
I love salami. There's just nothing better. But my husband insists that it can spoil quickly and refuses to let me put it on a tray as an appetizer. Is he right?
    Hostess in Pig, Kentucky

Dear Hostess,
Salami should be sliced while cold, but served at room temperature to get the full benefit of the flavor.
    Sophie

"Whoa! That was a whopper of a detail to conveniently forget. Makes me wonder what else she didn't tell me."

"I don't think she knows."

He drew his head back. "She doesn't know that her husband suspected her of poisoning his food?"

"He didn't want anyone to know. Humphrey took samples to a friend of his. Wolf doesn't sound particularly interested because the cause of death was definitely related to something Hollis inhaled. I think he said it probably triggered an underlying respiratory condition."

"Wolf's no dummy. If Kelsey noticed Hollis being careful about what he ate, she might have changed her method of getting rid of him." He was silent for a moment. "That certainly does change the picture. If she hires me, I'll have to have a little talk with Wolf. She's right about one thing. Wolf wouldn't be sniffing around bees unless he thought something else was going on."

Voices outside drew our attention. Alex dropped his arms, and we walked over to the kitchen door. No one was there.

"It's coming from the backyard," I said.

We hurried to the sunroom, where we spotted Bernie and Mars unloading coolers from a truck parked in the alley. With the gate open, we could see the hound dog logo of The Laughing Hound on the truck. Daisy raced around the backyard, happy to be home.

We walked out to help them. Bernie had brought stacks of cutting boards with grooves to catch juices from the meats. I carried them to a table next to the grill. Mars walked back to Bernie's house to fetch his grill. Francie and Duke came over through the gate between our properties. Nina heard Mars rolling Bernie's grill along the street and came back with him, loaded down with pitchers of some kind of cocktail.

I hurried back inside to slice pineapples to throw on the grill. I cut off the tops and the bottoms, then attacked the sides and removed the little brown eyes that remained on the pineapples. I cut them into lovely slices and tossed them into a bowl so Bernie could add them to the grill. In my opinion, they didn't need any seasoning because the heat would intensify the yummy sweetness. As I brought them out to the grill, Parker and Trula showed up carrying platters of cheeses and crackers, followed closely by

Humphrey, carrying a big pot of macaroni and cheese. His not-so-charming mother accompanied him.

"Humphrey!" I said. "You must have a gas stove. Hello, Mrs. Brown."

Her nostrils flared in disgust, and she muttered, "Good evening, Sophie."

"Actually, my house is entirely electric," said Humphrey, "but for obvious reasons, the funeral home has a generator, so I cooked this there."

Nina overheard him. She whispered to me, "I am not eating anything cooked in a funeral home!"

"Good idea," I whispered back. "He probably baked it in the crematorium."

From the look on her face, she did not appreciate my sarcasm.

Other neighbors began to arrive with their dogs and before we knew it, a party was in full swing with everyone pitching in.

Trula joined me at the beverage table. "Thank you so much for hosting this, Sophie. It's a brilliant way to use up the food that will spoil. Parker is a nut for cheese. He thinks cheese is a food group. We kept these in a cooler to be sure they'd be good, but I'm thrilled to get rid of them."

"It looks like quite an exotic assortment."

"It is." She lowered her voice. "I'm glad we have an alternative to Natasha's appetizer."

"I didn't see her arrive. What did she bring?" I tried to sound upbeat but was almost afraid to find out what she had concocted.

"Well, she glided in with Jay Charles on her arm!" She winked at me. "But you meant the food. She went to a lot of trouble to cut up a watermelon like a basket."

"Those are cute!"

"Not when they're filled with a watermelon, olive, and mushroom salad."

My eyes met hers. "No one will eat it. Ugh. At least she didn't add anchovies. One of us will have to distract her while the other one spoons it into a little trash bag so she'll think it was eaten."

"That's probably best . . ." Her voice trailed off.

At that very moment, I heard someone cry out in pain. From where we were standing, we had a perfect view of the little drama that unfolded when Lavinia Brown twisted her ankle and grabbed Jay Charles as she fell to the grass.

"Lavinia!" he cried.

She gazed up at him. "How silly of me. I fear I have broken my ankle."

Jay immediately knelt next to her and palpated her ankle.

Natasha edged up to Trula and me and hissed, "Did you see that? The nerve of that woman. She did that on purpose. Broken ankle, my fanny! He came with me!"

I felt sorry for Natasha. She was obnoxious and thought she was always right, but she continued struggling to achieve her dreams, no matter what. Most people would have given up by now, happy to have a successful local television show. And now she had set her sights on Jay, but she was being outsmarted by an older woman.

Trula elbowed me. I nodded and hurried off to find a trash bag while Lavinia held Natasha's attention.

Keeping a close eye on Natasha, I scooped a generous amount of the questionable salad into a trash bag, tied a knot in the top, and hustled it off to the garbage can just inside the gate.

When I returned, Lavinia was seated in a chair with her ankle up. Jay Charles attended her solicitously while Natasha stood over her like a vulture, saying, "It's not swelling."

I returned to Trula, who was stifling giggles. "Can you believe the two of them are fighting over Jay?" she asked.

"He's quite a catch, of course, but who would be that obvious?"

"I hope Natasha won't pull a stunt now to draw Jay's attention to her. At least I managed to *consume* some of her salad."

Trula's gaze shifted. "I'm surprised that Kelsey has the nerve to be here. So tragic about Hollis. Parker and I are shaken to the core."

"I invited Kelsey."

"*You* did?"

"She's had a very tragic life. You wouldn't believe what she has been through."

"Oh, I doubt that. She's even more of a threat now that she's a wealthy widow."

Why did Trula have to be such a snob? I couldn't help myself. "*I'm* single."

Trula snorted. "You're not chasing my husband, sweetheart. Kelsey had the nerve to call Parker and ask him to represent her. At least she's dressed decently tonight. I guess I'm overly sensitive because I've been spending a lot of time at the library. It breaks my heart every time I see Cindy there. She does a good job of hiding her feelings and keeping a stiff upper lip, but when I think how that young woman came into her life and ousted her like last week's leftovers, well, all I can say is that I hope some young Twinkie does the same to Kelsey someday so she'll know how it feels."

When she put it that way I understood why she disliked Kelsey so much. "I guess you spent a lot of time with Cindy?"

"Parker, Hollis, and Gage were law partners for a long time. We celebrated together and partied together. Of course we knew one another well. Now it's down to poor Parker. I don't know how he'll manage to handle their caseload all by himself." Trula whispered, "He's talking about bringing Alex on board!"

I didn't know if Alex would like that. He seemed to enjoy being his own boss and calling the shots. But maybe I was wrong about that. "Are you still volunteering at the library?"

"On Wednesdays. Promise you won't breathe a word of this, but I'm doing genealogical research into Parker's family. It's so hard to find a great gift for him. He's related to the Revolutionary War spy John Dixon. I thought it would be a wonderful gift to have his family tree painted by a local artist."

The name John Dixon sounded familiar to me. "Parker will love that. Who was John Dixon? The only one I know is the ghost on Prince Street."

"That's him! Can you imagine being related to someone who was so brave? Parker would fall apart on his first day as a spy. He definitely didn't get the bravery gene from his ancestors. I haven't found the genealogical link between them yet, but I still have some digging to do. I've gotten to know Jay a lot better, too. He's often there with me searching for information on his house." She paused and watched her husband talking with Kelsey. "Now, tell me why we're calling these charcuterie boards. If I recall my French correctly, and I think I do, charcuterie means processed meats like salamis and pâtés."

"I'm no French expert, but I believe you're right. We could call them storm boards if you like that better."

Trula laughed. "I have no objection to those fabulous steaks Bernie is grilling. And it looks like he has some lovely sausages and chicken on the grill, too. And I have to admit that I do like this sort of communal style of eating at long tables with boards of food bringing us all together. Such a fun change from formal dinners. It's sort of a pop-up dinner, isn't it? No one knows what will be served or who will be there."

She drifted away, and I had an awful feeling that she was looking for someone more interested in bashing Kelsey.

Madison sidled over to me and murmured, "Can you believe a woman Lavinia's age pulling that kind of stunt? I swear I would *die* before I did something like that to get a man's attention! I'm glad to see that Kelsey is appropriately dressed tonight. I saw her at the hardware store the other day and honest to goodness, the men couldn't take their eyes off of her blouse down to there and her skirt up to you know where." She laughed. "Listen to me. I'm beginning to sound like my grandmother!"

"Take the time to talk with Kelsey. You might like her more than you expect."

"That would be the gracious thing to do, wouldn't it? I'll go do that right now."

Jay Charles moseyed up and helped himself to a drink. "I'm so sorry that I haven't anything to contribute. I don't cook."

"Don't worry about that. It's all in good fun. Bernie needed to use up the meat he's cooking."

"Actually, it's kind of nice for me. Since my wife died, I eat mostly takeout. It's good, but not quite the same as a home-cooked meal. I hope you'll let me reciprocate some time by taking you out to dinner."

I made a mental note to include him for dinner at my house more often. "That's very kind, but not at all necessary."

"Sophie," he said, "I understand that you were the one who found Hollis in the street."

"I'm afraid so."

"Was he able to speak?"

"Yes, but he didn't say much. He was having difficulty breathing."

"No clue or hint as to what might have caused his condition?"

"Not really."

Jay rubbed the back of his neck and gazed at the ground.
"Hollis and I were friends for a long time. I was after him
for years to shed weight and exercise. If he'd had a heart attack, I would have said I had seen it coming. But I find the
circumstances around his death to be peculiar. I pulled
some strings and got a look at the autopsy report, which
definitely indicates inhalation of some kind of poison.
There are indications of an underlying issue that may have
made him more sensitive."

"That's what Wolf said."

"Sophie, Hollis wasn't an idiot. It's not difficult to imagine that anyone could mistakenly spray an aerosol insecticide in a manner that could blow back into one's face. But if
that happened, anyone would have stepped away for fresh
air, thus reducing the amount of exposure. Had Hollis inhaled a great deal of insecticide, it would have made him
sick, but probably wouldn't have killed him."

I understood where he was going with this line of
thought. "And wouldn't he have told the EMTs if that had
happened?"

"Exactly!" Jay beamed at me. "And he wouldn't have
sprayed bees in the dark, after the underground dinner."

"Not unless Kelsey was afraid and he did it to pacify
her. But she claims he came home, took a sleeping pill with
a drink, and went to bed."

"That sounds more like him. Hollis, for all his wonderful traits, was not much of a hands-on kind of guy. He was
a pick-up-the-phone type. Even when it was something as
easy as trimming bushes or raking leaves, Hollis preferred
to pay someone to do it." Jay licked his lips. "I hope you
don't think I'm criticizing Hollis. He was always very

busy. I was raised to do things for myself. More than once I pitched in because Cindy was undertaking something that Hollis should have done for her around the house."

"We all have our priorities." I paused for a moment as a thought occurred to me. "If Hollis sprayed the bees, wouldn't the cans still be in the trash?"

"How foolish of me. Of course! Excuse me, Sophie."

Jay hustled toward Kelsey. He gave her a big hug, and I was under the impression that he might be expressing his condolences.

The evening air was cooler than normal, probably a consequence of the storm that had passed through. Mars turned off the grill and built a fire in the outdoor fireplace, while I walked around lighting candles and lanterns.

There was no question in my mind that I preferred life with electricity. It wasn't even close. But at that very moment, in the company of good friends, with the scent of grilled meats and pineapple in the air, the crackling fire and flickering candles added a certain charm that electric lights couldn't match.

I was setting up the ice-cream sundae boards when Jay sidled over toward me. He whispered, "Kelsey confirms exactly what you told me. Hollis took a sleeping pill with a glass of Scotch and went up to bed."

Jay pulled out a pen and wrote something on the back of a paper napkin. "I'm going over to look through their trash. Call me if Kelsey leaves before I come back."

"Maybe you should take someone with you."

"I'll be fine."

"Mars!" I called. "Could you give me a hand?"

He ambled over with a tall, icy drink in his hand. "What do you think? I like the fire, even though it's the middle of the summer. Sort of like a campfire, it adds ambiance."

"Could you serve dessert?" I asked. "I'll be right back."

"Where are you going?"

"Shh. We don't want to draw any attention." As soon as the words came out of my mouth I regretted them. There were few things I could have said that would have intrigued him more.

Chapter 14

Dear Sophie,
My wife insists on having a refrigerator and a
freezer. I think that's a waste of money. Freezers
use a lot of juice!
    Electricity Miser in Humbug, Arizona

Dear Electricity Miser,
Those appliances can be electricity hogs, but you'll
save money by filling them up. Full refrigerators
and freezers stay cool longer and use less energy
than empty ones. If your freezer doesn't have much
in it, fill empty gallon bottles with water and put
them in the freezer to help keep it cool.
    Sophie

Jay whispered, "We're going to paw through the Habermans' trash."

Mars's head snapped up like someone lit a firecracker behind him. "I'm in! Nina can serve the dessert. Hey, Bernie!"

Good heavens, before I knew it, everyone except Kelsey would be digging through her trash. "Shh!"

Mars whispered to Bernie, and I knew I was licked.

Mars handed me his drink. "No one touches this. It's too good to throw out."

Armed with a lantern and flashlights, Jay, Mars, Bernie, and Daisy not so subtly left the dinner.

Nina joined me. I handed her a board. "Could you set this on the table, please?"

The large cutting board contained salted caramel ice cream, chocolate chocolate-chip ice cream, and vanilla bean ice cream in good-sized bowls, along with hot fudge sauce, strawberries, blueberries, chopped pecans, almond cookies, chocolate sandwich cookies with a creamy middle, and hazelnut-filled wafers. "Thanks for helping me serve. I love that everyone can take what they want. Sort of like an ice-cream bar, but it's at the table."

"I'm not serving unless you tell me what's going on."

Why did I have such nosy friends? I motioned her closer and told her what was happening.

Nina shuddered. "And I wasn't invited?"

"Really?" I whispered. "You want to dig through trash?"

In the glow of the lantern I saw her wrinkle her nose.

"Maybe not." She took the tray and brought it to the table, where I heard "oohs" and "aahs."

On the next large cutting board, I placed bowls of dulce de leche ice cream, mango sorbet, and hazelnut gelato. To that I added chopped walnuts and a bowl of caramel sauce. I placed handfuls of chocolate chip cookies, soft oatmeal cookies, and peanut butter cookies in between the bowls. I scattered banana and kiwi slices, as well as strawberries, in the remaining space.

Nina plucked a peanut butter cookie from the tray and noshed on it. "Nothing better than peanut butter," she muttered with a mouthful.

I was making the rounds with after-dinner decaf coffee and tea when Natasha stood up, raised a hand against her forehead like an overly dramatic star in an old movie, and said in an fake Southern accent, "Oh my! I feel faint." And with that, she crumpled to the floor.

Everyone moved their chairs away from her. She lay still as death.

Humphrey raced around the long table, wedged his hand under her neck, and started mouth-to-mouth resuscitation. On the other side of the table, away from the fire, they were lit mostly by the light of the lanterns. The crowd had stopped chattering. We waited in silence for Humphrey to revive her.

Suddenly, Natasha lifted her right hand and slid it along Humphrey's head, almost as though she were holding him in a romantic moment.

"Are they kissing?" asked Nina.

Humphrey had stopped taking breaths.

I heard a chuckle or two.

Humphrey finally pulled away but remained kneeling beside her.

Her eyes were still closed when she murmured, "Ohhh, Jay!"

"Can you sit up now, Natasha?" asked Humphrey.

She opened her eyes, looked straight at Humphrey in horror, and sucked in air. Natasha sat up and said, loud as could be, "I believe I passed out. What happened?"

Humphrey helped her stand, but I couldn't help noticing that she brushed his helpful hand off her arm the second she was on her feet. She ambled over to me, leaned toward my ear, and said, "Please tell me I didn't just kiss Humphrey."

I didn't have to tell her because at that moment, Jay and his entourage returned. Natasha looked seriously queasy.

Holding a pot of coffee, I walked over and sniffed them but didn't pick up any stinky garbage odors. "Well?"

"Surprisingly little trash," said Mars.

"What about the bee spray?"

Jay shook his head. "Not a single can."

I stared at the three of them for a long moment. "Then what did he inhale?"

"The cans could still be inside the house," said Mars.

Bernie shot me a look. "Or she could have gotten rid of them elsewhere."

I hated what they were thinking. Was Kelsey the poor young woman who seemed clueless and helpless? Or the calculating vixen that Trula and others thought? I had always imagined myself as a pretty good judge of character, but Kelsey had me confused. She could be a combination of the two. Softly I said, "Or someone else killed him."

Jay appeared skeptical.

"That's right, Soph," said Mars. "They came home from the underground dinner. An unknown assailant broke into the house and sprayed Hollis with bee spray, but Kelsey knows nothing about it."

I was sorely tempted to stick out my tongue at him. He didn't have to be so sarcastic. "I'm just exploring the possibilities." In a whisper I hissed, "She says she didn't kill him."

Mars tilted his head at me. "You bought that story about her horrendous childhood and now you're trying to side with her because there's nothing you love more than an underdog who needs your help."

There was no way I was going to agree with him. But as soon as the power returned, I would do some checking up on her background. Surely the murders of her aunt and sister had made the newspapers. I ought to be able to dig that up. And then it would be Mars eating crow.

Mars eyed the drink he had left. "I trust no one spit in this?"

"I'm tempted to now. What are you drinking?"

"Nina brought them. They're called A Day at the Beach. Apparently she made them because you're not going to the beach."

Bernie wrapped an arm around my shoulders. "Isn't it time you had a bite to eat?"

It was. I helped myself to steak, sausage, coleslaw, pineapple, some of the cheeses, and one of Nina's concoctions. Even though Mars scooted over to make room for me, I passed by him and wedged in next to Alex.

That put me right beside Natasha.

"I am so embarrassed that I could just curl up and expire on the spot. Did anyone notice?"

"Everyone." It was mean of me. But it was the truth. "Look at her."

"Who?"

"Humphrey's mother! Didn't you see that oh-I-twisted-my-ankle stunt she pulled earlier to get Jay's attention?"

"Is that why you suddenly crumpled to the floor? You thought you'd one-up her and seduce him with a kiss right in front of everyone?"

"You don't know how hard it is to get a man's attention these days. I'm as perfect as a woman can be, but I can't compete with someone like Kelsey. Look at Parker drooling over her. Bleah."

"Why, Natasha Smith."

"Shhh. You know I hate it when you use my last name. Seriously, though, wouldn't Jay and I make the perfect couple? I love those bow ties he wears, and he's just so gentlemanly with the most exquisite manners." She paused. "Sophie, I have finally figured it out."

"That Jay is perfect for you?"

Natasha tossed her hair over her shoulder. "That too, but I meant that I cannot believe I overlooked the obvious for so long. I suppose I've sort of been doing it all along with my show, but I always thought it was about being a domestic diva."

"It's not?" I tried the drink Nina had mixed and understood why Mars liked it so much.

"In a manner of speaking. I saw a book this morning by a nobody. Just a complete nobody! It's basically a picture book about entertaining. She sets up a glamorous photo of a tablescape for various events like holidays or a romantic dinner for two, and provides recipes for the food and the proper etiquette. I could do it in my sleep, Sophie. And I realized that books on how to entertain are how Martha got started!" She frowned at me. "Now don't go stealing this idea from me."

"Aren't you stealing it from Martha and the complete nobody?"

"No! That's entirely different." She sounded annoyed.

"So you're going to become a photographer?"

"Don't be ridiculous. It's about etiquette and lifestyle. Not just about recipes or entertaining, but that's part of it. It's bigger, though. It's about how you live your life. For instance, I notice that you still haven't dropped off a dish at Kelsey's. Very bad manners, Sophie."

I swallowed a melt-in-your-mouth tender bite of beef. "I presume you have already delivered your Coca-Cola cake?"

"Sophie! There was no electricity!"

Why, why, why had I sat down next to Natasha?

"You see," she said, "etiquette and manners are part of it, too. For instance, just like you, people don't know what to do when someone dies. I can tell them! I have the gorgeous house. All I have to do is show people how to live like me."

At that very moment, I sorely wanted to tell her off. "Excuse me, Natasha." I took my plate and drink and whispered to Alex, "Scoot over, please."

He didn't even ask why. I sat on the other side of him and planted a big smooch on his cheek.

If the light had been better, I suspect I might have seen him blush. He wasn't much for public affection.

Neighbors lingered, laughing and chatting. Kelsey probably felt it was too light-hearted for what she was going through, but I noticed that Francie had taken Kelsey under her wing.

Slowly our ranks diminished as neighbors headed home.

At midnight, when Alex offered to walk Kelsey to her house, Nina jumped up and said she'd go with them. She tugged at me. "Come on. Let's stretch our legs a little."

Jay joined us.

I had to admit that it felt like an adventure. The moon offered the most light. When a cloud passed over it, our world turned pitch-dark. Only a few houses on our street still had gas lanterns by their front doors. While they were charming, they didn't offer much light, and the flickering took us back a century. It was like walking the streets in an old movie set.

Inside the houses, we saw an occasional flashlight beam sweep past a window. It was totally creepy.

"Are you sure you're okay staying by yourself?" I asked Kelsey.

"You'll think I'm a total sap but sitting alone with a solitary candle sort of matches my mood. I think about my parents, and my sister. And about Hollis and Sassy. And for just a little while, it almost feels like they're with me, watching over me."

How sad. The poor woman had lost everyone she ever loved. Maybe I would want to sit by myself in the dark with a candle if I were in her shoes. Instead of fighting her thoughts and sadness, Kelsey faced it head-on. No one could know how they would deal with that situation.

We walked up to the Haberman house. Kelsey unlocked the door. She lighted a lantern that she had left on a console in the foyer.

It lit the small room, casting eerie shadows on the wall. Even our reflections in the mirror were spooky.

I was being silly. Why did darkness make everything seem sinister?

And at that moment, we heard a door creak.

Chapter 15

Dear Natasha,
My ex-husband has died. I'm not friends with his
new wife, but I spent more years with my husband
than she has. Much as I hate the old buzzard now,
I did once love him and am devastated by his
death. Is it appropriate for me to go to the funeral?
    Old Buzzard's Ex in Dead Mans Crossing,
    Indiana

Dear Old Buzzard's Ex,
You should absolutely attend the funeral. Take care
not to be ugly to anyone, especially the new wife.
Express your sympathy, but remember that you are
no longer a member of the family, and don't up-
stage the new wife.
    Natasha

We could have dealt with the eerie creaking if a door
hadn't slammed shut. Nina screamed like she had
seen the devil himself.

"A breeze must have caught the door," Alex said calmly.

Holding the lantern in her hands so that the candle caused shadows to flicker on her face, Kelsey said, "It sounded like the back door."

Jay and Alex didn't hesitate to rush toward the rear of the house. I was right behind them. We burst into the kitchen. The door was straight ahead.

It creaked again when Jay opened it. Alex shone his flashlight around the backyard. The beam crossed the gate to the alley, which hung open, gently swinging in the soft breeze.

Alex ran out in the yard.

Jay and I followed. The three of us stopped in the alley. I held my lantern high while Alex pointed the flashlight in both directions. "Someone was definitely in the house."

"We'd better search it." Jay led the way back into the yard.

"Definitely." Alex latched the gate securely. "It's unlikely anyone is still inside, but you never know."

We walked back to the house, where Kelsey and Nina waited in the foyer.

I told them what we saw. "Do you think we should call Wolf?"

"No!" Kelsey's eyes grew large. "Oh, please don't call him."

I tried to reason with her. "Kelsey, what do you think will happen if Alex and Jay find someone in the house? Besides, they'll barely be able to make out anything with only flashlights and lanterns. I can tell you one thing, there's no way I would sleep in this house tonight unless Wolf cleared it first."

"Okay," Kelsey whispered. "I hadn't thought about it that way." Kelsey murmured to Alex, "You do the talking, all right?"

*   *   *

Forty minutes later, Wolf had gone through the house and declared it safe.

We all reconvened in the elegant living room, which smacked of the nineteenth century. I could just imagine a family entertaining friends there by gaslight and candlelight.

Wolf sat down on a settee and bent forward toward Kelsey. "Do you have any idea who it could have been?"

She looked at Alex, who nodded.

"No."

"Is there a possibility that you left a door unlocked?" asked Wolf.

"I don't think so."

"Who else has keys to the house?"

Kelsey shrugged.

"Do you keep a spare key outside somewhere?"

"No."

Wolf always kept his cool. I often thought he would be a dangerous poker player. I suspected he was frustrated, but he didn't show it.

"Okay. I guess we're through here. Tomorrow in the light of day you should have a look around to see if anything is missing. If you find something is gone, let me know."

Kelsey nodded.

We all stood to leave. I walked over to Kelsey. "Are you certain you're okay sleeping here by yourself tonight? You're welcome to stay over at my house."

"Oh, darlin', that's so nice of you. I'll be fine. I've been through much worse. Thanks for walking me home. I'll see you in the morning, Alex."

We left her house and turned to walk to Jay's house next door, but he stopped us and said good night.

"You don't even have a flashlight. Let us walk you to your door," said Alex.

"That's not at all necessary. Thank you for offering."

"At least take a lantern," I offered, holding mine out to him.

"I can see fine. Thank you for a lovely evening, Sophie." He turned abruptly, hurried to his door, and let himself in. We heard the door lock clank. I watched the first-floor windows for the mellow glow of a candle or the beam of a flashlight but didn't see one.

"Did anyone else think that was odd?" asked Nina.

"It has to be black as pitch in there," I said.

Alex, who wasn't the gossipy type at all, looked up at the second-floor windows. "He didn't want us in his house."

"That's for sure!" said Wong.

Nina gasped. "I wonder what he's hiding!"

It probably wasn't a secret that Jay was hearing voices in his house and thought he had ghosts. But he had spoken to me about it privately as though he didn't want others to know. I studied the building. Surely the alleged ghosts couldn't be the reason he didn't want us to help him find his way inside. If I thought I had ghosts other than Mars's Aunt Faye, and I wasn't sure about her, I would certainly want some kind of light on. But everyone was different.

Wolf and Wong said good night, but I noticed that they took their time getting into their cars.

"I'm off then. Are you sure you two will be okay walking back by yourselves?" asked Alex.

"It's not even a full block," I said. "Nina and I will be fine. Besides, there are two cops sitting right there."

"What time is the Widow Haberman meeting with you tomorrow?" asked Nina.

Alex was silent for a moment. "Did you want to come?"

"Yes! Could I?" Nina asked enthusiastically.

Alex planted a kiss on her cheek. "No." He kissed me as well, but on the lips. "Thanks for dinner, Sophie. See you tomorrow."

Alex took off at a leisurely pace, as though he was enjoying the quiet night.

When Nina and I walked away, I noticed that Wolf and Wong didn't turn off our street until we were within yards of our homes.

"Do you feel like a time traveler?" asked Nina.

"A little bit. Especially in the Haberman drawing room."

"Sophie, I'm going to come right out and say it. Were you out of your mind to put Kelsey and Alex together?" asked Nina.

"What are you talking about?"

"The Widow Haberman will be looking for her next husband very soon. You handed her another Hollis, except much better looking."

"Don't be ridiculous."

"Consider yourself warned," said Nina.

"Have you been talking with Trula? She's very bitter about Kelsey marrying Hollis."

"For heaven's sake, Sophie! No one likes a husband thief."

"No, they don't. You're right about that. And on the surface at least, that's the way it appears. But don't you feel just a little bit sorry for her?"

"I do! She's had an awful life. Assuming that any of that wild story is true. For all we know, she was a perfectly average child who grew up in a nice suburb and her parents are still alive and living in the same Cape Cod with a white picket fence. But you're my best friend, and I'm telling you that she's willing to find solace in Alex's arms."

I laughed aloud. "Really? You don't know Alex better than that? Mr. Straight-Laced? I happen to know for a fact that lawyers cannot sleep with their clients. It's considered unethical, like shrinks sleeping with their patients. Alex may be sympathetic to her, he might even buy her lunch, but there's no way he will succumb to whatever siren-like charms she presents to him."

"Hmm. I suppose he is stronger than Mars in that respect."

"Oh! That's a low blow." Mars and Natasha had set up housekeeping together shortly after our divorce. A lot of people thought Natasha had stolen him from me. Of course, I knew what was happening in our marriage. Mars and I had put so much energy into our work that we seldom saw each other and drifted apart. We all coped with life's unfortunate twists in our own ways. Call me naïve, but I preferred to imagine that Natasha had been available when Mars and I split. "I thought you were my friend."

"I am. But you're not listening to me. Beware of Kelseys dressed as damsels in distress."

That made me laugh. When we reached my house, the kitchen was immaculate. We found Mars, Bernie, and Francie lounging in the backyard by the fire drinking Nina's cocktails.

Nina and I settled into chairs around the fire.

Bernie poured drinks for us. "What took you so long?"

Nina launched into a detailed explanation.

Mars said, "Jay thinks Hollis was murdered. He's a pathologist. I have to believe he knows what he's talking about."

"Jay and my husband have known each other since their med school days. Sometimes he makes me a little nervous," Nina chuckled, "because he's so proper. I've never seen him truly relaxed like we are now. He'd be sitting up straight and wearing a bow tie. But he has a brilliant mind."

"Have you spoken with Wolf about this?" asked Francie.

"He's concerned," I said. "I gather there are two big issues. Why are the bees inside the house dead while the outside bees are mostly alive? And how did Hollis manage to inhale enough of the pesticides to kill him unless there was some kind of foul play?"

Bernie relaxed on a chaise with his feet up. "He had a drink and took a sleeping pill before he went to bed. Some of those sleeping pills are pretty powerful. Could she, or someone else, have sprayed bee spray directly on him while he slept? Or would that wake a person?"

"Did you say, '*Or someone else*'?" I asked. "You're thinking Kelsey is having an affair?"

"It wouldn't be the first time the December half of a May—December romance bit the dust for that reason." Francie looked up at the stars. "Maybe he was waiting for her in the house tonight and panicked when he heard voices."

Chapter 16

Dear Natasha,
I was born and raised in the South. Recently, I received an invitation to a "bring your own meat" cookout. Did my mama overlook teaching me about this curious event when she taught me etiquette?
Foodie in Pie Town, New Mexico

Dear Foodie,
Natasha is still trying to catch her breath from the notion of a party to which guests bring their own meal. Your mama did not overlook anything in your education.
Natasha

Nina, who had been comfortably ensconced, jumped forward, nearly spilling her drink. "I bet you're exactly right! That makes so much sense. We ought to stake out her house to find out whom she's seeing. Then we'd know who murdered Hollis!"

I really hated to admit that Nina might be on to something. I desperately wanted to point out that even if she *was* having an affair, it didn't mean she or her lover had killed Hollis. But Hollis had stumbled out of their house very early in the morning. Who else would have been there at that hour except for Kelsey and possibly an accomplice? My heart sank. I really hadn't thought she was responsible for Hollis's death. And then out of nowhere, the obvious became horrifically clear to me.

"Cindy," I said. "That's who. What if Hollis didn't change the locks? She could still have a key to the house."

"I admit that she's angry enough with Hollis to do some harm," said Mars. "But he was Gavin's dad. For that reason alone, I can't see her killing him."

"And what about Kelsey?" asked Bernie. "Cindy lets herself into the Haberman house in the dead of night, sneaks into the master bedroom, but Kelsey doesn't wake up? Even when Cindy sprays her with bee spray?"

"Have any of you geniuses considered that Parker, Hollis, and Gage were law partners?" asked Francie. "And now Parker is the only one standing?"

"But Gage's death was an accident," Nina protested.

"Really?" Francie emptied the last of her drink. "How do you know that?"

"Parker!" shouted Nina. "Kelsey's lover is Parker!"

Bernie, Mars, and I broke into laughter.

"Staid old Parker?" chuckled Mars. "While we're imagining things, maybe she had an affair with Jay, too!"

It was closing in on two in the morning, and we were too tired to think straight. On that note, Mars put out the fire, and we all headed for our beds.

I expected to be exhausted after the party. But all I could think of was Kelsey. Some part of me just couldn't accept Kelsey as the black widow, swooping in on men to kill them and collect their estates. It happened. But surely Hollis hadn't been so susceptible that he fell for a scam like that. And I couldn't imagine Kelsey being that wicked. Nina's theory made sense. In fact, it was the only theory that made any sense—so far. I made up my mind to sleuth a little deeper. Like it or not, I believed Kelsey.

I drifted off, only to be awakened at just past three in the morning when bells rang, machines jumped back to life, and lights came on again. I turned over and slept, secure in the knowledge that life would be normal again when I woke.

In the morning, Nina and I slept late. When we rose, I fed Mochie salmon and made lattes for Nina and myself. Since we were technically on vacation, even if we weren't at the beach, we agreed to meet in an hour for brunch at a café on the waterfront.

I indulged in a long, hot shower, pinned my hair up to stay cool, and dressed in a turquoise twill skirt, white sleeveless blouse, and sandals. I missed having Daisy to take along but hoped she was having fun with Mars.

Nina and I met on the sidewalk in front of her house and walked down to the waterfront. It was a glorious day, without a cloud in the blue sky. We found a table with a red umbrella overlooking the Potomac River and truly felt like we were vacationing.

We both ordered their specialty fried chicken and waffles with butter and maple syrup. Decadent, but we *were* on vacation after all. Nina sipped coffee, I switched to hot black tea with milk, and we people-watched when we could tear our eyes away from the water.

When our waiter served our meal, I noticed that his nametag said, *Chadwick.* He was about Gavin's age, friendly and chatty, telling us chicken and waffles were his favorite dish.

I took a chance and said, "I hear you have a girlfriend."

He stopped dead. "Do I know you?"

"I don't think so. Gavin Haberman used to be a neighbor. I heard what happened. Are you grounded, too?"

He frowned at me. "Noooo."

"You didn't get caught when you snuck out in the middle of the night on Thursday? That was a lucky break! Don't worry, I won't mention that to Gavin's mom."

His brow furrowed. "Gosh, I hope not. I just got off being grounded. I'd hate to be grounded again, especially for something I didn't do." He started to walk away.

"Chadwick!" I called.

"Yes, ma'am?"

"Let me get this clear. You and Gavin didn't sneak out on Thursday night to meet up with your girlfriend?"

He stared at me with clear blue eyes. "I didn't go anywhere on Thursday night. I was still grounded. Excuse me." He hurried to another table, where a rude diner was holding his coffee mug in the air.

"What was that about?" asked Nina.

"Cindy told me that Gavin sneaked out with his buddy Chadwick on Thursday night after the underground dinner."

Nina was about to take a bite of chicken and stopped her fork midair. "I love Gavin. Bet he has his own girlfriend now, but he didn't want to tell Cindy."

I hoped she was right. But I wondered which one of them had lied. Had Gavin fabricated a story to tell his mother? Or had Cindy invented it for my benefit? I shook it off. Cindy had no reason to tell me a story about Gavin's misbehavior. In my eagerness to exonerate Kelsey, I was imagining killers everywhere.

On the way back, we couldn't help noticing a collection of funeral foods on Kelsey's doorstep.

"Do you think she doesn't know those are out here?" asked Nina.

"She's probably not home." Nevertheless, I banged the door knocker.

Kelsey opened the door. "Oh my goodness. Did you two bring all this food?"

"It was on your doorstep," said Nina.

Kelsey bit her upper lip. "No one is knocking. They don't want to talk to me. Everyone thinks I murdered Hollis. How can they be afraid of me but still bring food?"

Nina giggled, breaking the tension. "That's Southerners for you. Never let it be said that they didn't bring food in your time of need!"

We left Kelsey to find a way to fit it all in her fridge and strolled on to our houses.

Apparently news traveled fast among teens, even when one of them wasn't allowed to use his cell phone. When I got home, Gavin was sitting on the stoop outside my kitchen door.

"Hi, Gavin. Looking for a mowing job?"

"Not today." He looked up at me with fear. "Um, I heard you talked with Chadwick today."

"I did. He seems like a nice guy." I sat down on the stoop beside him.

Gavin shifted to face me. "The thing is that I didn't go anywhere with Chadwick that night. I lied to my mom. Maybe . . . maybe for old times' sake you could avoid mentioning that to her?"

"She'd be pretty upset if she knew you lied to her, huh?"

"Yeah." His lips tightened. "The divorce was really hard for her. I mean, Mom's still the greatest, but she's kinda tense. You know, hyper."

"So you don't want to upset her." I eyed him. "Aren't you grounded?"

"Technically."

I tried to hide a grin. "What exactly does that mean?"

"Okay, I'm grounded. But Mom doesn't understand. I can't tell her about it because she'll flip out."

About what? I waited to hear what he would say next.

"See, that night when I snuck out of the house, I went to my dad's house."

Oh no. Surely he hadn't murdered his dad. I held my breath.

"I saw him at the underground dinner, you know? And her, too. My mom calls her 'the one-who-shall-remain-nameless,' like she's evil and we can't even say her name. My dad tried to talk with me at the dinner, but I kept avoiding him. I would just walk away or pretend like he wasn't there."

He wiped his eyes with the backs of his fingers and whispered, "I didn't know he would be dead the next day."

I wrapped an arm around his shoulders. "No one could know that."

He buried his face in my shoulder and cried.

He lifted his head, sniffled, and wiped his eyes with the backs of his wrists.

"She knew. The one-who-shall-remain-nameless knew."

"Why would you think that?" I asked gently.

"Because I saw her that night."

Chapter 17

Dear Natasha,
Honeybees have so many problems. I don't want to be stung, but I want to help them thrive. I love clover. Who could possibly be against the gentle plant that produces luck in the form of four leaves? And I let dandelions grow, too, to help the honeybees. But my neighbor is outraged and has accused me of having a weed-infested yard. I think it's my business what I grow in my yard. What do you think?
  Bee's Knees in Clover, South Carolina

Dear Bee's Knees,
Have you lost your mind? Do you know how dandelions blow in the wind and spread? And they're near to impossible to eradicate. Clean up your yard, Bee's Knees!
  Natasha

"**Y**ou mean you saw Kelsey at the dinner?" I asked. "I saw her when I went to my dad's house. I guess I was spying."

"You guess?"

"I didn't know exactly what I would do when I got there. I thought I might knock on the door and talk to my dad. But then I was afraid *she* might answer the door, and that would have been awful. I couldn't take seeing her there where my mom should be."

A shiver went up my spine. I didn't want to report him for murder. "Did you have a key, Gavin?"

He nodded. "Sure. *I* lived there before she came along. It was my house. My yard. My tree house and my basketball hoop. But I didn't go in. I sat in the tree house until she left."

That caught me by surprise. "Kelsey left the house?"

"Yeah, the lights went out in the master bedroom. I thought they had gone to bed."

"But you didn't leave?"

"I know it's silly, but I spent a lot of time in the backyard as a kid. So I was kind of just sitting in my old tree house when she walked out of the house. I thought she had caught me, but she walked right on by like I didn't exist. I guess she didn't notice me in the dark."

"What time was that?"

Gavin shrugged in the "Who cares?" way that teenagers do. "I followed her."

"Gavin!"

"See? You said that just like my mom would have."

"Where did she go?"

"A house on Duke Street."

"And?"

"She went inside, and I started getting texts from my mom, who had discovered that I threw my comforter over pillows so it would look like I was asleep. So I finally went home."

"Then you lied to your mom."

"You don't know what it's been like, Mrs. Winston. I knew she'd flip out. And she'd have told my dad. He would have hated me for following the one-who-shall-remain-nameless. It was wrong to sneak out, but if they all knew I was spying on my dad, I would have been grounded until I was thirty-five."

They would have been upset for a lot of reasons. But Gavin didn't seem to realize the grave importance of what he'd just told me. Kelsey could have exposed Hollis to a pesticide and left the house. That would explain why she hadn't been impacted as severely as Hollis.

"Gavin, can you describe the house the one-who-shall-remain-nameless went to?"

"Sure. It was blue, and it had a weird door knocker in the shape of an upside-down octopus." He gazed at me. "Or are they right-side-up when their heads are down?"

That was more like the old Gavin I knew. "All right. I'm not going to tell your mom. But if she asks me, I'm not going to lie for you." That was fair, wasn't it?

"Deal. I can live with that. You think the one-who-shall-remain-nameless poisoned him and then left the house so she wouldn't have to sleep next to a dead man?"

Ewww! "Good grief, Gavin! I hope not. But if you remember anything else, you let me know. Okay?"

He stood up and nodded. "Thanks for not ratting on me." He looked away and didn't face me when he asked, "Are you on to her? Are you going to prove that she murdered my dad?"

I was at a total loss. How should I answer that? I stood up. "Wolf is looking into your dad's death, Gavin."

"I wish you were doing it. Would you if I asked you to?"

"Gavin, I'm not a professional. Wolf will get to the bottom of it."

"What if your dad married a bimbo and died under suspicious circumstances?"

Ouch! This kid knew how to reach a person's core. I already felt guilty for not convincing Hollis to go to the police about Kelsey poisoning him. Imagining that it had been my dad in Hollis's shoes was awful. I would have been like the determined bees that follow people for half a mile because they disturbed the nest. "I can't guarantee anything, Gavin. Is there anything else I should know?"

Gavin launched himself at me for a hug. He looked a little embarrassed when he stepped back. "I . . . uh, I'll let you know if I learn anything else." He turned and walked away.

"Gavin? Do *not* get involved in this. If you do, I'll tell your mother everything. I'm not kidding." If he was anything like Hollis, he wouldn't listen to me and would do what he wanted. *Not again.* I ran up to him and grabbed his arm. "Now you listen to me, Gavin Haberman. I'm serious. People who murder won't think twice about doing it again. You stay out of this."

He didn't seem to be cowed in the least. "Maybe I should just call your mom." At least it might not weigh on my conscience as much.

A hint of a grin crept onto his face. "She thinks the same thing I do. It's just a matter of catching the one-who-shall-remain-nameless." Gavin walked away.

It looked like I would be making another trip to the library this afternoon. And I wanted to know who lived in the blue house with the octopus on the door.

I unlocked the door to check on Mochie. He was sitting in the bay window in the kitchen, watching the street.

"Do you miss Daisy?" I asked.

Mochie purred but didn't seem particularly distressed about being home alone. Cats were cool about solitude.

I stroked him a few times, then locked up again and headed to the library, thinking that I was no better than Hollis. I had so wanted to believe that Kelsey didn't kill him. Everyone else suspected her. Everyone!

I turned the corner and rushed to the library. I pulled open the door and dashed inside. Cindy was in the office, talking with someone.

Impatient, I waited for her to finish. As I paced, I spied Trula and Jay in the special collections room.

Trula looked up from her work and waved me in.

I glanced back. Cindy was still busy. I stepped inside and asked, "How's the research going?"

Trula pretended to sag. "You won't believe this, but Jay's research and mine appear to be intersecting. He's making far better progress than I am, though."

"It appears," said Jay, "that Mr. Dixon resided in my house when he was a spy. At least for a time, as far as we can tell."

"Wow! That's so cool," I said. "I'd like to do some research on my house one day."

Trula raised her eyebrows and said, "I understand Kelsey is being represented by your Alex."

"We don't need cell phones in Old Town," I joked. "News moves at the speed of light."

"Well, it was just so obvious to everyone with a brain. Younger woman moves in on wealthy man in terrible physical condition and then he dies. I saw her buying those four cans of fogger at the hardware store only hours before Hollis died. She didn't even try to hide what she was doing."

I blinked at Trula. "You saw her buying fogger? You mean, like bug bombs? The kind you set off inside your house?"

"That's exactly my point. Who buys foggers to kill bees?"

"Someone who has them inside the house," I said.

"Sophie! When are you and Alex tying the knot? You're already defending his clients. You might as well be a team." She pointed at the four-carat rock on her finger.

I ignored her silliness, mostly because the presence of foggers sealed up the whole scenario and made more sense than bee spray. "I presume you told Wolf this information?"

Trula slapped a hand on her chest. "I have never liked being a tattletale." She turned to Jay. "Hah! I would have made a terrible spy. But I do believe it's my duty to report something as crucial as this, don't you?"

"When did you tell Wolf?"

"This morning. Honestly, with the storm and Parker making such a fuss about those cheeses, it just went right out of my head."

"Tell me what you saw."

"It was all quite innocent. I happened to be in the hardware store—"

"What were you buying?" I asked.

She licked her lips. "Silver polish. I never allow my silver to tarnish. And I happened to see Kelsey buying bug bombs. I remember it because I was appalled. I mean, bugs in the house?" She squished up her face in disgust. "Speaking of silver, I wonder if Kelsey even has any to put out for the post-funeral lunch. I haven't heard a thing about a memorial service for poor Hollis. Have you?"

"I don't think they've released his body yet."

Trula flipped her hand. "This should be interesting. I wonder if she'll be arrested before then. Who would make the arrangements? Oh! There's Cindy now. I need to speak to her anyway. I've lost my purse!"

It was probably a terrible breach of Southern etiquette,

but I shot out the door before Trula even finished speaking. I said very quietly to Cindy, "We need to talk about Gavin right now."

Trula was breathless when she arrived. "Cindy, sweetheart, is there a lost and found in the library? I think I left my purse here yesterday, but I don't see it anywhere."

Cindy took everything in stride. Calmly she said, "Trula, we keep the lost and found box behind the circulation desk. Ask if you can have a look. Sophie, follow me."

Trula didn't let her go, though. "Cindy, will you be hosting the memorial service for Hollis in the event that Kelsey is already in the slammer? I'm wondering when and to whom I should bring a casserole. It would be so awkward to bring it to Hollis's murderer. That has to be a major breach of etiquette."

Cindy's mouth opened and closed repeatedly like a fish out of water. She didn't even manage to say "excuse us." She simply turned and propelled me to a private room.

Cindy took a deep breath. "What is she talking about? Have they arrested Kelsey?"

"No, she's just speculating. You know how Southerners are about funerals."

"I think people are forgetting that Hollis was once very dear to me. They think his death hasn't impacted me one bit, which isn't the case at all."

"I'm sorry. I guess so many people have bad divorces that they forget some people love their ex-husbands."

"That's right! Like you and Mars. Goodness, but he would be devastated if anything happened to you." She placed her hands over her eyes briefly. "Trula drives me up a wall. She acted like I was the bee's knees when I was married to Hollis. Once we separated, she treated me like dirt. It was as though she couldn't be bothered with me once I wasn't attached to Hollis. And now she's doing all this genealogy research and suddenly I'm the queen bee again. She introduced me to someone as a *dear old friend*! If I'm ever like that, I hope you'll knock some sense into me." She huffed in dismay. "So what has Gavin done now?"

I tried to choose my words carefully. "He's such a wonderful kid. He thinks Kelsey murdered Hollis."

Cindy was clearly unimpressed. "So do I. So does Trula and everyone else in Old Town. What's wrong with that?"

"I'm afraid he's going to try to spy on her or snoop around."

"That boy." Cindy shook her head. "He's been a surprise since the day he was conceived. I didn't think I could have children. Hollis and I tried and tried. We went to experts and they put us through tests, but it just never happened. And then one day, when we least expected it, I was pregnant. We spoiled him terribly. Who wouldn't? We knew he was the only child we would ever have."

"He turned out pretty great in spite of that."

"I like to think so."

"I just don't want him playing sleuth and getting into trouble."

"Thanks for the heads-up, Sophie. I'll keep an eye on him." She left the room and was immediately accosted by Trula.

I strode out of the library into the sunshine. I had done everything I could. Something strange had been going on with Hollis, and it was beginning to seem that the more curious it got, the more I was drawn into his drama.

I strolled along, deep in thought, but when I reached the hardware store, I couldn't help going inside. I found the section with foggers and studied them. Kelsey had stood right here contemplating which brand to buy to kill Hollis. It was chilling to the core. I looked up the aisle and down the other way. Where had Trula been to see Kelsey's purchase?

"May I help you?" asked an elderly gentleman whom I recognized as a part-owner of the store.

"My friend Trula Dixon was raving about the silver polish she bought here the other day."

"She must be mistaken. Perhaps she bought silver polish elsewhere. I recall Mrs. Dixon's purchase quite well. She bought four cans of fogger. I remember because we had a run on them that day. Mrs. Haberman purchased some, too."

Chapter 18

Dear Sophie,
My mom took in her nieces and raised them with
her own children until her death. Do we list them
as survivors, or is it only appropriate to mention
those who were actually born to her or adopted?
*   Oldest Sister in Looneyville, Oregon*

Dear Oldest Sister,
By all means include the children whom she raised
as her own. They will be pleased, and she undoubt-
edly would be, too.
*   Sophie*

"Trula Dixon?" I asked to be absolutely certain we were talking about the same person.

"Yes, ma'am. Four cans, just like Mrs. Haberman. We joked about it because we can go months without selling one can of the stuff. And those two ladies wiped us out within minutes."

He must have thought I'd lost my mind because I just

stood there thinking wild thoughts about Trula. "Thank you. You've been very helpful."

I wandered out, feeling a little bit dazed. Trula. Was there some kind of rift between Parker and Hollis? Did Parker have a reason to want to knock off Hollis? Maybe we had been too quick to laugh off the possibility that Parker had gotten rid of both of his law partners, Hollis and Gage. Was Trula helping him?

Who would have information about Gage's death besides Madison? Pondering that, I turned off King Street and headed for Duke Street. There were quite a few blue houses in Old Town, but I couldn't recall having seen an octopus door knocker. I found the place within fifteen minutes.

It was a narrow older house. The oval plaque designating it as a historical building was proudly displayed on the wood wall. A single dormer window jutted from a roof that slanted a bit too much and appeared to be in need of repair. Next to the stairs that led to the front door, a basement window no larger than one foot by one foot was beside a door so tiny that a hobbit couldn't have fit inside. It must have replaced the original ice cellar door. The mail slot in the front door meant there was no mailbox with a name on it.

The house shared walls with the houses on the left and the right. The house on the right was significantly larger and three stories tall. I counted the number of houses to the corner and walked around the block to see if there was an alley.

I was in luck. Maybe the rear of the house would give me a clue about the owner or tenant. I counted again to make sure I had the correct house from the rear. I was about two narrow houses away when a Mustang with a rusted-out driver's side door whipped by me. Angus Bogdanoff was driving it.

That couldn't have been a coincidence. Was it Francie who had suggested that Kelsey was having an affair? Maybe she was right.

I continued to the small parking pad from which the car had emerged. The rear of the house was white and much more modern than the front, which wasn't all that unusual in Old Town. But I was certain it was the same house because of the shabby roof and the fact that the next house over was taller.

I didn't know exactly what I had expected to find, but it sure wasn't this. Kelsey mentioned visiting Angus in the hospital the day he had been stung. Had she gone to his house during the daytime, I might have assumed she was bringing him food or checking on him. But she went there by herself at night after her husband went to bed and was probably fast asleep.

I stared at the rear of the house, trying to put it all together. Hollis had suspected Kelsey of poisoning him. Maybe she was on to him and switched to another type of poison.

There had been two problems with the bee spray. It was difficult to imagine that Hollis wouldn't have awakened if Kelsey had sprayed it in his face while he slept. And even Jay Charles had said it was unlikely a few whiffs of it would have killed him. But bug bombs were another thing entirely. If they had been set off while Hollis was fast asleep, maybe he could have inhaled too much of the stuff.

How long had Kelsey been seeing Angus? Had she met him when he was hired as the Haberman handyman, or had she known him all along? Had she married Hollis for his money, planning to murder him and make a life with Angus?

It was too depressing to imagine this had been a grand scheme and they had actually managed to pull it off. Poor Hollis. She had sucked him right into her arms and then stung him. The woman I hadn't wanted to imagine doing something like that had ruined the lives of a happy family. Hollis was gone, and things would never be the same for Cindy or Gavin.

I was turning to leave when I heard a scream and a crash. Unless I missed my guess, they came from Angus's house. I ran through the parking pad and short backyard. "Hello?" I called. I listened but didn't hear anything. "Hello? Do you need help?"

I heard a low moan and the sound of knocking. *Thunk, thunk, thunk.* I stepped back and examined the rear of the building. It was tiny. There was a back door and only one window on the first floor. The basement was underground on this side.

"Where are you? Do you need help?"

More thunking. The old townhouse butted directly against the houses beside it. There was no access on either side. "I'm going around to the front," I yelled as loud as I could.

I ran along the alley and around the corner, wishing I could call 911 while I ran. In front of the house, I dashed up the few stairs to the front door and knocked with the octopus. "Hello? Can you hear me?"

I heard the thunking again, this time quite faint. I didn't waste any more time and called 911. "I don't actually know if this is an emergency," I blathered. "But I heard a crash and a scream, and someone makes a knocking sound when I call out." I gave her the address and knelt to see through the tiny window to the basement. It was too dark to make out anything.

"I've called for help," I shouted. I paced in front of the house, hoping someone would arrive soon. When a police car drew up, I ran to it, delighted to find Wong inside.

She moved quickly but calmly as I explained what had happened.

"Weird knocker," she muttered before banging it. "Police!"

The strange thunking sound came again.

"You know who lives here?" she asked.

"I think it's Angus Bogdanoff."

"So it's probably Angus making that banging noise?"

"I saw him drive away."

She threw me a curious glance. "When we get Angus or whoever out of there, we're going to have a little talk about what you're doing here."

The ambulance arrived next. Since she didn't know what she might find, Wong called for backup. The entire process took far too long in my opinion. They finally opened the front door.

Wong pointed at me. "Stay out here, Sophie. I mean it. You hear me?"

I was itching to go inside with them, but I understood that it could be dangerous and that I could interfere, making their job more difficult, so I waited by the front door. A crowd was gathering on the sidewalk in front of the house.

I could hear them talking inside.

"Where are you?"

"Tap again!"

The next thing I knew, an EMT fetched a stretcher.

Wong finally returned to the stoop. "It's the Haberman kid."

"Gavin? Is he okay?" It was a stupid question. If he was fine they wouldn't need a stretcher.

"It appears that he was hiding in a closet and fell through a rotted hatch to the basement."

They were bringing him through. Wong and I left the stoop and stood aside. Gauze wrapped Gavin's head, but blood had seeped through. "Noooo," I breathed.

"You have his mom's number?" asked Wong.

I nodded and pulled up the number for the library on my phone.

Wong called Cindy and informed her about Gavin's accident. I heard Cindy scream through the phone.

I walked over to the stretcher and took Gavin's hand in mine. His eyes were closed. The angle of his leg made me wince. I leaned over him. "Gavin, it's Sophie Winston. You'll be fine. We've called your mom, and she'll meet you at the hospital. You're going to be okay, kiddo."

His fingers tightened on mine, and I knew he'd heard me.

Wong and I stood by and watched as he was loaded into the ambulance. It drove away, and the crowd dispersed.

"Now," said Wong. "Suppose you tell me what Gavin was doing in a closet in this house and how you happened to be outside. Please tell me you weren't waiting for him."

I told her the whole story about Gavin following Kelsey to Angus's house. "And it appears Gavin may have been correct all along. I can't think of a good reason for Kelsey to come here in the dark of night when she should have been at home in bed with Hollis."

"I'll notify Wolf," she said. "I imagine he'll want to talk with you."

I left her there to deal with finding Angus and notifying him that they had entered his house. I walked home slowly, sick about Gavin and angry with Kelsey.

Nina was standing on the sidewalk in front of my house. "Where have you been?"

We went inside. I told her all about it while I poured tall glasses of iced tea. I handed her one, slugged mine down, and refilled my glass. Not at all ladylike.

"It's all so obvious," said Nina. "Kelsey must have thought no one would see her go to Angus's house."

I hated to concede that everyone else was right, but it certainly looked that way. "I'm going over to the hospital. I didn't like the way Gavin looked."

"What was he thinking going into someone's home like that?"

"Probably the same thing I was. He wanted to know who lived there."

Nina and I drove to the hospital, parked, and hurried to the emergency room. We found Cindy in no time.

She waited by herself, crying, a knotted tissue in her hand. She hugged both of us. "I can't believe this happened. They're taking him to surgery!"

"His leg is broken?" I asked.

She sniffed and nodded. "You knew, Sophie. You warned me about this. I didn't even have time to talk with him about not getting involved. He was supposed to be at home!"

"How's his head?" I asked.

"He has a concussion. They said he fell through a trap door and hit an old brick half wall in the basement before he fell to the stone floor."

"Is there anything we can do?" asked Nina.

"I don't know. My head is spinning. Oh! Yes, Gavin is blood type AB, which is the rarest blood type. They said only three or four percent of the population has AB positive and that if I know anyone with that blood type, I should ask them to donate."

Cindy looked at us hopefully.

"Gosh, I'm so sorry. I'm type A," I said.

Cindy nodded. "Me too."

"I'm type O . . ." Nina didn't finish because a woman who bore an amazing resemblance to Cindy rushed through the door. Cindy ran to her. They held each other and sobbed.

"I'm guessing that's a sister," said Nina.

Immediately behind them, Parker, Trula, and Madison

showed up. Cindy hugged them as though they were a receiving line. Everyone asked how Gavin was doing and what had happened to him.

The door opened again and more people rushed in. It was apparent that other members of Cindy's family had arrived.

We asked Cindy to keep us informed and left her to explain everything to her family.

When I was parking the car in my garage, Nina said, "People are still leaving food on Kelsey's doorstep. I guess I'd better buy something."

Does one bring funeral food to a murderer, I wondered? Was there an etiquette rule for that? Probably not. Besides, she hadn't been convicted or even arrested.

Nina hurried off. I went inside and poured myself another tall glass of iced tea. I carried it back to my tiny home office.

Mochie ambled along and jumped up to my desk when I sat down at the computer. I needed Kelsey's maiden name. I could just ask her, of course. But that might make her clam up. Alex would probably have it, but I knew him well enough to know that he would treat any information he had like it was gold in Fort Knox. And sneaking a peek in his office just wasn't my style. It was important to him to keep his clients' business private.

I tried an online record search of marriage licenses under Hollis's name but didn't turn up anything. It required the exact city where the license was issued. They could have gotten it outside of Alexandria.

Besides, what if Kelsey had changed her name? If her stories were true, she had been on the run from the police when she was a teen. I typed in *murder Delilah Jean.* While there were a surprising number of hits, none of them seemed right or referred to a person called Delilah Jean, which I thought fairly distinctive. Kelsey said she was eleven years old at time. I guessed at the year and typed it in along with the name *Delilah Jean* and *murder*.

To my amazement, a website with dedications to those who had lost their lives to domestic violence popped up. And there it was.

In memory of our beloved mother Delilah Jean Doshutt, who was taken from us by her abusive ex-husband. Let no one forget her name or her love for her children and nieces.

It was a simple jump to the obituary, which listed after the names of her six children, "her nieces Kayla Brooks and Kelsey Brooks."

Brooks wasn't an uncommon family name. I could only hope that the very sad deaths of Kelsey and Kayla's parents made their obituaries stand out somehow. A quick Google of the girls' names turned up their parents' obituaries. But more interestingly, it also led me to an article about the death of Kelsey Brooks.

Chapter 19

Dear Sophie,
What is the difference between gelato and ice cream? My husband says gelato is Italian for ice cream, but there's no other difference. I say that the texture is different. Who wins this argument?
Smart Wife in Treat, Arkansas

Dear Smart Wife,
You're both right! Gelato is Italian for ice cream. But there is indeed a textural difference. Gelato contains less fat and less air, which makes it denser than ice cream. It's served at a warmer temperature than ice cream, too, which gives it a softness.
Sophie

I hit the link as fast as I could.

Double Murder in Fairview
Kelsey Brooks, the teen who disappeared from
Fairview in June, was strangled Friday night on

the very day she was returned to the custody of her relative, Sassy Green. Green's boyfriend, Wayne Khropinki, strangled the girl when she refused his sexual advances. The victim's sister, Kayla, also a juvenile, allegedly attacked Khropinki, hitting him repeatedly on the head with a cast-iron kettle. Khropinki died at the scene from his wounds. Kayla Brooks is sought by authorities for questioning.

It had been awful hearing about it when Kelsey told us what happened, yet it was shocking all over again to read about it. Kelsey had told us the basics. But she hadn't mentioned that she changed her name to that of her dead sister. Kelsey, really Kayla, had also conveniently omitted the fact that she had killed her sister's murderer.

A little breathless, I sat back in my chair. Kelsey had murdered before.

It was probably justified in order to protect her little sister. I couldn't even imagine the horror of being in a situation like that. But there was no doubt in my mind that I would have done the same for my sister.

It had happened over a decade ago. Would the police still be searching for Kelsey? Did she even know they were looking for her? Probably.

A sharp prosecutor would make her out to be a murderess. Which she was. The circumstances were horrific and had she gone to trial, she probably would have been exonerated for defending her sister. But she had run, tried to disappear, and been successful at it.

Or had she? Had she told Hollis? Was that why he was afraid she was poisoning his food? Because he knew that she had killed a man? Maybe he found out about it online just as I had. Which brought up the question—Who else knew?

If she thought she could be arrested and tried for murder, which, as far as I knew was a distinct possibility because there was no statute of limitations on murder, then she was a fine target for blackmail. And anyone who knew Delilah Jean's name could find out about Wayne's murder just as easily as I had by following the obituaries.

There I was again, trying to find reasons to imagine that someone else had killed Hollis. Why couldn't I accept that everything pointed to Kelsey?

I put the computer to sleep and returned to my kitchen, where Kelsey was looking through the window of my kitchen door.

Now that I knew she was a murderess, I wasn't sure about letting her into my house when I was alone. I didn't even have Daisy with me. True, Daisy would have kissed her, but I wouldn't have felt quite as vulnerable. As much as I didn't want to believe that Kelsey had murdered Hollis, I also didn't want to put myself in jeopardy. I grabbed my purse and pretended to be leaving the house.

Slinging my purse over my shoulder, I opened the kitchen door. "Hi! I'm just on my way out."

"Maybe I could walk with you?" she asked.

I looked into her eyes and thought I was being incredibly stupid for even imagining that she would harm me. Locking the door behind me, I said, "Sure. Have you been to the new gelato place?"

She threw me a slightly embarrassed glance. "Not yet. To be honest, I don't know what gelato *is*."

"It's like ice cream. I bet you'll love it."

"Okay. I could use a little treat. Sophie, I want to thank you for hooking me up with Alex. I finally feel like I have someone, besides you, on my side. He was so nice to me."

"He's a good attorney, too."

"When I got home, somebody called the house about

Gavin. Do you know anything about it? It's not like I can call Cindy. She'd probably hang up on me."

I nodded. "He's in the hospital. Cindy already knows about it."

We had arrived at the gelato place, a tiny hole-in-the-wall with a couple of tables out on the sidewalk. I chose the blackberry flavor, and Kelsey opted for hazelnut.

"Did Wolf search your house?"

"Yes, it was awful. But they didn't find anything of interest. It's not like Hollis was shot and there was blood everywhere. They took the food in the fridge, including some funeral food that people had brought. Can you imagine? Natasha said I better make sure the police give the containers back or there will be some very angry people."

With cones in hand, I led the way to an outdoor table. Kelsey would learn the truth sooner or later, so I thought it was best to be forthright with her. "Gavin followed you to Angus's house the night Hollis died."

She swallowed hard and blanched. "Oh no! What was he doing there? I didn't see him."

I couldn't exactly say it was because he thought she murdered his father. I played it safe. "I don't know. I'm not sure Gavin knows. From what I can gather, he didn't want to see Hollis or do things with him after his parents separated. That night at the underground dinner, he saw his dad, and it sounds like he had conflicting feelings about that. Maybe he really missed Hollis a lot and was hurt?"

"Hollis missed him, too. On the way home from the underground dinner, Hollis could not stop talking about how Gavin had avoided him all night. He tried and tried to talk to Gavin, but he just walked away. It's all so sad. I can't believe he followed me. Why on earth would he do that?"

I wanted to ask, why on earth did you go to see Angus? But I licked my gelato and said, "I think he went to Angus's house today to find out who lived there. I have no idea what possessed him to enter the house. Apparently there's some kind of hatch to the basement in a closet? It gave way and he tumbled down."

Kelsey closed her eyes in pain. When she opened them again, she didn't look at me. "It's so pretty here in Old Town. I love the flowers and the old houses with all their little nooks and crannies and interesting features. But underneath all the pleasantries, the people are all the same. They have problems, and fears, and sorrow. You know, when you don't have any money, and Lord knows I've been in that position most of my life, you think money will solve everything. I'll grant you it does take away one worry. But in the end, it doesn't solve all your problems. Maybe that's why people like Madison despise me. They're afraid of *being* me. They're afraid they'll lose everything they have and be like me."

Initially I was taken aback by her theory. But as I considered it, I thought she might be right.

"I wish I could do something for Gavin," she said. "Hollis would go to see him, of course, but I don't dare do that. Cindy would have me thrown out."

"They're asking for blood donations from people with type AB-positive blood. Any chance that's what you have?"

"Oh my gosh! I do. I can do that for him. Would you send flowers to a boy?"

"Flowers are never wrong. Tell them they're for a teenaged boy, and I bet they can come up with something baseball themed. Maybe you can find someone who makes those cute arrangements that look like dog faces. I bet he'd love that."

Kelsey held her head at an angle and leisurely licked a

drizzle of melting gelato. "Sophie, you've been very kind to me, so I'm going to come right out and tell you the truth. Alex told me not to talk, but I have nothing to hide about that night. I did go to see Angus."

She paused to finish eating her gelato. "Angus and I dated before I met Hollis. Eventually the relationship kind of fizzled. It wasn't a big deal. But then I was in a really awful car accident." She took a deep breath like she was going to say something that was hard for her. "Sophie, I've been alone for a long time. I don't have a sister or a mom, or anyone I can call if I need help. When I was released from the hospital, Angus came over and took care of me. It wasn't romantic or anything. It was one friend helping out another. And I was a mess. He changed gross bandages for me and drove me to doctor's appointments. I don't honestly know what I would have done without him. I recovered, and he met a girl he liked, and we hardly ever saw each other anymore. I went to Parker about legal issues regarding the accident and that was when I met Hollis."

So far her story rang true to me.

"After I married Hollis, I didn't have any connection with Angus anymore. Then one day, I ran into him on King Street. He had moved to Old Town and was looking for a job. I wanted to throw him a little work. I haven't ever been in a position to help someone else that way before." She sat back, seemingly comfortable with herself. "We needed a handyman because Hollis was busy and not inclined to do things around the house, so it seemed like a perfect fit. But then, as time went on, Angus started wanting to get cozy, if you know what I mean. I told him I was married and that he needed to find someone else."

The corners of her mouth tightened. "The day Angus was stung, I went to the hospital to check on him. He was so pathetic, begging me to come back to him. I was adamant that it was *not* going to happen. But that night, I was worried about him. You saw how terrible he looked with that swollen eye." She stuck out the tip of her tongue. "So when Hollis went to bed, I walked over to Angus's house. His face and hands were all swollen. That eye was still swelled shut, and he had stings just everywhere. He could barely handle the remote with his hands because they were so puffy. So I cooked him dinner, cleaned up the kitchen, and did some laundry for him. It was the least I could do. After all, it was our bees that stung him!"

She placed her elbows on the table and leaned her forehead into her hands. "I never dreamed that anything would happen to Hollis while I was out. I left him snoring happily in the bedroom." She looked up at me. "I didn't want Hollis to know I had gone to Angus's house. He would have jumped to the wrong conclusions like everyone else will. Angus needed a hand, and he had been so good to me when I needed help that . . . well, I guess you could say I felt like I owed him for being there when I needed someone."

I sat back and wondered what I would have done. I didn't have to ponder it long. I would have done the same thing if it had been Mars who was stung. "What time did you go home?"

"It must have been around three thirty in the morning when I left Angus's place. The door to our master bedroom was closed. I didn't want to wake Hollis, so I showered in the guest bathroom. When I got out, I quietly opened the door and went into the master bedroom, but Hollis wasn't there. I put on my nightgown and bathrobe and was looking for him when I saw lights flashing on the street. And you know how it went from there. I thought someone had had a car accident."

There was one major item she hadn't mentioned. I couldn't help wondering why. "You didn't smell anything funny when you came home?"

"I did. But it wasn't very strong downstairs or in the guest bathroom. It was the kind of thing when you wonder what that funny smell is, but then you walk away and don't really notice it as much. But it was very strong in the master bedroom."

The door had been closed. If Kelsey had placed all four foggers in the master bedroom while Hollis slept with the door closed, he would have inhaled far too much.

I wanted to believe her. I wanted to think that she had tried to be kind to Angus and hadn't killed Hollis. On the face of it, I didn't see any holes in her story. On the other hand, she had spent years on the run, perfecting the art of lying about who she was. And there was another problem. That story could be one hundred percent accurate, but it didn't mean she hadn't set off four foggers in the bedroom and left the house.

"Kelsey," I said softly, "there's more bad news."

She looked at me in alarm.

"Someone saw you buying the foggers."

She licked her lips. "It was the bees. They managed to get inside the house. Hollis told me to buy four cans of that bug bomb stuff. I didn't tell the cops that yet. They would have handcuffed me and carted me off."

"Wait. I'm not following you. Are you saying that Hollis set them off?"

Her brow furrowed. "No, maybe. I don't know," she wailed. "What I do know is that they're gone."

"Gone?"

"I've looked everywhere. I can't imagine what happened to them."

"But this doesn't make any sense. Do you think Hollis set them off before the dinner last night?"

"No, I remember seeing them on the kitchen counter before we left."

"So what you're saying is that Wolf doesn't know yet

that you bought foggers and that they're gone. Did you also buy bee spray?" I asked.

"No, Angus said he thought they were getting into the house, so Hollis told me to buy foggers. You know the hardware store will tell the cops that I bought foggers right before Hollis died. They'll think I did it intending to murder him!"

Unfortunately, that was exactly what they would think. It all fit together. "Or maybe they'll think you bought the foggers to kill the bees in your house. That's what any rational person would have done."

"He died from something he inhaled. What if it was from the foggers?" Kelsey looked like she felt sick.

I looked into her eyes. "Did you set off the foggers?"

In a tremulous voice, she shouted, "No!"

A few people nearby turned to gaze at us.

I didn't know what to say. She had laid out a perfect setup for murdering Hollis. "Thank you for telling me what happened that night, Kelsey."

She placed her hand on top of mine. "Thank you for believing me."

I'd never felt like such a crumb.

Chapter 20

Dear Sophie,
My sister-in-law has suggested throwing a party to
which the guests bring their own cookout meat.
I'm baffled by this and feel one ought not extend an
invitation if one doesn't intend to feed the guests.
Horrified Hostess in Turkey, Texas

Dear Horrified Hostess,
The concept of a potluck has been around for a
long time. However, you'll note the difference. At a
potluck, one brings a dish to be shared by all. The
bring-your-own-beef idea arose among college stu-
dents, all living on a budget. In such a case, it is
perfectly reasonable for friends to agree to such an
event. But if you are hosting a party, then you are
indeed expected to provide the food and beverages.
Sophie

Kelsey left to place an order for flowers and donate
blood.

I strolled home, wondering if it was possible that Kelsey

was innocent when everything pointed to her as Hollis's killer.

A tall, white-haired woman stood across the street from the Haberman house. As I approached her, I recognized Humphrey's mother, Lavinia Brown. I briefly considered crossing the street to avoid her, but I knew that would be wrong, no matter how much I wanted to.

Pasting a smile on my face, I said, "Good afternoon, Mrs. Brown."

She eyed me with steely aloofness. "What are you doing here?"

Really? The woman sounded like she thought she owned the town. "I live on this street."

"In one of these big old houses?"

"Yes."

One of her eyebrows arched. Honestly, the woman didn't need to dress up for Halloween.

"Which house belongs to Dr. Charles?"

"The one with the gray door across the street."

And just like that, without so much as a thank you, she turned and stalked away. I hoped Humphrey would never introduce any girlfriends or prospective wives to his mother. She could kill the deal without a single word.

I watched as she walked to the corner and crossed the street. Putting her out of my mind, I hurried home lest she catch up with me.

Mochie met me at the kitchen door, complaining about an empty food bowl. I scooped him up and cuddled him. He tolerated me for a minute, then wrestled to be put down. He ran straight to his food bowl and flipped it with his paw so it banged against the counter.

"I got the message, Mochie. How does chicken in aspic sound?"

His tail twitched. I took that as approval.

When he was eating, I pondered what I should bring to

Kelsey's house. They would probably release Hollis's body soon. I decided on funeral potatoes because they were always popular. The shredded hash browns needed to thaw first, so I took the bag out of the freezer and popped it into the fridge.

The truth was that my mind was totally on Kelsey. I made a crust for a tart and while it was in the oven, I sat down at the kitchen table and made a list. Mars was the one who usually did that, but this time, he seemed sure that Kelsey had killed Hollis.

I began the list with Cindy. I didn't write anything beside her name. She was angry in many ways as a result of the divorce. And I had heard her threaten him. They had threatened each other actually, but he was the one who was dead.

Next I wrote, *Angus—jealousy.* If Angus was still in love with Kelsey, he might have murdered Hollis to get him out of the way. If Kelsey's story was true, he might have even seen it as a way to financial security if he thought Kelsey would inherit Hollis's money and marry him. There was the issue of his beestings, though. He might have been incapacitated. On the other hand, I wasn't ready to write him off.

As I pondered the possibility that Angus was the killer, I realized that the timing wasn't quite right, either. If Kelsey was with him that night, when could he have set off foggers in the house? Kelsey would have to be involved for Angus to have killed Hollis. I struck his name from the list, then added it back *+Kelsey.*

Trula and Parker fell into a category all their own. If Gage hadn't died suspiciously, I wouldn't have considered them at all. Then again, Trula had lied about buying silver polish at the hardware store. Very curious. I jotted down *Talk to Madison.*

It wasn't much of a list, but it was a place to start. I took the tart crust out of the oven and set it on a rack to cool. Still thinking about who else might have murdered Hollis, I heated cream and watched chopped chocolate melt into it. There was something soothing about stirring the melting bits. I poured the chocolate truffle filling into the tart pan and set the tart on a rack to cool. I checked the time. Unless I missed my guess, Trula might be at the library.

I locked up and walked over to the library. Sure enough, Jay and Trula were in the special collections room.

When I entered, Trula was saying, "I just don't understand how this can be. I wish we had some of his DNA to test."

Jay said, "Can you imagine how much easier genealogy will be in the future? You'll be able to enter a saliva swab in a machine and all your ancestors will pop up on a chart."

"I wish we had that now," Trula grumbled. "I don't suppose they'd let me dig up his father for a DNA sample."

"What's going on here?" I asked. "It sounds very intriguing. Whose grave are you planning to rob, Trula?"

"I'm joking, of course. I thought I had Parker's ancestry sewn up. But we just found out that the lineage stops because the sole offspring of John Dixon died at age fifteen in the Battle of Eutaw Springs. I'd like to jump over him and dig up his dad to test his DNA."

"Weren't there a lot of unacknowledged children back in the day?" I asked.

"Of course. But how would I know with whom John may have dallied?"

"Good question." I looked at the vast array of resources available to them. "It could be something as obscure as a veiled remark in a letter." I stared at the pile of books in front of Trula. "You know, it's not all that different from searching online. Computers are quicker, of course, but sometimes one thing leads to another."

Jay raised his eyebrows. "Sounds like you've done this before."

"Hasn't everyone sleuthed online?" I asked. "Any word on Gavin, Trula?"

"Not since we were there earlier. Cindy was a mess. Poor thing. When I think of all she's been through."

"It was nice of you, Parker, and Madison to go to the hospital."

"We had to! I don't see much of Cindy and Madison anymore, but we were all very close when our husbands opened the law firm. I remember how thrilled Cindy was to be pregnant. I carried little Gavin around in my arms back in the day. He was a very sweet child." She glanced at her watch. "I can't believe I've been here so long. The time flew by. Forgive me, Sophie, but I have to pick up Parker. He has AB-positive blood, so he went over to make a donation. See you soon." She flicked her hand in a quick wave and left.

Jay stared after her. "Did she have that right? Gavin is type AB-positive?"

"That's what his mother told us. I can't imagine they would be asking for blood donations of that type if it weren't accurate."

Jay's eyes widened. "Hollis wasn't Gavin's father."

Chapter 21

Dear Natasha,
I hate bringing my lovely casserole dishes to repasts
and potlucks because they invariably disappear.
How does one mark them so they will find their
way back home?
          Not Made of Money in Sandwich,
          Massachusetts

Dear Not Made of Money,
The proper way to identify your glass casserole
dish is to etch your name into it. This can be done
with glass etching cream, which is available at craft
stores.
          Natasha

"How do you know that? Did he tell you?" I asked.
"A type O father cannot produce a type AB child."

"You know for sure that Hollis was type O?"

"It's on his medical records."

"So who can produce an AB child?"

"That depends on the mother's blood type, but practically anyone could produce an AB child with the exception of a type O."

"Cindy had an affair!" I blurted.

Jay nodded. "Most likely. Though she could have been inseminated."

"Maybe that was what Hollis meant. They were fighting at the underground dinner and he said something like 'Do you really want to open that can of worms?'"

"So he knew. He was a good father to Gavin. I never would have imagined that Gavin wasn't Hollis's child."

I whispered lest a library employee overhear me. "Do you think she could have killed Hollis so he wouldn't tell Gavin the truth?"

"Anything is possible, but word around town is that Kelsey was the one who murdered him because *she* was having an affair. Poor Hollis! He knew how to pick unfaithful women." Jay drummed his fingers on the table. "What intrigues me about this whole thing is the method of death. It's a very hands-off way to kill someone. Similar to poisoning food, a favorite of women. I suppose one can't draw definite conclusions about the gender of the killer from the method of death, but I'm sure you can see what I mean. There's something sneakily civilized about setting off poisons that would eventually disperse as opposed to slamming someone over the head. No blood, no mess, no confrontations."

"You've been giving this a lot of thought."

"Death and its causes are things I ponder professionally on a regular basis."

"Of course. How silly of me. Do you have any other observations about Hollis's death?"

"I do. I hope Kelsey has a good lawyer."

I was about to leave but stopped to ask him one more question. "Do you know anything about Gage Jenkins's death?"

He nodded. "Drowning. As I recall, they found alcohol, but no drugs."

Nothing new there. "Still hearing voices?"

"I'm sorry to say that I am."

"What do they say?" I asked.

"I can't tell. It's sort of like whispering."

"Would you like me come over and listen with you sometime?"

"Oh no! I wouldn't dream of imposing on you. I'll figure this out."

"Call me if you change your mind." I left the building, wondering where Madison might be at that time of day. She'd said something about staying home too much. I thought I'd take a chance and walk over.

Madison's house stood three stories tall with elegant blue-gray double front doors. There were no front steps, only a tiny railing on each side of the door. The house almost merged with the brick sidewalk, a testament to its age. I glanced at the plaque that verified it as a historic building. It had been built in 1840. The ornate door knocker looked to be pewter. I lifted the handle and banged it.

I could hear someone rustling inside. Madison opened the door. "Sophie!"

"Please forgive me for just dropping by. I was out and thought I'd check on you."

"How thoughtful of you. Won't you come in?"

Madison closed the door behind me and led me to a charming family room off the kitchen. Original ceiling beams had been uncovered and left open on display. French doors led to a patio and garden outside.

I perched on a sofa. "At the underground dinner the other night, you mentioned how lonely you were."

"Oh, you sweet thing! I'm sure you have better things to do than worry about me."

"Are you still thinking about selling? This is a wonderful house."

"I change my mind every single day. Have you heard anything about Gavin?"

"Not yet."

"It was almost like old times today. Of course, Gage and Hollis weren't there, but the feeling was. The compassion we used to have resurfaced for just a little while. Gavin is younger than my children. He was a late baby for Cindy." She grinned. "They were so excited when Gavin was born. Gage and I used to joke that he would grow up thinking he was Prince Gavin. There was nothing they wouldn't do for that little boy."

"You must have gone through a lot together."

She nodded. "We shared joys and sorrows for a long, long time. Makes me melancholy to think about it. Those were the days. Halloween costumes and birthday parties . . ."

"You must miss Gage terribly."

"I do. You know what I miss the most? Just talking with him. He was so intelligent and had amazingly varied interests."

"Alex is so obnoxious. He never talks about his cases."

Madison laughed. "I know exactly what you mean. Gage had the perfect poker face. He'd be working on a prominent case, and I wouldn't know a thing about it until I saw Gage's name in the newspaper. I guess that's why I still don't understand what happened the night he died. It was so unlike him. It was the worst night of my life." She stood up. In a congested tone, she asked, "Where are my manners? Would you like a Coke?"

"I'm fine, thank you."

She sniffled and grabbed a tissue before sitting down again. "Working late was the norm for Gage. I'd grown used to it. He was a workaholic. Ridiculously conscientious and he took such pride in his profession." She massaged a spot over her eyebrow. "He usually phoned, though, if he would be later than nine or ten. Around eleven, I started calling him. He didn't answer the phone at the office or his cell phone. I thought maybe something was wrong at the office, so I walked over. It was nearly midnight. The doors were locked, and it appeared to be closed up for the night. I called Hollis and Parker. Hollis had planned to meet Gage for a drink after work. By the time I called him, Hollis was home in bed. He said Gage had never shown up. I phoned the police and reported Gage missing, of course. The police verified the information with Hollis and the bartender. It was like Gage had simply vanished. The kids and I were out of our minds with worry. And then he turned up in the Potomac River. I still don't know how that happened. I suppose I never will." She wadded the tissue in her hand tightly. "Oh, Sophie. This wasn't how it was supposed to be!"

I leaned toward her. "Madison, does it seem odd to you that both Gage and Hollis have died?"

"I thought I was the only one who would consider that. The thought certainly crossed my mind. But it's evident that Kelsey knocked off Hollis. Haven't you heard? She's having an affair with their handyman."

"I have heard that. So you don't think there could be a connection between Gage's death and Hollis's?"

"I don't see how."

I threw a barbed question her way. "Doesn't Parker stand to gain a lot as the last man standing?"

Madison drew a quick breath. "I suppose he does. Are you suggesting that he murdered both of them?"

"I'm not suggesting anything. It's just odd that two lawyers from the same firm have died so unexpectedly."

"Another one of life's weird twists, I guess."

I nodded and rose to leave. "Do you happen to have a list of the waitstaff at the underground dinner? I've been looking for a lovely blond waitress who did such a wonderful job serving." I fibbed a little. "I'd like to add her to my list of people to call when I need servers at events." It wasn't entirely a lie. I really might call her if things worked out. But the truth was that I wanted to know what her little conversation with Parker was about.

Madison walked over to a desk and pulled out a list. "I hired them through an agency—Let Us Serve You. But I think I know who you were talking about. Ponytail, no makeup but adorable?"

"That sounds like her."

"Fawn, I think. Yes, Fawn Fitzhugh."

"Thanks, Madison. Keep me posted if you hear anything about Gavin, okay?"

She walked me to the door, saying, "Of course. Thanks for dropping by."

I walked out into the heat again, thinking *that* had been a big bomb. It was probably a long shot, but it still worried me that Hollis and Gage had both died under unusual circumstances. I was only a couple of blocks away from Alex's office. I hoofed it over there.

Located on the first floor of an old building that had once been a home, Alex's office was the epitome of Old Town elegance with oriental carpets and swagged Colonial-style window valences.

His receptionist was not at her desk. I poked my head into his office. "Anyone home?"

He looked up from his computer. "Hi! What are you up to?" He rose and circled the desk to kiss me.

"You're going to have a hard battle defending Kelsey."

"Uh-oh. Sophie, don't get involved."

"Too late." I plopped down in a leather chair while he perched on the edge of his desk.

"I don't want to fight about this, Sophie. You know I can't tell you anything."

"I'm not here about Kelsey. What do you know about Parker, Hollis, and Gage?"

Alex focused at me. "It's a respected firm."

"And?"

"You think there's a connection between Hollis's death and Gage's?"

"Could be. I haven't run across anything specific, though. Any rumors out there?"

"There was a lot of talk about Gage's death. It was bizarrely out of character for him. Kind of like me getting loaded and falling into the river. It just wasn't very likely to happen. Gage was a worthy opponent. Always the gentleman. He was an old-school lawyer. No histrionics in court, just good, competent representation. I admit that I'm precise and particular, but I don't even compare to Gage, who was absolutely meticulous."

"Any possibility that he had a drinking problem?"

"In my experience that can be an easy thing to hide— for a while anyway. He wasn't the kind of guy to wear his emotions on his sleeve. Not like Hollis."

"So if he was under a lot of stress, he might have turned to booze to help him relax?"

"Could be, but that's just idle speculation." He grinned at me. "What are you up to, Sophie Winston? Don't you usually throw these wacky theories around with your friends?"

"Everyone thinks Kelsey is guilty. She bought foggers. She left the house when Hollis went to bed, and she went to the home of a previous boyfriend. Doesn't look good, Counselor. Add in that she changed her name to that of her deceased sister, and cap it all off with the fact that she killed someone in the past, and the prosecution has a slam dunk."

I'd never seen that expression on Alex's face before. He rubbed the back of his neck and then gazed at me in what appeared to be astonishment.

"What makes you think she changed her name and killed someone before?"

"I *have* a computer."

"You found that online?" Now he looked worried.

"Yup, right there for the whole world to see."

Alex sat in the chair opposite me, leaned his elbows on his knees, and looked me in the eyes. "Then why do you want to help her?"

"I don't think she killed Hollis. It's just a feeling that I get when I'm with her. Besides, Kelsey has street smarts. She evaded the law and made her own way in the world. If she had wanted to kill Hollis, she wouldn't have left such an obvious trail. The last time she killed someone, she took off and started a new life. She didn't do that this time. Her marriage to Hollis must have been like a dream come true. I don't think she would kill the font of her new comfortable life."

"I believe I have severely underestimated you." Alex grinned at me.

"You're just saying that because I don't think your client is guilty. If she goes to trial, even such a brilliant lawyer as yourself will have trouble convincing a jury of her innocence."

He leaned his head back and laughed, which was a huge relief to me. We had argued far too many times about local murders. I understood that he couldn't talk about his clients. That was fine with me. But we invariably butted heads when I thought his client was guilty.

Even though the door was open, Alex's receptionist knocked. "Your four o'clock appointment is here."

I jumped to my feet. "Dinner tonight?" I asked.

"Rain check?"

"Sure." I pecked him on the cheek and walked out into the reception area. His next client was a buxom brunette with a wasp waist and legs like a giraffe. If I'd been the jealous type, I would have been worried.

I strolled home, enjoying the leisurely feeling of not having to work. I stopped by the grocery store, where I purchased a large flank steak. The green grocer was having a sale on beautiful huge strawberries. I couldn't resist buying a couple of packages.

I took them home, washed them, and dabbed them dry with paper towels. I hulled them, cut them in half lengthwise, and arranged them in circles of decreasing size on the tart. I whipped some cream with just a little bit of sugar and vanilla. After filling a pastry bag with the cream, I piped a decorative border of cream around the top edge.

I slid it into the fridge and took out the flank steak. I measured bourbon, canola oil, smoked paprika, salt, and pepper into a bowl and whisked until the liquids had emulsified and no longer separated. After smashing each garlic clove with the flat side of a large knife, I removed the skins, minced them, and added them to the liquid, which I poured over the meat.

Just as I finished, my cell phone chimed. I glanced at it to see what was going on. Nina had texted, **Library. Come quick!**

I slid the marinating meat into the refrigerator, checked on Mochie, who slept soundly, and rushed out the door, stopping to lock it behind me. I had never been much of a runner, but I attempted to half jog straight to the library. I was panting like crazy when I saw a police car was parked outside. When I staggered closer, I recognized Wolf's unmarked vehicle, too.

I wanted to run up the steps, but I wobbled up them instead. A crowd had gathered around the entrance to the special records room. Saying "excuse me" repeatedly, I wormed my way through the people who had gathered. Nina spotted me and waved me inside.

Wong and Wolf kneeled on the floor in front of a bookcase. Both of them wore gloves.

Jay hovered nearby. He wore his trademark red bow tie and looked very distinguished, but there was no mistaking the shock on his face.

"What happened?" I whispered to Nina.

"Jay found four empty bottles of fogger hidden behind old books."

Chapter 22

Dear Sophie,
I'm not much of a cook, but I would like to bring
something to a family who just lost a loved one.
I'm at a loss about what to give them. Could you
make some suggestions?
    Clueless in Deadmans Corner, Maine

Dear Clueless,
So many people focus on lunch and dinner dishes,
that something the family can grab and eat for break-
fast is often appreciated. Coffeecake, muffins, and
the like are readily available at bakeries. One fam-
ily I know was thrilled to receive a small Christmas
tree complete with lights and ornaments because
they couldn't focus on the upcoming holiday.
    Sophie

"Cindy!" I whispered to her. Who else would hide the murder weapon in the library? I had put her name at the top of my list of suspects. Poor Gavin! What would happen to him? His father was dead, and if his mother went to prison . . .

So Kelsey had been telling the truth. Unless, of course, someone was trying to frame Cindy.

"In one way," Nina said, "it was a brilliant move. It could have gone undiscovered for years."

"Or she could have removed them around Halloween when the hubbub about bees and foggers and Hollis's death weren't foremost in everyone's thoughts. If she had thrown them in a Dumpster somewhere then, no one would have given them any thought."

Nina tugged me toward Jay. "You're in here every day. How come you didn't notice these sooner?" she whispered.

Wolf looked up at us. I got the feeling he wanted to know the answer to that question, too.

"They keep collections of pamphlets—things that were sold, advertisements, and such down on that shelf. They aren't directly related to my line of research."

Wolf got to his feet. "What exactly are you researching?"

Jay shot me a desperate glance. "The history of my house."

That appeared to satisfy Wolf. There was no need for him to know about the ghostly voices Jay was hearing.

"Are they the missing foggers from the Haberman house?" I asked Wolf.

"That would be my guess. I can't think of any other good reason to stash empty foggers in a library. Anyone else would have thrown them into the trash," said Wolf. "But this isn't like finding blood on a knife that we can link directly to the victim. Unless there are fingerprints on the cans, it might be hard to prove that they are the foggers used in Hollis's death."

Unless, I thought, the accused happened to be a very popular librarian.

Additional police officers showed up and it was beginning to get crowded. "I think it's time to make our exit," I said to Nina.

She was reluctant to leave but finally acquiesced. "I can't believe it could have been Cindy. She's always so gentle and kind. I was certain Kelsey had killed Hollis."

On the walk home, I filled her in on the entire saga of that night as Kelsey had relayed it to me. "So she was with Angus, but only to be nice and help him out."

Nina stopped in her tracks. "That could have been me!"

"What do you mean?"

"It's the kind of thing I would do for an old friend." She looked at me with a gleam in her eyes. "We really ought to bring Angus something, don't you think?"

"You mean you want to pump him and verify what Kelsey told me?"

Nina feigned innocence. "*Moi?* Would I do that?"

"Why do I think it's not a coincidence that we're across the street from Big Daddy's Bakery?"

"I do love his cupcakes."

We crossed the street and bought two half-dozen boxes of cupcakes. One for Angus, and one for us. Nina selected peanut butter with chocolate buttercream, chocolate with chocolate frosting, vanilla with vanilla buttercream, strawberry with a lovely pink frosting, and two salted caramel cupcakes for each box because she knew we would both want one. Nina wasn't a half a cupcake kind of person except in emergencies.

Armed with our excuse to visit, we walked down to Duke Street.

The two of us strolled up the stairs to the stoop at Angus's front door, and I banged the octopus knocker.

There was no answer.

"I have to do this. I never saw an octopus door knocker."
Nina raised her hand and grasped the octopus head. She
shuddered. "It's a little creepy." She banged it loud enough
to alert the entire neighborhood.

"I guess he's not home. We'll have to try again later." I
walked down the steps.

"Sophie . . ." Nina's voice was shaky. "The door's not
locked."

I looked up at her. "Nina!"

She had already opened the door. "Angus!" she sang.
"We brought you some goodies."

By the time I reached the landing, she was already inside
Angus's house.

"Nina!" I hissed. "Get out of there."

"It's not breaking and entering if the door isn't locked."

"Actually, I think it is. And if it's not, then it's certainly
trespassing."

"It's decorated in early man cave."

"What does that mean?" I asked from the stoop.

"Sports stuff."

"Will you get out of there?"

There was a long silence. Too long. "Nina?"

"Sophie!" she screamed.

I dashed inside, thinking the worst. Someone must have
caught her inside the house. She interrupted a burglary or
something. "Nina! Where are you?"

The house was very narrow. It wasn't difficult to locate
her. She stood near the doors of the living room that led to
a brick patio. Angus lay at her feet.

I gasped at the sight of him. "Noooo!"

His hands curled limply near his neck. There was no
sign of blood.

Nina grabbed my arm with a trembling hand. In the
other hand, she still held the bag containing boxes of cupcakes.

I was pretty sure Angus wouldn't be eating any more cupcakes. My hands quivered, too, as I punched 911 on my cell phone as fast as I could. The dispatcher asked if I hadn't called about the same address earlier that day. I assured her this was a separate event.

I handed the phone to Nina and walked around Angus's body. I knelt on the floor, reached for his neck, and tried to find a pulse. He was already cold. I had little hope of finding any sign of life but continued to search for a pulse and realized that his neck bore the imprint of something used to choke him.

"How can you touch him?" asked Nina.

"If he has a pulse, we need to do CPR. Maybe we should anyway." I debated between rolling him over to try CPR and leaving him exactly as he was so I wouldn't mess with the evidence. In the end, it was his cold skin that made me decide to wait for the authorities. "I think he was choked to death."

It wasn't long before we heard sirens. I rushed to the front door so they would know which house it was. A young police officer I hadn't met before arrived at the same time as the EMTs. The name tag on his shirt said *Mc-Graw*. He took a long look at Angus. For a minute, I thought McGraw might be sick. He regained his composure and pulled Nina and me aside while the EMTs calmly set to work.

When we told him our names, he wrote them down before looking at us curiously. "Why do your names sound familiar?"

Uh-oh. "We're friends of Wolf Fleischman," I explained.

I saw the spark of recognition in his face. "Ohhh. Yes, that's why I've heard of you. Addresses, please?"

Suddenly I realized how spoiled I had become because

Wolf and Wong knew me so well. They didn't have to ask for my personal details. They knew where to find me.

"Name of the victim?"

"Angus Bogdanoff," I said. That was more than we knew the last time we called 911 for him.

"He lived here?"

"Yes."

"How did you know the victim?"

"We didn't know him well. We helped him a couple of days ago when he was stung by bees."

"How was it that you found him? He doesn't look like he could answer the door."

I sucked in a breath.

Nina held up the bag of cupcake boxes. "We brought him a treat. We knocked on the door. When he didn't respond, we got worried about him, opened the door, and found him sprawled on the floor." Nina responded so smoothly that it frightened me a bit. It wasn't a lie, of course, but we really had no cause to go inside the house.

"And then?"

"And then Sophie called 911," she said.

One of the EMTs walked up and very quietly said, "I'm calling the medical examiner."

The cop blanched.

When the EMT moved away, I said, "Call Wolf. This is his case."

"That's not protocol." McGraw stared at me for a moment. "Why do you think this is Wolf's case when it hasn't been assigned yet?"

"Because I'm pretty sure it's directly related to the death of Hollis Haberman, which is Wolf's case."

His eyes grew large. "If you don't mind, I'm going to follow protocol, but that's good to know."

"Can we go now?" I asked.

"Maybe you better hang around a little longer."

McGraw walked away and phoned someone out of our earshot.

"I don't see any ropes," whispered Nina.

It was a small house. "Unless the killer took it upstairs or left it out on the patio, he probably took it with him." I didn't see anything that looked heavy and bloody lying around.

I sidled into the kitchen. Careful not to touch anything, I searched for signs of blood or anything unusual. There were stacks of empty pizza boxes on the counter along with a jar of instant coffee, a six-pack of sodas, and a bag of barbecue-flavored potato chips. Empty beer bottles cluttered the recycling bin. Angus hadn't been a health food fanatic.

I edged around the counter to what would normally be a dining area and stubbed my toe on something hard. I cried out and everyone looked over at me.

Even though my big toe throbbed, I said, "Sorry. I'm fine." I glanced down at the culprit. It looked like a cast-iron ball with a flat bottom and a handle on top. Next to it was a set of dumbbells in graduating sizes. And hanging off of some of them were small chains. "Officer McGraw," I called.

He walked over to me and nodded. He squatted near them, his arms on his knees, and eyed them. "Thanks, Sophie. I think you're on to something here."

Wolf walked up behind him. "She has a good instinct for things like this."

I wasn't about to tell him I had literally stumbled into the mother lode of murder weapons. "What are the chains for?"

"They make the weight heavier as you lift it," Wolf explained.

Nina and I ran through our story again for Wolf.

"Hollis and his handyman," mused Wolf. "You two can take off. I'll stop by if I have any questions."

Nina grabbed my hand and tugged me out of there like a locomotive. When we reached the sidewalk, she stopped and sucked in huge gasps of air. "That poor man. Can you imagine? He probably thought, *I'll have a beer and watch some ESPN, then take a nap.* He had no idea what was coming."

"Maybe. Maybe not."

"He thought he was going to be murdered today? Seriously? Sophie, you've gone round the bend."

"That's not what I meant. I don't think some stranger barged into Angus's home and choked him. Look around. If you were burglarizing a house, is this the one you would have picked?"

"I see your point. The shabbiest house in the neighborhood probably isn't where you'd find gold coins or something worth stealing. Somehow, he must have been more involved in Hollis's murder than we know."

"He might have had a hunch that he needed to watch his back."

"Well, he didn't do a very good job of that!" she said.

We started walking back to our block.

"Angus's death points at Kelsey," said Nina.

"You mean because a dead man can't deny what she told me?"

"Exactly."

I didn't want to agree with her, but Angus's demise *was* very convenient for Kelsey in that regard. Too convenient.

My cell phone buzzed. I glanced at it while we walked. It was a text from Mars.

Have news. On way to your house.

"Mars says he has news. He'll meet us at my place."

Nina lifted the cupcake bag she still carried. "I'm bringing dessert."

In spite of the grisly scene we had left, I was getting hungry. When I unlocked my front door, I heard a voice behind me.

"Where have you been?" asked Francie. "I've been waiting for you to come home."

The three of us and her dog, Duke, entered the foyer.

I stopped myself from reminding her that I had a cell phone and she could have called me. "Is everything okay?"

"I know who killed Hollis."

Chapter 23

Dear Sophie,
When we recently had a death in the family, I
hosted the repass, as well as out-of-town guests.
My dear cousin brought a salad in the plastic gro-
cery store container where she had clearly assem-
bled it at the salad bar. My aunt flipped out and
accused her mother of not teaching her any funeral
etiquette. As much as I love my aunt, I sorely
wanted a quick comeback to help my cousin save
face. What can I say the next time this happens?
     Mad as a Wet Hen in Smackover, Arkansas

Dear Mad as a Wet Hen,
You could tell your aunt that while it might be
poor etiquette to bring a salad bar contribution to
a repass, it's absolutely barbaric manners to men-
tion it. Good manners means always making oth-
ers feel comfortable.
     Sophie

Francie had our full attention. So much so that Nina shrieked at the sound of a pinging against the window in the kitchen door.

It was Mars. I unlocked the door and Daisy bounded in. She circled around me, prancing and wagging her entire rear end. "I missed you, too, Daisy!" She licked my face and calmed down when I hugged her. Speaking to Mars, I said, "Francie knows who killed Hollis."

"Me too," said Mars. "And it's not who you think!"

Simultaneously, Francie said, "Cindy!" as Mars said, "Jay!"

Nina sighed. "I need a drink."

"Me too." I felt like I'd walked all over Old Town. I boiled water and salt in a large pot and tossed in quartered red-skinned potatoes. Nina whipped up icy piña coladas in the blender and poured them into tall hurricane glasses.

Francie helped Mars set the table with a cheerful yellow and red tablecloth.

Nina collapsed onto the banquette and told Francie and Mars about finding Angus.

"Angus is dead?" Mars retrieved forks and knives. "That changes everything. There has to be a connection."

I pulled yellow Fiestaware plates from the cabinet, as well as rectangular white serving dishes. I set out a cutting board loaded with cheeses, olives, water crackers, and salami for us to nosh on while dinner cooked. Then I removed the marinated flank steak from the refrigerator and set it on the counter.

"Where's Bernie?" I asked.

Mars groaned. "Ever since the power came back on he's been at the restaurant. They have food to throw out and orders to place, and people are lining up at the door, sick of peanut butter sandwiches. Until I moved in with Bernie, I had no idea restaurants were so much work. When you eat at one, it all seems so simple and organized. They cook, you order, eat, and pay."

"Maybe they'll make up some of the lost revenue," said Nina.

"Ladies first," said Mars to Francie.

"Thank you, dear. Do you remember how awful I felt because I broke the news about Hollis's death to Cindy? Hah! She acted like it was the first she had heard of it, but I just found out from my friend Frieda, who works as a volunteer at the hospital, that Cindy was at the hospital to see Hollis by six in the morning! Now why would she have misled me that way unless she had something to hide?"

I stopped slicing a juicy rosy-red German Johnson tomato from my garden. "Things are beginning to look bad for Cindy. Could she have somehow entered the house and set off the bug bombs? She would have been waiting to hear that he had died. Someone must have notified her that he was in the hospital. She went to see him, and either before or after that, she removed the foggers and hid them in the library, where Jay found them."

"Now hold on," said Mars. "Jay found the foggers? That might not have been a coincidence. It could have been Jay who stashed them there. Get this—Hollis recommended an investment to Jay that crashed and burned. Jay lost a huge amount of money and was furious with Hollis."

"I've never seen Jay be furious in my entire life," said Nina. "He's always well-mannered and polite."

Mars cocked his head. "Really? People who are polite can't get angry?"

"Some people hide their emotions," said Francie. "They let their anger build up until it just explodes. Maybe that's what happened. Jay held it in for so long that he couldn't contain himself anymore and finally murdered Hollis."

"Who told you this?" I asked Mars. "Did he lose enough

money to impact his life? Will he have to retire later or sell his home?"

"He was acting very odd about us walking him to his house," said Nina.

"You're kidding," said Mars. "That's now the measure of a killer?"

"Even Alex thought he was behaving oddly." I added olive oil to the bowl.

In a resigned voice, Nina said, "Jay never should have invested so much of his savings. My husband said he may never recover financially."

"You *knew* about this but you never told us?" I glared at her before scooting the tomatoes into the bowl, sprinkling them with salt and pepper, and turning them gently.

"My husband told me. I didn't mention it because Jay didn't murder Hollis."

"And how do you know that?" asked Mars.

"He's not the type." Nina spread cheese on a cracker.

"I suppose I am the type?" asked Mars.

"Apparently not. If you were, you'd have murdered Natasha a long time ago."

"Okay, you two." I placed the flank steak on a broiler pan, turned on the boiler, which heated immediately, and slid in the steak, carefully watching the time. "So what we're saying is that while we can't eliminate Kelsey as a suspect, we now have two more viable suspects—Jay and Cindy." I checked the potatoes with a fork to be sure they were cooked through and poured off the water. Adding a knob of butter, three tablespoons of cream cheese, and a splash of milk, I began to mash them furiously with an old-fashioned potato masher.

"Right." Mars sipped his drink. "They both had motives and opportunity."

Minutes later, I pulled out the steak, placed a mound of home-style mashed potatoes with the skins on each plate, and brought them to the table. Nina carried the tomato salad to the table, Mars sliced the flank steak and set the entire cutting board on the table so everyone could help themselves, and we sat down to eat.

Francie worked her fingers uncomfortably. "There is one other person I believe we may have overlooked. Mind you, I don't think he did it, but we'd be foolish not to consider him. I'm talking about Gavin."

Nina almost spilled her drink. "Francie! He's just a kid."

"Hollis ruined life as Gavin knew it." Francie's lips drew tight. "I don't want to think he killed his father, but did you see him at the underground dinner? He ran from Hollis every time he came near. It was terribly sad. Gavin already admitted being there that night. And he certainly had the ability to hide the foggers at the library where his mother works."

"But Gavin was in the hospital and couldn't have murdered Angus," I pointed out.

"Mmm, good." Mars swallowed a bite. "I wonder if Cindy left Gavin's side today. If she didn't, then we could rule her out in Angus's murder."

Nina speared a tomato. "The only person who could possibly have a motive for murdering Angus is Kelsey. She didn't want him exposing her for killing Hollis. He knew what she had done, and he would have talked eventually."

I still didn't want to believe it was Kelsey. "That would be easy enough to find out. She was going to give blood when I left her this afternoon. If she went to the hospital and donated blood, then she wouldn't have had the time to get back to Angus's and kill him."

"I bet there's a way to verify that," said Francie.

"Wolf can probably get that information." They all looked at me. "If I ask nicely, he might tell me. Sometimes I'm surprised by what he shares."

"Don't flatter yourself, Soph." Mars helped himself to

more potatoes. "Wolf's no pushover. If he gives you information, it's for a reason. It means it's something he wants you to know."

I saw the look that passed between Francie and Nina. Mars and I got along well, but we could easily fall into obnoxious bantering.

"There's another person we haven't considered. What about Parker?" I asked.

"What possible motive could he have?" Francie cut a tomato on her plate.

"Money?" I looked around at them. "Wouldn't that be an incentive to get rid of partners?"

Nina giggled. "I can't see staid old Parker sneaking into Hollis's house at night and setting off bug bombs. I'm sorry, but that image cracks me up."

"Maybe he's out of money. Or maybe Hollis and Gage were planning to leave? Is there such a thing as partner insurance?" I gasped. "Would Parker get money when Gage and Hollis died?" I asked.

Everyone stopped eating and stared at me.

"I always wondered about Gage's death," said Francie. "He was a young fuddy-duddy. Jay Charles is proper and dignified, but Gage was simply a bore."

Mars put down his fork. "You might be on to something, Sophie. But how would we find out more?"

"I talked to Madison about Gage, and she's still wondering about his death, too. I can ask Alex about the insurance angle," I offered.

"Francie," asked Nina. "How close are you to Trula?"

Francie nearly choked on her food. "That pompous egotist? I will not listen to her babble about Parker and her ancestry. Those poor people are probably flipping in their graves in shock that they're her claim to fame. I've never heard her express an interest in anything else."

We all snickered a little at Francie's assessment of Trula.

"Well, I guess that leaves me to have a chat with her," said Nina.

"Find out if they knew Angus. Maybe he did some work for them," I said.

At that moment, I looked up to see Natasha standing outside the kitchen door, watching us. I hopped up, opened the door, and invited her to join us.

"Thank you, Sophie. It would have been nice to receive an invitation."

Natasha chose a seat directly opposite Mars. I brought a plate, napkin, and silverware to the table for her.

"I've just come from the Habermans. That house needs so much work. It's dreadfully old-fashioned. I hope Kelsey will update it and rip out that ancient interior." She looked over at me. "And I'm furious with Wolf! He took my entire Coca-Cola cake for testing. Can you even imagine? I bet they're eating it down at the police station as I speak. Now I'm going to have to bake another one. I hear it was Hollis's favorite."

Mars finally gazed at her. "You do realize that he won't be there to enjoy it?"

"How do you manage without me to tell you what to do?" asked Natasha. "One brings dishes the deceased enjoyed to a repass."

"Repast," Mars corrected.

"I've never heard that." Nina scowled at her. "And before you say something derogatory about my upbringing, my mama taught me etiquette from day one. In North Carolina they take it very seriously."

Francie shook her head. "That's just silly. One should be grateful and welcome any dish at a repast." She giggled. "Can't you just see the bereaved standing at the door with a list of approved dishes and turning people away? Preposterous!"

"You people act like a *repass*," she emphasized her pronunciation and glared at Mars, "is just a haphazard thing. No wonder so many of them are slapdash." Natasha frowned as she poked at a slice of beef on her plate.

"Um, I hate to tell you this, but a funeral isn't something most people plan well in advance," said Nina. "Death is often unexpected. Like Hollis's death, for instance."

"Oh, Nina. I fear your mother did not do a good job with etiquette, after all. All funerals and memorial services should be at least a week to ten days after the demise of the person so the event can be properly planned. You have to choose the color scheme, order favors, and pick meaningful flowers. Not to mention hiring a videographer. They are not always readily available, you know."

"Are you sure you're not confusing a repast with a wedding?" I asked. "A color scheme and favors? Really?"

Natasha clasped a hand to her chest. "Bless you, Sophie. You do try. Did you cook this dinner? It's so . . . interesting." She speared a tomato and held it up in the air to examine it.

I'd had about enough of her snide remarks. What had gotten into her? "So how are things going with Jay Charles?"

She froze and shot me a look of daggers. "I'm sure I don't know what you mean." She glanced at Mars out of the corner of her eye.

"I ran into Humphrey's mother on the street today. She was looking at his house." It was probably mean of me to say. But it was true.

"She wasn't! She has been chasing him ever since the underground dinner. I don't know what he could possibly want with an older woman."

"You mean when he has you around?" asked Francie.

Natasha flashed her an irritated look. "Sophie, I hope you have your contribution to the bereaved Haberman household ready. I've let everyone know that Kelsey will be receiving tomorrow." She turned in Nina's direction. "Don't bother bringing anything store-bought."

"Who made you the funeral director?" spat Francie. "Nina can bring whatever she pleases."

"I'm trying to save her from embarrassment, Francie. There's simply no excuse for stopping by the store for something. You show you care by cooking a dish from the heart. Every good Southerner has a funereal recipe that she can whip up at a moment's notice."

"I suppose you have one?" asked Francie drily.

"Absolutely. I keep a Coca-Cola cake in my freezer at all times."

"Nina, we can bring crudités," said Francie. "Natasha won't know if it came from a store or if we broke off every little bit of broccoli with our own delicate hands."

Natasha's eyes flashed. "Crudités are out of vogue. You see, this is why I have to tell you these things. Being old is no excuse for poor manners."

Francie howled with laughter.

Chapter 24

Dear Sophie,
A coworker's husband was murdered recently. Un-
fortunately, I had problems of my own at the time
and wasn't able to prepare a casserole to drop by.
Now it's ten days later. Is it too late to bring her
food?
      Better Late Than Never in Opportunity,
      Montana

Dear Better Late Than Never,
The sad truth is that a great deal of food is thrown
out because everyone rushes to bring it immedi-
ately. The family will still be grieving and may ap-
preciate your kind gesture even more now that the
other food is gone.
      Sophie

At eleven the next morning, I made funeral potatoes to bring to Kelsey. They were amazingly easy to make and they were always popular thanks to the cheesy rich-ness of the potatoes. So she wouldn't have to worry about returning the pan, I baked them in a very sturdy disposable baking pan. It wasn't as pretty as a ceramic casserole dish, but it would be a lot less hassle for Kelsey.

At noon, I popped aluminum foil over the top to keep it warm and walked down the street to Kelsey's home. I banged the fox-head door knocker.

When Lavinia Brown opened the door, for a moment I thought I had the wrong house.

"Oh. It's you," she said.

What was wrong with that woman? I said hello and stepped inside. "Is Humphrey here?"

"He's working today. I came over with Jay. Someone left a casserole on his doorstep by mistake."

"How odd." I swept past her into the dining room, where Natasha had decked out the table with a black tablecloth again. If I recalled correctly, Natasha had gone through a couple of black decorating phases.

A small group of people, including Jay and Kelsey, had gathered around one dish.

"Did someone bring something yummy?" I asked.

"We're trying to figure out what it is," replied Jay. "It was left on my doorstep by mistake." He scooped a little bit out and placed it on a plate. He dipped a fork into it.

"Is it rice or noodles?" asked Kelsey.

"Hard to tell." Jay tasted the tiniest bit. "Oh! Spicy! I think it just cleared out my sinuses."

Unidentifiable food that was spicy? I knew who had cooked it—Natasha. But she knew perfectly well which house was the Habermans'. Leaving the dish at Jay's house had not been a mistake. What was she up to now?

I made room on the table for my funeral potatoes. Behind me someone said, "Those smell good." I knew the voice—Wolf.

I turned around. "I hope they'll taste good. You'll have to try them and tell me."

"I'm not sure I should eat anything. I'm not here as a bereaved."

"Why are you here? I heard you didn't find much when you searched the house."

"Sometimes it's interesting to see who shows up."

"I give you permission to eat some of my potatoes. And really"—I gestured toward the laden table—"there's plenty of food. Most of it will end up in the trash if people don't eat."

"True. I'll keep that in mind."

"Any word on Gavin?"

"He's going home today. He'll be fine. The surgery on his leg went very well. He just needs some downtime to recuperate."

"Did you have a chance to talk with him?" I smiled at Jay and moved out of the way so he could try my potatoes.

Wolf shook his head. "He and his mom lawyered up fast."

"So Kelsey is off the hook!" I whispered.

"Whoa. Don't go jumping to conclusions yet. Everything, except the foggers hidden in the library, still points at Kelsey."

I wasn't about to say it aloud, but I had a hunch I knew why he said that. Kelsey could have planted the foggers to implicate Cindy.

Madison sidled up to us. "Wolf, I'm so glad to see you here. I'd been debating about calling you, and when I heard about the bug bombs in the library, well, I knew I had to say something. I've known Cindy for a very long time and she's a dear, but Sophie and I heard a scathing discussion between Cindy and Hollis at the underground dinner."

Wolf focused on Madison intently. "Sophie mentioned that. I'd like to know what you recall, though. Sometimes people remember different things."

"Hollis practically threatened to behead her!"

Wolf didn't even flinch.

"It was horrid. And, Sophie, did you get the idea that there's some kind of family secret? Didn't Hollis warn her against opening a can of worms or something?"

"Thank you, Madison," said Wolf. "If you recall anything else, please let me know. Even if you don't think it's important."

"There is one more thing," she said. Madison brushed her hair out of her face and took a deep breath. "I just didn't think anything of it at the time. Since Gage's death I haven't been sleeping well. I'm sure you understand. I close my eyes and have nightmares. It's awful. Anyway, when I can't sleep, it's far worse to be at home, so I walk around town. After the underground dinner, I expected to be wiped out. But sleep eluded me, so I went out for a walk. You know how beautiful Old Town is at night. Anyway, I was a block away from here when I saw Cindy run by."

"Are you sure it was her?" asked Wolf.

"Definitely. She's so thin and delicate. She was dressed in black, wearing leggings I think. She was on the other side of the street, and I wasn't about to yell out her name and wake everyone up. But she ran by and kept going right down the street."

"Thank you, Madison." Wolf appeared grim to me. "I appreciate your coming forward with that information."

"I had to. It was meaningless at the time, but now . . . And I'll do some digging to see if I can find out that Haberman family secret."

Madison drifted over to the table and picked up a plate.

I could hear Natasha whining to Kelsey, "Entirely too many people are dropping by with food. If this continues, no one will bring anything for the real repass after Hollis is buried."

I whispered softly to Wolf, "I think I may know that

family secret. Follow me." I walked straight to Dr. Jay Charles. "Could I tear you away for a couple of minutes, please?"

"Why certainly, Sophie. Your potatoes were smashing!"

I beckoned the two of them out to the back porch. The first thing I did was look for the bees. They were gone and a temporary patch was in the spot they had invaded.

"Jay, would you please tell Wolf about Gavin's blood type?"

His eyebrows shot up. "Yes, of course. Hollis was not Gavin's biological father." He went on to explain about their incompatible blood types.

Wolf pulled a small pad out of his coat pocket and wrote down the details. "Are you sure about this?"

"I haven't seen Gavin's chart, but apparently they asked for type AB-positive donations."

Wolf's eyes met mine. "One more little thing." I tried to phrase my request so it wouldn't sound like it was a favor for me to verify the information. "Kelsey was with me early in the afternoon yesterday. From there, she went to donate blood and order a flower arrangement for Gavin. If she did donate blood, she would have been tied up for a while."

"So she wouldn't have been able to kill Angus," said Jay. "She might have an alibi!"

Wolf took off in a hurry after that. Jay went back inside, saying something about trying a Coca-Cola cake. I was about to join him when a plump, fiftyish woman opened the gate to the backyard with her hands full.

I jogged out to help her and took a Crock-Pot out of her hands.

"Thank you so much," she said. "I couldn't find a parking spot on the street. I hope I don't get towed."

Scents of chicken wafted to me from the covered Crock-Pot. "Something smells good."

"It's my family's go-to dish when someone dies. It's homemade chicken noodle soup. I know that seems like it should be for a cold or the flu, and it works great for those, too, but so often the bereaved just can't choke down food. Soup is easy to swallow and digest."

"And what's that you're carrying?"

"Hollis's favorite." Tears welled in her eyes. "I'll never make deviled eggs again without remembering him. Every time we had a little celebration at the office, Hollis asked for these. I think he could have eaten a platter of them all by himself."

"You worked with Hollis?"

"I'm Lisa Bar," she said, as though that should mean something to me. "I miss him so much. He was the best boss I ever had. I was with him for over twenty years. We were more than coworkers. What do they call it? Work-husband and work-wife? He was always there for me, you know?"

"Nice to meet you, Lisa. Even under these terrible circumstances. I'm Sophie Winston."

We walked across the grass and up the porch steps. She held the back door open for me. We walked through the kitchen to the dining room, where I placed the Crock-Pot of soup on an antique mahogany buffet where it could be plugged in. Kelsey directed me to soup bowls.

"No need," said Lisa. "No one wants to do dishes at a time like this. I brought bowls." She held up a clear plastic bag of disposable bowls and another with plastic spoons.

Natasha swooped in like an irate hawk and plucked them away from her. "Were you raised in a barn?"

Lisa's eyes grew wide and she cringed.

Fortunately, Natasha disappeared into the kitchen.

I placed my hand on Lisa's arm. "I'm so sorry. Don't mind her."

"I feel like I've committed a most egregious faux pas!" She trembled slightly.

"How do I get rid of her?" asked Kelsey. "She's been ordering me around since the day after Hollis died." Kelsey leaned toward us. "She insisted on a red coffin with a white lining that was totally reminiscent of vampires. I'm telling you, if they had put Hollis in that thing, it would have brought him back to life."

Lisa gasped. "Hollis would have flipped out. He had such genteel taste. What did you do?"

"I came home, called Humphrey, and told him to cancel everything. They haven't even turned Hollis over to the funeral home yet, anyway. Now, my aunt Delilah Jean would have loved that red coffin. She couldn't get enough red. Her walls were red, her hair was red, and she always drove a red car."

"Well, I apologize for any breach of etiquette," muttered Lisa. "I've brought those bowls to a dozen bereaved families. Now I'm terribly embarrassed. Imagine what those people think of me."

Kelsey hugged Lisa. "They think you are considerate, and I'm certain they were as grateful as I am."

"Kelsey"—Lisa smiled at her sadly—"I know a lot of people are close to Cindy and weren't as welcoming as they might have been. But, honey, you made Hollis very happy. When he met you, it was like he got a second wind."

Kelsey burst into tears. "Thank you," she rasped. "Thank you for telling me that."

Feeling a bit like a third wheel, I backed away to give them time together. Natasha seized me by the arm and propelled me into the kitchen, where Madison appeared to be studying the goodies on the counter.

"I baked a casserole for Jay, but someone brought it over here!" hissed Natasha.

Madison ambled over. "Maybe he can't eat an entire casserole by himself."

"It hadn't even been touched!"

"Did you leave it on his doorstep?" I asked.

"He doesn't answer his door. Don't you think that's odd? I'm certain he was home."

So it was the spicy casserole as I had suspected. "He thinks someone left it at his house by mistake."

Madison grinned. "So what are you doing bringing Jay casseroles, anyway? I thought you were trying to reconcile with Mars."

"Don't you think Jay would be perfect for me? We're both so proper and well-mannered."

Madison pointed toward the dining room. "Maybe you'd better get him away from that woman then."

We looked to see what she was talking about. Humphrey's mother fed Jay a taste of something on her plate.

"That's not proper etiquette at all!" Natasha stalked toward the two of them.

"Ohhh, Madison," I said. "What have you done?"

She laughed and immediately placed her hand over her mouth. "I can't believe I'm laughing at a repast. How dreadful of me."

I spied Lisa standing alone for a moment and excused myself to talk with her. "That was a really nice thing to say to Kelsey."

Lisa helped herself to cake. "Oh, but it was true. The divorce was really ugly. It wasn't the first time Hollis and Cindy had butted heads. No marriage is perfect, but they had some rocky times. That's for sure."

I sucked up my courage and asked what I was dying to know. "Is there any speculation at your office about who might have murdered Hollis?"

Chapter 25

Dear Sophie,
I was appalled when I washed a glass potluck
casserole dish and found the person had etched her
name into the bottom with a fancy script. It said,
"Do not steal. This belongs to Sara Murgatroid."
Is this the appropriate way to mark a dish?
  Blown Away in Surprise, New York

Dear Blown Away,
It sounds to me like Sara Murgatroid has lost a lot
of her dishes in the past. Personally, I think it's far
easier and certainly more friendly to simply stick
an address label on the bottom.
  Sophie

Lisa moaned. "We can't talk about anything else. You can imagine the atmosphere. First Gage and now Hollis? It's insane. Everyone is whispering theories."

"Any possibility that there's a connection between the two deaths?" I asked.

Lisa looked around and motioned me out to the porch, saying in a loud voice, "I really need to get back to the office."

I followed her onto the porch.

She gazed out over the backyard. "Something was wrong. I'm not sure what it was, but right before Gage died it was as if a cloud of gloom descended on the office. The thing is, I don't have anything concrete. No letters or visits from suspicious people, nothing like that. Just a feeling in the air."

She rambled on about how much she loved working for Hollis and what a great sense of humor he'd had. I nodded and smiled appropriately, but I wasn't really listening anymore.

"Lisa," I interrupted, "do you think there could have been a problem between the partners?"

She shook her head. "I never heard a cross word between them. They were consummate professionals. Gentlemen. I'm sure you know what I mean. But Gage's death was so unexpected. Just between us, and I don't mean this in a cruel way, if Hollis had had too much to drink and had fallen into the river, I would have said, 'Well, that's Hollis.' He did things in a big way. But Gage wasn't the type. I guess it could happen to anybody. I've been known to have a drink or two too many myself."

"What about clients? Was there anyone who was angry with Hollis?"

"Clients aren't always happy with the outcomes of their cases, but I don't know of anyone who had it in for Hollis. I didn't hear anyone threaten him or anything." She gazed at me intently. "These are the same things that the cop asked me."

Must have been Wolf asking questions. "*Someone* had it in for Hollis."

She looked around and whispered, "You didn't hear it from me, but Cindy isn't always the angel she seems."

Lisa hurried down the stairs and out to the gate. Only then did she stop to look back at me. She didn't wave. She closed the gate, and a few seconds later I heard an engine start.

What did that mean? We all had our moments, of course. And the divorce had been ugly. Maybe that was what she had in mind. She had probably overheard Hollis's side of some angry discussions. Or maybe when Cindy called Hollis's office she had been less than congenial to Lisa. Funny how things had shifted in Cindy's direction.

Instead of going back inside the Haberman house, I left through the gate and walked along the alley to the street. No matter who had murdered Hollis, it was a good bet he or she had arrived and left this way. I gazed around, looking for anything out of place. Wolf would have collected anything suspicious, so I didn't expect to find much, but even eagle-eyed cops could miss something. The trouble was that even if Cindy, Kelsey, or Angus had dropped an item, it would be meaningless. All three of them had legitimate reasons for being in the alley behind the house.

I walked a few blocks to Alex's law firm. His assistant waved me into his office. Alex studied something on his computer. He held a Tupperware bowl in one hand. The other hand held a fork poised over it.

"I'm interrupting your lunch."

"I'm always happy to see you." He set the bowl down and came around his desk for a quick kiss. "Are you bringing me good news about Kelsey?"

"I have a question." I peered into the Tupperware bowl. "Is that chicken salad? Did you make it yourself?"

"I won't take offense at your implication that I'm not capable of cooking for myself. My assistant had some kind of party with girlfriends and brought me the leftovers for lunch."

"I wasn't implying that you can't cook. I just see you barbecuing, not cutting up pretty grapes and little chunks of chicken. That was very nice of her. Looks good."

"I presume that wasn't the question you had in mind?"

I shot him an annoyed look. "Do law firms carry insurance on the lawyers?"

"Some of them do. It's called key person insurance. A lot of companies carry it. It's not just for lawyers. The idea is to cover the firm in case a prime moneymaker dies."

"Really? I thought that was a long shot. So Parker might have lucked into insurance proceeds for the deaths of Gage and Hollis?"

"I don't know if they had key person insurance." He paused and grinned at me. "But it might be interesting to find out."

"Trula said Parker was thinking of asking you to join the firm."

"He might. We're having a little meeting over drinks tonight."

I froze. Would Alex be the next to die? "And?"

"If he makes an offer, I'll probably turn him down. Frankly, I'm happy doing my own thing. There are times when I wish I had a team of paralegals to help me, but mostly I'm happy with my professional life the way things are."

Watching his response carefully, I added, "And you don't know what's going on over there?"

He showed no emotion whatsoever. Very quietly he said, "There's that, too."

"I'm glad, but do you think you could ask about key person insurance during your meeting?"

"Sneak it into the conversation? Sure."

"It's beginning to look like Cindy might be behind Hollis's death, but I still can't help wondering about Parker."

His eyes narrowed. "Other than an insurance motive, do you have any leads? Any reason to think Parker was involved with the deaths?"

"No," I said glumly.

"Any gossip about Angus's death yet?"

"You're worried that Kelsey will be blamed?"

"Sure I am. Chances are that Angus's death was completely unrelated to Hollis's demise, but any reasonable person would have to question it. Not only because they were murdered so close together in time, but because Angus worked for Hollis."

"There's a good possibility that Kelsey was giving blood when Angus was killed. The time frame between seeing him alive and finding him dead is fairly narrow. I've asked Wolf to find out if Kelsey gave blood like she said she would."

Alex tilted his head and glared at me. "Gee, thanks."

"What's wrong?"

"What if she wasn't giving blood just then? And what was she doing running around giving blood when her husband just died and she's under suspicion for his murder?" He looked away and muttered, "Who does that?"

A sigh shuddered out of me. "The not-so-ugly stepmother of a child who was injured and has an exceedingly rare blood type that she shares with him but not with his father."

His gaze whipped back to me. "What?"

"She gave blood for Gavin, who it turns out is not Hollis's biological kid."

He very slowly massaged a spot over his left eyebrow and a grin grew on his face. "Does Gavin know this?"

"I don't think so."

"Poor kid. So who is the dad?"

"Gavin is about fourteen. I guess you'd have to ask Cindy."

"Whoa."

I could almost see the cogs turning in Alex's brain. "Let me guess. If they indict Kelsey, then you'll throw this news in their faces to cast doubt in the minds of the jury?"

"Maybe. That's a whopper of a tidbit. Cindy is always so soft-spoken and quiet. I never imagined she could have a wild side."

"Before you get too excited, Jay Charles mentioned that she might have been inseminated. Could be that Hollis couldn't have children."

He grimaced. "Good point. I should not jump to conclusions." He grinned again. "But this does have potential."

When I left Alex's office, he had forgotten all about the remaining chicken salad. I stopped in the doorway to look back at him. He sat at his desk, staring at the chair I had occupied and tapping his right forefinger on the desktop.

I strolled back and spent a quiet evening at home. But Hollis and Angus were always in my thoughts.

Just before two in the morning, Mochie woke me by jumping over me. He sprang from my bed to the floor. I groaned and turned over. My eyes closed, I became aware of a faint tapping sound, not unlike a dripping faucet. I wasn't one for sleeping with a pillow over my head to block out sounds and lights. Grumpily, I shuffled into the bathroom. The faucets weren't dripping and the pinging continued.

I returned to the hallway and looked around. Where had Mochie gone? He knew where that annoying noise was coming from. The old stairs creaked under my feet as I walked down to the first floor. Yawning, I stumbled into the kitchen and checked the sink. Nothing dripping there. I peered out the window. Everything seemed quiet out on the street.

The sound stopped and Mochie mewed. I followed his voice into the sunroom. A dark figure stood at the door looking in.

Chapter 26

Dear Sophie,
What's a repass? My cousin died and everyone is
talking about a repass.
        Clueless in Little Hope, Texas

Dear Clueless,
Your relatives' accents may have led you astray.
The correct spelling is repast with a T. It is a gath-
ering of friends and family after a funeral or a
memorial service. However, in the South, it is well-
known as a repass. The T is dropped.
        Sophie

I shrieked, more from surprise than fear.
"Sophie! It's me, Kelsey!"

I flicked on the lights and unlocked the door. "Is something wrong? Are you okay?"

She thrust an envelope at me. "I have to leave. Will you look after the house for me?"

"Where are you going?"

"It's better if you don't know."

"I don't understand."

"They're going to arrest me. Please?" She waggled the envelope. "There are things you don't know."

"You mean about you killing Wayne?"

Her eyes opened wide. "If you know about that, then the cops have found out, too."

"Maybe not. They might not know that you had an aunt named Delilah Jean."

She sucked in the cool night air and released it. "It's not just that. They'll murder me, too, if I stay."

"Who?"

"I wish I knew."

"Come inside, Kelsey. I'll make you a cup of tea and we'll talk."

She glanced around. "I can't. Please help me out?" She shoved the envelope at me again. "They're following me. I've heard them. I know they're out there."

Reluctantly I took the envelope. "They? You think there's more than one person?"

"It sounds like it to me. I've heard them."

"Heard them?"

She nodded. "They're watching me."

"Kelsey, why do you think someone wants to murder you, too?"

"You're a smart woman, Sophie. It's very simple. The two men in my life were murdered, Hollis and Angus. I'm certain that I'm next. Whoever murdered Hollis probably thought I was in the house, lying in bed right next to him that night. How do I know that I wasn't the intended target?"

That thought hadn't even occurred to me. "But when the lights were out, you weren't afraid to be home alone."

"I was so devastated by Hollis's death that I hadn't thought it through. At that time, I didn't want to live without him. That kind of despair clouds your mind and erases fear and logic."

I felt for her. She had been all alone in anguish in that big house with no electricity. "Do you have an admirer? Someone who might think if he got rid of them that you would be available?"

"Not really. Parker has been coming around a lot, but I think that's because he feels an obligation, being Hollis's partner and all."

Chills ran down my spine. Trula had been worried about Parker falling for Kelsey. "Please come inside. Let's talk about this."

She hugged me ferociously. "I'll be back. Don't worry about me. I know how to disappear. It's not the first time I've had to do it."

She let go of me and ran into the darkness of my yard. "Kelsey!" I shouted in a whisper.

But she was gone.

I locked the door and returned to the kitchen. In the darkness, I put on the kettle for tea. While it cooked, I peered out the bay window at the street. Everything seemed calm. No one lurked outside, not that I could see anyway. The crickets chirped, happy that it was summer and that I had planted a garden for them to feast upon.

I flicked on a soft light. Poor Kelsey. The problem was that she didn't have any great alibis for Hollis's death. She could easily have set off the foggers before she left the house. That's what the prosecution would say. I could just hear it. "The defendant set off the bug bombs, then left the house to see her lover, hoping to use him as an alibi." Now that the finger of guilt had swung in Cindy's direction, I had expected Kelsey to be more confident. But Kelsey had said something that threw the entire situation in another direction.

I was lifting the kettle to pour water into my mug when I heard tapping on the glass door. Kelsey! She had changed her mind and come back. I decided against turning on the outside light, lest she be running from someone who was following her.

I peered out the window. "Nina?" Unlocking the door, I asked, "What are you doing here?"

She pulled her silk robe tighter. "Couldn't sleep. I saw your light on and thought you might be eating something good."

"Tea?"

"Peach schnapps for me." Nina disappeared into the dining room for a couple of minutes and returned with an etched cordial glass that contained a clear liquid. "Anything to nosh?"

"Leftover chocolate truffle tart."

"Oh, perfect for a snack in the wee hours. Got any extra whipped cream?"

"You bet." I cut two slices and placed them on Marlborough Sprays dessert plates. I spooned whipped cream into a small crystal bowl and set it on the table, along with the tart, forks, and napkins.

"What's that?" Nina eyed the envelope Kelsey had given me.

I sat down and sipped my tea. "Kelsey ran away. She stopped by and gave me this envelope before she ran off into the night."

"You're kidding me! What's in it?"

"Haven't opened it yet." I picked it up and pried the seal open. A stack of cash was the first thing I noticed.

"Whoa!" Nina seized the money and started to count.

Meanwhile, I took out a letter written in a precisely controlled, girlish handwriting. I read aloud.

Dear Sophie,
I want to thank you for standing by me in my time
of need. You'll never know how much I appreciate

your friendship. Unfortunately, everything seems to be stacked against me. I understand how bad my situation appears. I did not murder Hollis. He was the best thing that ever happened to me. Without him, I feel like life will never be happy again. I have no choice but to leave. I hope to return soon, but sometimes murders go unsolved for years. I hope that won't be the case for Hollis or Angus. I didn't kill Angus, either, nor do I know who did. But you can surely understand why it would be dangerous for me to remain in Old Town at this time. I don't know who is after me. I'm enclosing some money. Please pay Alex whatever he needs to continue my representation. The key to the house is also enclosed. I would be so appreciative if you kept an eye on things during my absence. When the killer of Hollis and Angus is arrested, please tie a white scarf onto the back of the bench just outside the mock lighthouse at the marina to let me know it is safe to return. Thank you for believing in me.

   Hugs,
   Kelsey
PS. Please water the plants.

"The plants?" yelped Nina. "She's on the run from the cops and a killer, and she's worried about watering the plants?"

"It's funny, but I think it indicates two things. One, she really is planning to return. Otherwise, she wouldn't care about the plants. And two, she's telling the truth. If she had spent a lot of time making up a story, her mind wouldn't have been on withering plants."

Nina spewed schnapps and grabbed a napkin. In a mockingly placid tone, she said, "Why, of course. Because murderers don't like plants. We can do away with juries. We'll put defendants on the stand and pretend that we're going to hurt a plant. If they protest, they're innocent!"

"Very funny. I still think she's telling the truth. Think about it, Nina. She could have disappeared the night Hollis died."

"But if she disappeared, she wouldn't have inherited the money."

"She pointed out that the two men in her life had been killed, so I asked if she had any admirers." I leaned toward Nina. "She said Parker had been hanging around. At the underground dinner, Trula asked me how to get rid of a strumpet without getting caught."

"She was just joking."

"That's what I thought, too. But now I wonder . . ."

"If she meant to kill Kelsey, then she's not much of a murderer because she killed the wrong person twice."

"But what if it were Parker who was jealous of Hollis?"

Nina took a big bite of tart. She wasn't laughing anymore. She swallowed and waved her fork as she spoke. "So Parker killed both Hollis and Angus so he could be with Kelsey? In that case, Kelsey has nothing to fear. Trula would be next.

"Or maybe Trula meant to get rid of Kelsey by killing Hollis and framing Kelsey," said Nina. "Maybe she saw Hollis as collateral damage. Or maybe she didn't like him for some reason."

"She's very judgmental. Sometimes she's worse than Natasha. Trula has been spending a lot of time in the library, too. She could have planted the foggers there."

"*Bssst.*" Nina made a buzzer sound as though I had gotten the wrong answer. "But then she would have been framing the wrong person." Nina picked up the envelope and shook out the key. Her eyes met mine. "I suppose we really ought to check on the house in the morning."

"That would be the friendly thing to do."

"After all, who knows what kind of condition those plants are in?"

At eight in the morning, Nina showed up at my kitchen door dressed entirely in black. She wore a scoop neck T-shirt with black golf shorts and black sneakers.

"You do realize that black is for nighttime surveillance?"

She poured herself a mug of coffee and doctored it with sugar and milk. "Seemed appropriate anyway. Are you ready to go?"

Mochie had eaten his breakfast of chicken stew for cats and was engaged in cleaning his fur. Leaving him to his morning bath, we left. I took care to lock the door behind us.

Our street was quiet. I assumed most people were already in their offices. We ambled over to the Habermans' house. A casserole had been left at the door. Nina swooped it up and sniffed. "King Ranch Chicken Casserole. Smells delicious."

I unlocked the door, feeling more than a little bit odd to be entering someone else's home.

Nina barged ahead. I found her in the kitchen, ready to stab a spoon into the casserole.

"You can't eat that!"

"I don't see why not. It's not as though Kelsey will be eating it."

"It wasn't meant for you. Besides, how do you know that the killer didn't prepare it?"

"The killer has excellent taste. This is the kind of casserole dish you would leave."

I recognized the red ruffled edge. "It's Emile Henry stoneware."

"See?" Nina lifted the casserole and read the name appended to the bottom. "It's from Bonnie and Barry Seltenfelder."

"Do you know them?"

"No."

"There you go. Put it in the fridge."

She sounded a little miffed and took a very deep sniff of it before stashing it in the crowded refrigerator.

I was more interested in the fact that Kelsey had bothered to clean up the kitchen before she left. The counters were clear. I peeked in the dining room. The tablecloth had been changed, and the dishes were stacked as if ready for another onslaught of visitors.

In the light of day, it was a beautiful house. Not a hint of anything sinister caught my attention. I stepped onto the porch, where the bees had been. They hadn't returned, but the wall and ceiling still needed a permanent repair.

I sucked in the fresh morning air and gazed around. What could have happened to scare Kelsey? I couldn't help feeling that her departure had been very abrupt. And sort of late in the game. Of course, in the beginning, only Hollis had been murdered. So what was it about Angus's death that had terrified Kelsey and made her believe she might be next?

"Sophie!" Nina's voice held a note of excitement.

I returned to the kitchen and locked the door behind me. "Where are you?"

"In the living room."

I walked through the dining room to what I imagined would have been called the parlor. Nina had opened a glass door and stood with her back to me.

As I neared her, she stepped aside so we could both see the narrow passage between the Haberman house and Jay Charles's house. A brick wall separated the properties. Someone had cleverly omitted some bricks in a diamond shape, probably for air circulation.

It was a small private garden. In the middle, red bricks were laid in a herringbone pattern. Comfy benches and an oversized outdoor chair offered seating. But two giant pots containing tree roses had been tipped over and broken. Soil had been scattered across the brick patio.

Chapter 27

Dear Natasha,
My aunt Beatrice was the official funeral maven.
She was the first to show up and the last to leave.
She helped with funeral arrangements, told people
which foods to bring, washed dishes, selected the
hymns, and wrote the obituaries. Are there people
who do that for a living? It would make life so
much easier.
Need Help in Monks Misery, Maryland

Dear Need Help,
There are funeral event planners, funeral consul-
tants, and funeral event coordinators who can do
exactly what you're describing.
Natasha

"I hope these aren't the plants Kelsey was hoping we would water," said Nina.

"Oy. Somebody made a mess out there." I stepped outside. Whoever had done it had left a shoeprint in the middle of the dirt. "Guess we'd better notify Wolf."

I called him on my cell phone. While we waited for him to arrive, Nina and I had a quick look around the house, but everything else was in order.

"Think Kelsey heard someone out there last night and that's what spooked her?" asked Nina.

"That would be my guess."

Wolf went through the house again and took a close look at the damage to the garden. "Don't clean this up yet. I'd like to get someone over here to take photographs of that shoeprint. Is there any way you can get in touch with Kelsey?"

Bashfully, I told him about the white cloth I was supposed to tie on a bench.

To my surprise, Wolf smiled. "That Kelsey is one smart lady."

"Are you going to put out an all-points bulletin on her to find her?" asked Nina.

Wolf gave her the look of a patient parent. "She's not under arrest, Nina. I'm not happy that she skipped town. But it's not illegal for her to leave. Not yet anyway."

While we waited for the crime scene crew to arrive, someone banged the door knocker. Since Wolf was with us, I didn't hesitate to open the door.

Jay Charles stood on the stoop. "Sophie!" He blinked in surprise. "I didn't expect to see you here. Is Kelsey all right? I recognized Wolf parking on the street."

"Please come in. I suspect he'd like to know if you heard any noises last night."

Jay stiffened. Whispering, he asked, "You didn't tell him about the ghost voices, did you?"

I was pretty sure I had tried not to mention that to anyone. "No. Have you made any progress?"

A flush of pink crept up his face. "I can't believe that I, a man who makes a living looking for facts—concrete facts from which one can draw conclusions—am even discussing ghosts. I admit the research on my house has been fascinating, though. I wish the building could speak to me. It saw so many tragedies and intrigues, as well as happy times."

"So you no longer think you have ghosts?" I inquired.

He took a deep breath and beamed. "During the Revolutionary War, the house belonged to a Molly Jones. Molly's husband was killed by the British, leaving her a very angry, but wealthy young widow. In retaliation, she hosted formal dinner parties where spies could meet to pass on information. Apparently, some of the spies would leave information with her. She hung a pink petticoat out to dry with the laundry as a signal that she had information to be picked up."

"Amazing!" I said. "How exciting to know that information that passed through your home may have helped the country!"

"I'm told women weren't respected at the time, so they were generally overlooked as sources of news and secrets. They think that's how Molly managed to keep it up without being suspected."

"Do you think Molly is haunting your house?" I asked.

Jay cocked his head and lifted his shoulders. "I'm still not completely sold on the existence of ghosts. I haven't discussed this with many people, mostly discreet historians. I don't want it getting out that I've gone loony! However, it has been suggested by some that the murmurings I hear may be from Molly and her guests. It's true that I only hear them in my dining room. The odd thing is that I never heard them until recently. Certainly not when my wife was living. We'd have discussed anything that unusual."

"Would you feel better if I came over and listened the next time you hear them? I'd be happy to do that."

"I couldn't impose on you. It only happens late at night."

"It wouldn't be an imposition at all. It's not as though I live far away. I would be interested in hearing Molly and her friends."

"Thank you for your offer. You're very kind."

Wolf strode up. "Good morning, Dr. Charles. Did you hear any unusual noises last night?"

Jay shot me a desperate glance, which I interpreted to mean that he hoped I wouldn't mention the ghosts. "As a matter of fact I did. It was well past midnight, probably around one in the morning. It sounded like something crashed and broke out on the street. I sat up in bed but didn't hear anything more, so I went back to sleep."

I had no idea what Wolf was thinking, but I couldn't help thinking Jay wasn't particularly helpful. After all, we already knew it had happened. Jay hadn't provided any information of interest other than the time that it happened.

Jay followed Wolf to the little side garden where the pots had smashed.

"Wow. They're a good distance apart. I guess the sound of the first pot breaking woke me and then I heard the second one," said Jay. "If Gavin still lived here I would think it might have been some kind of prank by youngsters."

"Have you noticed anyone lurking around on the street or in the alley behind your house?" asked Wolf.

"No, but I must admit that I haven't been on the lookout for anything of the sort. A lot of people came here to the Habermans' yesterday since Natasha informed us we had to come. So there was a good bit of traffic. Anyone would have blended in. I didn't know half the people in attendance."

"Did Hollis mention to you that he feared his food was being poisoned?"

Jay stared at Wolf wide-eyed. "He thought Kelsey was trying to kill him? He never breathed a word about it to me." Jay staggered to a sofa in the living room and sank onto it. "Roughly a year ago, Hollis told me about an investment that was going to skyrocket. I should have recognized that he wasn't a terrific source of investment advice. After all, he was a lawyer, not a broker. Anyway, I put a lot of my money into it and took a very bad financial hit when it crashed and burned. Hollis lost money, too. And now that I know he was afraid someone was poisoning him, I can't help but wonder if he recommended the investment to someone else who lost everything and killed him in revenge."

Wolf observed Jay quietly. "Did you murder Hollis?"

A flicker of shock crossed Jay's face. But he recovered immediately. In a subdued tone, he said, "No. Hollis was my friend. He made a bad call, but I was the one who greedily invested far too much on something speculative at best. No one forced me to make that investment. I was shattered for a few days, but Hollis lost a bundle, too. He meant well."

He spoke so calmly and rationally that I believed him. I thought Wolf must, too. Surely a murderer wouldn't be so elegantly composed.

The door knocker sounded again. I opened the door to the crime scene crew. Nina, Jay, and I spent the next hour watching them. As far as I could tell, they didn't find anything of particular interest.

One of them climbed into Gavin's tree house. He came out grinning from ear to ear. "That takes me back. I wish I could sit up there reading comic books and listening to the birds. I bagged a couple of candy bar wrappers, but I doubt that anyone who would break huge flowerpots would have taken the time to have a snack in the tree house."

After they left, Jay brought over two large planters for

the rose trees. The three of us repotted them and hoped for the best. Kelsey could always change the pots when she came home if she didn't like them.

I locked up Kelsey's house, then Nina and I went home to change out of our dusty clothes. We met again in half an hour to walk down to the waterfront in search of the bench where I was supposed to leave an all-clear sign for Kelsey.

The mock lighthouse was part of a waterfront restaurant. People rested on four double-length benches in an open area in front of the lighthouse with the Potomac River merely feet away. I noted how easy it would have been for Gage to fall into the river unnoticed.

"Which one do you suppose it is?" asked Nina.

"Good question." We walked around them all, looking for some sign.

It wasn't until I stood with my back to the mock lighthouse and gazed out at the water that I spotted a camera mounted high on a pole and aimed right at me.

On a hunch, I pulled out my phone and searched the Internet for webcams in Old Town. Sure enough, I found one at the marina and saw myself in the image.

"Look at this." I beckoned to Nina.

She checked the image and looked up at the camera. "Wolf is right. Kelsey is pretty sharp."

Nina and I waved at the camera, just in case Kelsey was watching.

"I guess it's that first bench." I looked forward to the day we could hang a white scarf there.

On the way back we stopped for barbecued chicken sandwiches. The first people I saw when we entered the area of outdoor tables were Humphrey and his mother. It was too late to dodge them. I smiled sweetly, waved, and steered Nina to a table on the other side.

"What's with you?" asked Nina.

"Humphrey's mother is oddly rude to me. I have no idea why she doesn't like me, but she actually told me to leave her son alone!"

"Aah. Once upon a time he was crazy mad for you. Maybe his feelings have returned."

"That's all I need."

After we ordered, Humphrey dropped by our table. Pale and wan, he pulled out a chair and sat down with us.

But before he could say anything, Nina demanded, "So what's your mother's problem with Sophie?"

Poor Humphrey. I didn't think he could be any paler. A red flush grew on his cheeks and the tips of his ears. "Has she been unfriendly?"

"Don't worry about it, Humphrey." I patted his poor little pale hand. "She'll be going home soon anyway."

"Maybe. She might stay longer. She has taken a real interest in Jay."

"But she's much older than Jay. She could almost be his mother!" Nina's brow creased in disbelief.

"Love knows no age, Nina." Humphrey leaned toward me. "I'm sorry if she was rude, Sophie. Do you remember a girl in high school named Brandi Truett?"

The name rang a bell with me. "A loud redhead?"

"That's the one. My mother wanted to bring Brandi with her to match us up—a horrifically misguided love match. Can you imagine me with her?"

"No, I can't. But that was back in tenth grade. She's probably gorgeous now."

"Not so much. I saw her the last time I visited my mom. She talks like a foghorn."

Nina laughed so hard she almost spit a gulp of her soda.

"At the time, I just wanted Mom to stop trying to match us up, so I may have mentioned that you have ruined me for all other women."

Nina laughed even harder.

"I didn't think about what might happen if Mom actually saw you. And I might have reminded her of my interest in you when she suggested she bring Brandi with her on this visit."

At least it wasn't some etiquette breach or hateful thing I had said or done. "All is forgiven. I shall bear this burden with grace now that I know I'm saving you from Foghorn Brandi."

"Thanks for being a good sport. I have to get back to Mom, but I wanted to know if you think Natasha is secretly in love with me."

Nina laughed so hard that she actually gasped for air. I hoped she wouldn't fall off her chair. I delicately kicked her under the table.

Dear heaven! I hated to let Humphrey down. But as usual, I guessed it was better to tell him the truth. "Probably not."

"My mother says Natasha is exhibiting all the signs of infatuation."

Uh oh. Was this how his mother intended to get rid of her rival for Jay's interest?

"Sophie, you can't imagine how she kissed me at your dinner the other night. I've never been kissed like that in my life. It was . . . full of passion!"

"Honey, I think she may have been confused when she collapsed." There, that was a nice way of putting it. It allowed him to save face.

"Well, she sure wasn't confused when she woke up and kissed me. She wouldn't let go of my head."

I would have to take another tack. "Have you heard from her since then?"

"She was at the gathering for Hollis, but she was very busy introducing my mom around."

I suspected that what seemed like a generous and kind thing to Humphrey was in reality Natasha's way of steering his mother away from Jay. I seized the mention of Hollis as an excuse to change the subject. Wolf had already provided answers, but I was desperate to distract Humphrey. "Did your friend ever give you the result on the poison tests?"

"I should have called you with them. I apologize, Sophie."

"And?"

"They tested for rat poison, ethanol, which is in antifreeze, a couple of drugs known to cause breathing difficulties, belladonna, and arsenic. That's hardly a comprehensive test. I understand Wolf has ordered additional testing. But so far the mac and cheese, the meatball sandwich, the cheesecake, the pasta Alfredo, and the doughnuts came up clean."

"In other words, we still don't have a definitive answer."

"Right. But some of the most common poisons have been ruled out. I'd better get back to Mom. If you see Natasha, tell her I send my best."

I shook out of my thoughts about Hollis and poisons. "If you want Natasha, I suggest you wear bow ties."

Humphrey stood up. "Women find them sexy?"

"I can't speak for all women, but apparently Natasha does."

"Thanks for the tip, Soph."

Humphrey returned to his table about the time our sandwiches arrived.

I looked at Nina. "So it appears that Hollis was probably wrong about Kelsey poisoning him."

"But the important thing is that he was afraid he was being poisoned. That indicates some kind of problem in his life. He thought someone was after him," she said as she lifted her sandwich and eyed it.

"What if it wasn't Kelsey he was afraid of? Could Cindy

have poisoned Hollis's food?" I stared at my barbecued chicken sandwich. "Seems unlikely."

Something didn't add up. Kelsey had Hollis on a heart-healthy diet. Unless the cops took all the fattening food from Kelsey's refrigerator, there wasn't anything like cheese-cake or doughnuts or meatball sandwiches at her house. "How could I have been so stupid?"

Nina gazed at me as she chewed.

"Don't you see? Kelsey had Hollis on a diet. She wanted him alive. She wanted him to be healthy. The foods he gave me were lunch foods that *he* must have bought. He was cheating on his diet."

I smacked my hand flat on the table. "It wasn't Kelsey whom Hollis feared might poison him. It was someone at work!"

Chapter 28

Dear Natasha,
I am a barbecue fanatic. My wife says I'm not sup-
posed to pick up a sandwich or a rib with my
hands in a restaurant. What? I have to get takeout
or grill it myself to enjoy my meat?
Messy Guy in Seven Devils, North Carolina

Dear Messy Guy,
Get a napkin. And a fork and knife. When eating
in a public place one is not allowed to gross out
other diners.
Natasha

"We've been chasing the wrong branch of Hollis's life. I have thought all along that Parker stood to gain something from Hollis's death. Everyone suspected Hollis's young wife, but his problem was at the office."

Nina stopped eating for a moment and whispered, "You can't be serious. You think Parker murdered Hollis? What about Gage?"

I nodded, then spoke in a very low voice so I wouldn't

be overheard. "Possibly. Oh my gosh! Parker is always drooling over Kelsey. Trula mentioned that she was worried about it."

Nina gulped her soda. "He wouldn't have had to murder Gage for that."

"Maybe he needed money." I looked up to see Mars, Daisy, and Bernie headed our way.

Daisy pulled at her leash when she saw me. I hugged her like crazy while she wagged all over. She made a point of sitting next to me and leaning against my legs.

Mars and Bernie sat down with us. When they ordered, I asked for plain shredded chicken and water for Daisy.

When the waitress left, I spilled the news in a very hushed voice.

"Parker? Think he'd have the guts to kill someone?" asked Bernie.

Mars grabbed one of my extra paper napkins and pulled out a pen. "Let's consider this logically. What do we know for sure?"

"Whoever murdered Hollis had a key, unless Kelsey left the door open on purpose," I said.

"Kelsey and Parker together!" said Nina. "That fits. She could have let him in. They had to get rid of Angus, too, if they wanted to be together."

"Wouldn't Gavin have seen Parker?" I asked. "Unless Parker used the front door," I mused.

"Nina is right. It does fit," said Mars. "But it could also have been Trula."

"You're speculating again," said Bernie.

I thought aloud. "We know that Hollis was on a heart-healthy diet. I saw their refrigerator. The food Hollis brought me for testing definitely didn't come from there."

"Unless Kelsey threw everything out," said Bernie.

Mars scowled. "So someone had a key, set off the foggers inside the house, and left."

"And the foggers were found at the library," Nina added.

"Possibly to cast suspicion on Cindy," said Mars.

I wiped my hands with sanitizer. "Trula bought foggers but lied about it to me. She claimed that she bought silver polish." I finally bit into my sandwich.

"Sounds like Trula was in on it," said Nina. "Why would she lie about something like that?"

"Maybe Trula did it by herself," said Mars.

"But why murder Hollis if she wanted to get rid of Kelsey?" I asked.

"Mistake," Bernie suggested. "It was dark. Or she just didn't care. Maybe she thought Hollis would survive since he was so much larger than Kelsey."

"And that's why Kelsey ran away?" I asked. "She's afraid Trula will kill her next?"

"Kelsey's gone?" Mars and Bernie chimed in unison.

I filled them in on the details.

"Then she probably suspects one of them," said Nina. "Maybe she's like us and doesn't know which one to suspect."

"I still have a key to the house where I lived with Natasha," said Mars.

Nina and Bernie grinned. "Are you plotting something nefarious?"

"No! I'm pointing out that Cindy and Gavin might still have keys to Hollis's house. Or some other friends of theirs who housesat or took care of the house while they were gone."

"Just like the key Kelsey left for me." I took another bite of my sandwich.

"Okay," said Mars, "we've got Parker by himself, Parker with Kelsey, Trula by herself, or Parker with Trula?"

"What would be the point of Parker and Trula murdering Hollis together?" asked Bernie.

"Why would Parker and Kelsey have killed Gage?" I sipped my iced tea.

The waitress brought their orders. Daisy snarfed her chicken but stayed by my side.

Bernie said, "Maybe Gage's death was really just a stupid accident and not tied to Hollis's murder at all."

"I was at Alex's office yesterday," I said. "His assistant had brought him leftover food from home. It would have been easy for someone to bring Hollis food. Or to poison it when no one was looking."

Bernie's gaze met mine. "You said Trula lied about buying fogger. But no cans of fogger were found at the Haberman house. Right?"

We all stopped eating and focused on Bernie. "The general belief is that Cindy retrieved the cans of fogger and hid them in the library."

"Which," I added, "Trula could easily have done because she was spending a lot of time there researching Parker's ancestors."

"So why lie about buying fogger? Unless Trula was involved or trying to shield Parker, she had no reason to lie about her purchase. It almost points a finger of guilt at her," said Bernie.

"Too bad we don't have a way of knowing whether Trula or Parker went out that night after the underground dinner." Mars picked up his iced tea glass.

"Wait a minute," I reached over to pat Daisy. "Someone else was lying, too. Cindy said she was home all night, worrying about Gavin because he slipped out the window and sneaked out. But Madison saw Cindy out running that night."

"Very intriguing," said Nina. "Once again, why would either of them lie about it unless they had something to cover up? My money is on Cindy because of the foggers in the library."

"I think I may pay Hollis's assistant a visit right now. When she was leaving yesterday, she said something about Cindy not being as sweet as she seems."

I gave my favorite dog in the world a big hug before leaving. Then I walked straight over to Dixon, Haberman, and Jenkins.

The law firm appeared to occupy an entire building. Typical red brick on the outside, it looked to be three stories tall. The only indication of the business inside was a discreet brass sign with the firm name on it. I used the door knocker, but tried the handle, too, since most businesses expected one to walk right in.

A well-dressed woman with her hair pinned up in a bun sat at a desk in the foyer. "May I help you?" she asked with a smile.

"I'm Sophie Winston. I'd like to see Lisa, please?"

A shadow darkened her face. "May I tell her what this is about?"

"I met her yesterday at Hollis's house."

"Oh, thank heaven. I'll tell you, it hasn't been easy having to tell his clients that he's dead. I dread it every time someone walks in the door."

A talker! I loved her already. I held out my hand to shake hers. "I'm Sophie, and you're . . . ?"

"Bettina Gregory. I'm actually the office manager, but we have some people out on vacation and the receptionist is due to give birth any minute now. We're all waiting to hear from her husband." She gazed at me curiously. "Why have I heard of you?" She gasped. Whispering, she asked, "Are you looking into Hollis's murder?"

"As a matter of fact I am. Is there anything I should know?"

She shifted uncomfortably and studied the desk as if she were thinking. She pulled a sticky sheet off a pad and wrote on it. Handing it to me, she said, "Lisa is upstairs and to the right. You can't miss her office. It still has Hollis's name next to the door."

I walked up the stairs, as creaky and aged as my own at home, and read the slip of paper: *1/2 hour. Big Daddy's Bakery.*

I tucked it into my purse carefully so it wouldn't slip out. Bettina was obviously worried about something or someone.

At the top of the staircase, I turned right and found the brass sign that said HOLLIS HABERMAN. I knocked on the open door and stepped inside.

Lisa looked up from her work. "Sophie! What a nice surprise."

"I hope I'm not interrupting. I wanted to ask you a couple of questions about Hollis."

"Sure. Won't you sit down? Or would you like to see his office?"

"I'd love that!"

She showed me into a sunny office with two large windows facing the street. The walls were a light caramel beige. A very large oak desk dominated the space. Awards and framed diplomas covered the wall in back of the desk. A photo of Kelsey in her wedding dress and one of Gavin in a basketball uniform sat on the desktop.

"What will happen to you now that Hollis is gone?" I asked.

"There's a lot to tie up. I'll be very busy for a while, making sure the firm doesn't overlook anything that Hollis was working on. And then, well, I hope we'll have a new attorney who might want me to stay and work with him or her."

I tried to steer her to talking about Cindy. "Great picture of Gavin! I notice there aren't any of Cindy."

"There were once, but they're long gone."

"You made a comment about her yesterday. . . ."

Lisa examined her fingers and twisted her wedding band. She walked over to her office and closed the door to the hallway. On her return she said, "Everyone thought Cindy was the sweet one. Sometimes it aggravated me because it was Hollis who was kind and caring. Hollis put up with a lot from her. It wasn't like she beat him or anything, but . . . she had an affair with Parker."

All I could think of was Gavin's AB-positive blood type. "When was that?"

"I don't know the exact dates. It might be going on right now for all I know. But it was a big blow to Hollis. He wanted to leave her a long time ago, but it seemed like there was always some reason to stay in the marriage. He just dragged his feet on it."

"So Hollis knew that she was sleeping with Parker?"

"Most definitely."

"Does Trula know about this affair?"

"Either she doesn't know or she puts on a very good act. Between the two of us, I don't know why she would stay with him if she knew about it. I've always suspected that they kept it a secret from her."

"Hollis didn't tell her."

"Oh no! We discussed that. He said ruining one marriage was enough."

"But it must have impacted his relationship with Parker, too."

"It did. Everyone always says what a lovely firm this is and how everyone gets along so well, but there are undercurrents of unhappiness."

"Are you the only one who knew?"

She nodded. "I told you, Hollis and I were like workspouses. I knew a lot."

"How did he find out about Cindy and Parker?"

Lisa curled her lips inward like she didn't want to say it.

But I knew. "Gavin. He found out when Gavin didn't have the right blood type."

"You know about that?"

I nodded. "I didn't know who the father was, though. Since you knew Hollis so well, did Kelsey have him on a diet?"

"Hollis was the worst dieter ever. He was always sneaking food. He lived for meatball subs and cheesecake. Poor Kelsey was trying so hard to feed him healthy foods, but he was always noshing on something bad for him."

She walked around the desk and opened a side drawer. She crooked a finger at me.

I peered into it. Candy bars on top of candy bars! "Did people bring him food from home, too?"

"Of course. We all loved him. Bettina makes the world's best cheesecake, and she knew how much he loved it. She brought him a slice every time she baked it."

I reached out for her hand and clutched it in mine. "Thank you for telling me all this about Hollis. I can feel what a loss he is to you and the other people who work here. It warms my heart to know how much he was loved."

I left the office and walked down the stairs, holding on to the railing because I was a little misty-eyed. I hadn't known Hollis all that well, but now I wished I had.

I didn't encounter anyone else on my way out. I checked my watch and hurried toward King Street.

Chapter 29

Dear Natasha,
At our last family funeral, half my cousins were
chewing gum like cows chewing their cud. I like to
have died from embarrassment. How do I avoid that
at the next funeral in our family?
    Brought Up Right in Possum Grape, Arkansas

Dear Brought Up Right,
I feel your pain. At the next funeral, choose a fam-
ily member to hold a spittoon and collect gum
from the boorish side of the family.
    Natasha

I knew Big Daddy's Bakery fairly well and spotted Bettina right away. She had taken a table partly hidden in the back.

I bought a box of pastries and indulged in a cup of hot tea in spite of the heat outside. I brought them over to her table and sat down. "Thank you for meeting with me."

She was an attractive woman with even features in an oval face. But her lips pulled back into thin lines. She spoke in a very low voice. "I have no reason to think this has anything to do with the murders."

Murders? Plural? I waited for her to continue.

"You know that guy Angus who died?"

I nodded.

"I came back to the office one night around nine o'clock because I'd left my cell phone there by mistake. I heard voices. You know how it is when it's so quiet at night? Everything seems slightly amplified?" She closed her eyes in pain and huffed air out of her mouth. "It was wrong of me, I know. I don't know why I did it. Self-preservation? Some kind of weird instinct? But I hid. I turned off the lights and pretended I wasn't there. And then I waited to see who left the building. It was Angus. Parker left a few minutes later."

"Have you told the police?"

"No. Wouldn't they think that was meaningless?"

"You thought enough of it to tell *me*. And you made sure you didn't talk about it in the office."

"It doesn't mean Parker killed him," she said. "For all I know they could have been talking about the plumbing in Parker's house."

"But you don't really think that or you wouldn't be telling me all this."

She hid her face in her hands briefly. "Parker is a very generous person. He's been so good to me and trusts me completely. He's always giving clients a break on their bills, especially women without a lot of money. Neither Hollis nor Gage ever did that."

"A break?"

"Sure, he writes off part of what they owe. I think that's so kind and wonderful of him. I was a single mom for a long time. I know what it's like to count every penny and be broke before payday."

"Do you think Angus might have been a client?"

"I can't tell you who is or isn't a client." She shook her head in the negative, though, which told me all I needed to know.

I watched her carefully. While it was a possibility that Parker was doing Angus a favor, it seemed obvious to me that Bettina didn't really believe that. If she hadn't been suspicious, she wouldn't have hidden and spied on her boss. "I've heard from someone else in the firm that the atmosphere changed after Gage died."

"It was a huge blow to us all. Gage was the consummate Southern gentleman. He was sort of nerdy—an intellectual. Sometimes I thought it irritated Parker that Gage was more scholarly and precise than Parker. I think in a way, Parker wanted to be Gage. Hollis, on the other hand, was the jolly one. The warm guy who made jokes and smiled a lot."

"Other than being sad about Gage's death, did you notice any changes?"

"You mean other than Madison poking around? Poor thing. She just could not accept that Gage fell into the water and drowned."

"What did she think happened to him?"

"I honestly don't know. I guess she thought someone had killed him. She wanted names of clients who might have had a beef with Gage. But that's all confidential information. We can't just hand that out."

"Do you know someone named Fawn Fitzhugh?"

I caught a glint of recognition in her eyes. "I'm really not allowed to say who was or wasn't a client."

"But she wasn't an employee?"

"No, that I'm certain about," she said.

"Did someone have a beef with Gage?"

"With Mr. Perfect? Hardly."

"How about his coworkers?"

"You want me to say that I think Parker murdered Hollis."

"Not at all! I'm after the truth. Someone killed Hollis and Angus, and you were obviously somewhat wary or you wouldn't have hidden in the office when you went back for your phone."

"I don't want to be next." She seized her purse and ran out of the bakery in such a frenzy that everyone in the shop watched her leave.

I sat back and sipped my tea. I had thought that Cindy suffered from the divorce. She was certainly bitter about it for someone who had had an affair. Gavin's true parentage must have been the can of worms Hollis had referred to when they argued at the underground dinner. But why murder him? If Cindy wanted to be with Parker, then it was Trula they would have to get rid of. Cindy was already divorced from Hollis.

Still, it was good to know there was a connection between Parker and Angus. It probably didn't mean anything, but maybe it did. Meeting alone in the office at night *was* a little bit odd. There could have been a leak, and Angus was kind enough to come fix it after hours. We certainly couldn't ask him.

Poor Kelsey. She had married into a spiderweb. I didn't have any answers yet, but everything kept going back to the same group of people, the ones involved with the law firm—Cindy, Parker, Trula, and I guessed I should add Madison.

I took my box of pastries and headed down the street to The Laughing Hound. I walked past the host and through the restaurant to Bernie's office.

His desk was piled with papers. He looked up when I rapped on the open door.

"Soph! Come on in. I'm just setting up the employee schedule."

"Sorry to interrupt your work. I came by to see if you've heard of a waitress named Fawn Fitzhugh."

"Fawn! Everybody loves Fawn." He glanced down at the paper in front of him. "I should give her a call. Wonder where she's working these days."

"Do you know where I can find her?"

He typed on his keyboard and looked at his computer screen. "The last place I have for her is on Fayette Street." He jotted down the address and handed it to me. "I hope she's not in trouble."

"Not at all. I overheard her in a brief but tense exchange with Parker. I'm wondering what that was about."

"Tell her to give me a call. I could use Fawn around here."

I blew Bernie a kiss and hoofed it over to Fayette Street.

Fawn lived in a large house that had been divided into four apartments. The name *Fitzhugh* was on a little nameplate next to the door. I rapped on the red front door and tried the handle. It swung open.

Her apartment was on the second floor. I walked upstairs and knocked. "Fawn?"

An older woman opened the door of the other unit. "Haven't seen her in days."

"Thank you." I walked back downstairs, out of the building, and crossed the street. By my calculations, the big bay window on the second floor belonged to Fawn's apartment. I could have sworn I saw her looking out. But just like a ghost, when I blinked, she was gone.

I returned to her apartment building. I found a tiny notepad in my purse and wrote, *Bernie said to tell you to call him. He has a job for you. Would like to talk with you, please. Sophie Winston.* I left my address and phone number. I shoved the paper underneath her door and left.

Maybe it was time to pay Gavin a visit. I made a quick

phone call to get Cindy's new address. I had planned to share the pastries with friends, but they were the perfect thing to bring to Gavin. I walked the five blocks to their apartment.

It was in a very pricy and in-demand neighborhood. Someone had converted a white brick two-story building into apartments. In spite of the excellent location, when I walked up to the door I couldn't help feeling as though it wasn't as fabulous as their house had been. No wonder Gavin wanted to sit in his tree house and pretend he still lived there.

The front door opened without a buzzer, and I found their apartment in the back on the left. I rapped on the door.

Cindy opened it. "Sophie! What are you doing here?"

I held up the bakery box. "I thought I'd check on Gavin. How's he doing?"

"He's miserable. I guess I can't blame him." She showed me into a white bedroom with green linens and teenage boy décor. He was propped up on the bed playing a game on a TV when we walked in.

"Hi, Gavin! How are you feeling?"

His forehead was wrapped in a bandage, and his leg was in a cast. Poor kid!

"Mrs. Winston! Have the police arrested Kelsey yet?" he asked.

"No, honey. They haven't."

"What's taking them so long?"

I looked at Cindy, unsure how much I should tell him. I tried to keep it simple. "You know that guy Angus whose house you were in?"

"I hope *you're* not going to lecture me, too."

"How did you get in there, anyway?" I asked.

Gavin shrugged like only a teen can. "The door was unlocked."

"Do you walk into every house with an unlocked door?"

He made a face. "No."

"Gavin, he was *inside* the house. He could have had you arrested for trespassing. Even worse, he could have clobbered you, thinking you were a thief."

He turned his head away. "You sound like my mom."

"What did you expect to find in his house?"

"I don't know. His name?"

"His name was Angus Bogdanoff. Does that help you?"

"No. Why did the one-who-shall-remain-nameless go there?"

"As it turns out, she was once in a mess kind of like you are in now. And he was very kind to her and helped her out. So when he was stung by all those bees, she felt like she owed him and went over there to help him when he wasn't well."

The expression on Gavin's face softened. "That doesn't mean she didn't murder my dad."

"You're right about that. I brought you some goodies from Big Daddy's to make you feel better."

"Thanks. Hey, Mrs. Winston? I'm sorry I messed up. I should have listened to you."

I gave him a big hug. "Gavin, sweetheart, everybody makes mistakes. But you probably should listen to your mom."

He grabbed my arm. "You'll prove that she did it, won't you? I can't do it now that I'm stuck here with a broken leg. You have to do it for me. Promise?"

I looked into his young eyes. I knew how desperately he wanted the villain in his life to be the killer of his father. "I promise you that I'll do my best to find your dad's murderer."

"Gavin," said Cindy, "did you reach Chadwick yet?"

"He hasn't called me. I'll be okay. I'm not a baby."

Cindy smiled at me and closed the door to Gavin's room behind us.

"I have a meeting at the library tomorrow night. I'm hoping his friend can come over and stay with him while I'm gone."

"Would you like me to stay with Gavin?"

"I'd *love* it! But he'd claim you were a babysitter and be angry with me."

She gestured toward the living room sofa, which was clearly being used for a bed. I didn't see any other doors, except to a bathroom. They had moved to a one-bedroom apartment.

"Besides, I was going to give you a call. We're planning the fall fund-raiser, and we just don't have any brilliant ideas. I was hoping you might come to the meeting to help us brainstorm."

"The meeting is tomorrow?"

"Tomorrow night. I'm afraid it's quite late. Not until nine fifteen because the library closes at nine. We're a busy group of people, and it's so hard to find a good time to meet. We have learned through trial and error that meeting while the library is open is pure chaos."

"I'd love to come. How are you doing, Cindy?"

"I'm worn-out. Wolf has been by to interview me twice. Of course, that only agitates Gavin. I understand I'm the prime suspect now, even though I didn't do it."

"Do you have an alibi for that night?"

"Are you kidding me? You think I murdered Hollis, too?"

In a conciliatory tone, I tried to make amends. "Cindy, that's not what I said. You were here all night, waiting for Gavin to come home, right?"

She averted her gaze and looked toward the floor. "No one was here with me to corroborate that. I can't prove it!"

I was thinking of the way she had pretended not to know that Hollis was in the hospital. I played dumb. "Did Kelsey call you to tell you what happened to Hollis?"

Cindy sank onto the sofa and buried her face in her hands. Her voice was muffled when she said, "It's all going to come out eventually, isn't it? No matter how hard I try, someone will ferret out the truth. I was trying to protect Gavin."

I sat down next to her, worried about Gavin. "What are you talking about?"

She faced me, her normally placid expression distorted into one of grief. "I told you Gavin sneaked out that night. I assumed he was with his friend. But early in the morning, around five o'clock, I think, a neighbor called and said an ambulance was at my old house and she thought they were loading Hollis into it." She winced when she said, "I was scared to death that Gavin had done something terrible. I went straight to Hollis's house. No one was home, so I let myself in with my old key. I could smell the lingering fumes. I found the four foggers in the master bedroom. I . . . I thought Gavin had set them off. So I took them and hid them in the library, where no one would find them. Then I went to the hospital. Everyone there was talking about Hollis and his bizarre symptoms. I was so afraid that Gavin had tried to kill his dad." She winced. "I can't believe I'm saying that about my own child. He's not like that. You know what a sweet person he is. He was just so disturbed that night at the underground dinner. Seeing Kelsey there with his dad upset him. No, it angered him. And that's partly my fault. I shouldn't have taken him to the dinner to begin with. And I could have been more nurturing of a relationship with Hollis. Instead, I festered in my own misery, blaming everything on Kelsey, and that impacted poor Gavin. It was wrong of me to take glee in bashing Kelsey in front of him." She rubbed her eyes. "Seriously, Sophie, no one ever goes through the items on that shelf in the library. They could have been hidden there for a decade without anyone knowing."

"Is that what you told Wolf?"

"No. I'd sooner go to prison for a murder I didn't commit than have Gavin stand trial for murder."

I figured most moms would feel that way. "You're a good mother, Cindy. But you probably ought to come clean and explain this to Wolf. He's really a very perceptive and understanding guy."

"Maybe you're right." Her eyes met mine and she whispered, "But what if Gavin did it?"

"You said the truth would eventually come out. I suppose he could have waited until Kelsey left, then set off . . . No! If Gavin had set off the bombs, he wouldn't have been able to follow Kelsey to Angus's house. He could have returned and set them off." I peered at her. "Would Gavin even know what a fogger was? Seems like a fourteen-year-old who was angry would have hit Hollis over the head with something heavy. Gavin isn't strong enough to have overpowered Hollis. And to be frank, I think Gavin might have broken down and cried if he got that close to Hollis."

"You have more faith in my child than I do! But you're probably right. I hadn't thought about it that way."

I wondered if I was sitting with a killer. One who was making a fuss about her son to distract me from her own involvement. "Let me get this straight. You were out running in the dark?"

She gave me a quizzical look. "No, it was dawn when I went over to Hollis's house."

I searched her expression. Was she lying? "What if I told you that someone saw you?"

Cindy's eyes opened wide. "Then I would be highly suspicious of that person because it's not true. Not at all. I did not set off those foggers."

I tested her ability to lie with a straight face. I didn't know quite how to ask, so I just blurted it out. "Cindy, is Gavin's biological father actually Parker?"

Chapter 30

Dear Sophie,
My wife follows some dame named Natasha who
told me I have to eat barbecue with a fork and
knife if I'm in public. I think she's got a screw
loose. Who does that?
        Messy Guy in Seven Devils, North Carolina

Dear Messy Guy,
You may indeed use your hands to eat sandwiches
and ribs in informal public restaurants. However,
in a formal setting, one uses a fork and knife, even
if the host was inconsiderate enough to serve sand-
wiches or large sloppy ribs.
        Sophie

Cindy's eyes went wide, and she turned to look at Gavin's closed door. "Why on earth would you think that?" she whispered.

"His blood type. Hollis was type O."

"Please don't say anything. Gavin doesn't know." She shook her head. "I never imagined that this would crop up. Never!" She turned into an itching and scratching mess and blathered. "What do I do now? Is this common knowledge? I'll have to tell him before someone else does. Gavin will hate me. Hollis wanted to tell him when he was little so it wouldn't be a big shock later on."

I sat and watched her.

"Trula!" she said. "I forgot about her. She never knew. At least I don't think Parker ever confessed to her."

"You had an affair?"

"It sounds so awful when you put it that way. Hollis couldn't have children, so when I became pregnant, the cat was out of the bag, so to speak. We almost divorced then. We were living in a small apartment. Nicer than this, now that I think about it. Hollis moved out. But Parker didn't want to leave Trula and marry me so Gavin would have a family. The truth was that he didn't want to leave Trula's money. It was a nightmare. Eventually, Hollis came around and accepted Gavin as his own. For all his faults, he was a very good dad and loved Gavin dearly."

"You broke off your relationship with Parker?"

She stopped talking and chewed on her upper lip. "Mostly. Hollis and I had our arguments over the years."

I got her meaning. She and Parker were still in touch, if not consistently. I thanked her and left her to figure out how to handle telling Gavin the truth.

As I walked home, I mentally ticked off people whom I thought did not kill Hollis. Kelsey was at the top of my list. She had married into a tangled mess. I felt confident that Gavin hadn't killed Hollis, either. The timing didn't work well if he followed Kelsey that night. Jay had been so calm and reasonable about his beef with Hollis that I didn't think he had done it, either. Plus, I couldn't help thinking about the method of death. Someone must have known about the bees and the foggers that Kelsey bought.

Parker and Trula had moved into top position as suspects

in my mind. But one thing bothered me—why had Madison lied about seeing Cindy out running that night? Or why had Cindy lied about not being out and about?

I could call Madison and see if she would meet me for a cup of coffee. It was getting to be mid-afternoon. Maybe she would prefer an early cocktail. I was digging for my phone in my purse when I looked over and saw her across the street. "Madison!" I waved at her.

She met me at the corner.

"Could I interest you in a cup of coffee?"

"Sure. I could use a little pick-me-up."

We entered a nearby coffee shop and selected a table in the back. When we had lattes in front of us, I said, "I wanted to ask you a few questions about Cindy, Parker, and Trula. You know them so well."

"Do you think one of them murdered Hollis?"

"I don't know. But I can't tell if Cindy is lying to me, and I certainly can't ask Trula about Parker!"

"So what do you want to know?" She sipped her latte.

"How were things in the beginning? Was everyone agreeable? Were they always friends? Or were there problems?"

She took a deep breath and sighed. "In the beginning, everyone got along fine. Trula was always the busy socialite, telling everyone about their grand heritage and Old Town ancestors. I was busy with the kids, and Cindy was busy working and taking care of Gavin. The guys hammered out the division of work. I think it was set up so that office bills, rent, assistants, and such got paid off the top and then they prorated the payment the guys got so that if one brought in more money, then he made more money. We knew that Hollis and Cindy weren't always happy, and then one day, Cindy was out of the scene entirely when they divorced. I do know for a fact from Gage that Hollis bought out her share of the house. So Cindy may be living in a little one-bedroom apartment, but she's sitting on a pile of dough. I feel terrible for her every time I see her, but it's her choice."

"So the rumors that Hollis got everything in the divorce are wrong?"

"I imagine he wound up with a considerable amount, but I think Cindy has been milking it a little bit, pretending to be broke when she's not."

"How about Parker and Trula?"

"They're the kind of couple where each is happy to do his own thing. Trula has a lot of interests and Parker is busy with work, and that arrangement seems to suit them."

"Trula was worried about Kelsey, and I couldn't help noticing Parker gravitating toward her."

"Really? I have always thought that Parker was one of those sort of nerdy guys. The kind who didn't have a date for the prom. And that he felt a need to make up for it as an adult. He definitely likes women."

"Did he ever proposition you?"

Madison stared at me in silence. "How could you possibly have guessed that? It was a long time ago. I told Gage, who must have had a word with Parker, because he never tried again. In fact, now that I think about it, he pretty much left me alone after that. He was very sweet when Gage died, though—coming around and taking care of insurance and that sort of thing."

"Do you think Parker could have been after Kelsey? Maybe he propositioned her, but Hollis wasn't as kind about it as Gage?"

Madison's eyes widened. "What about the foggers in the library? I thought the police were on to Cindy."

"Maybe Trula put them there. Or Parker placed them in the room when Trula was doing research."

Madison gasped. "To point a finger of guilt at Trula! I never thought of that."

I got a little bit daring. "Or what if Parker was having an affair with Cindy?"

Madison thought for a moment. "She's very beautiful. Maybe that's why they divorced. Oh my word! Maybe Kelsey wasn't the one who broke up their marriage!"

"Did you know Angus Bogdanoff?" I asked.

"I never even heard of him until he was murdered. All I know is what I read in the newspapers."

"So he didn't work for the law firm?"

"I don't think so. Wasn't he a handyman? Sophie, I'm getting the feeling that you think Kelsey didn't kill Hollis."

"Everything seems to be leading back to the law firm. I just haven't managed to uncover the right link. Sort of like you were with Gage's death. At least we know for sure that Hollis's death wasn't accidental."

"*I* know that Gage's death wasn't an accident. Keep me posted, okay?"

I promised I would. We left the coffee shop.

Madison headed for the grocery store.

I checked my watch. Would Trula be at the library? I veered in that direction. Parker was the one I really ought to talk to. But if he had murdered Hollis and Gage, that was best done in the company of more people or in a very public setting.

I trotted up the stairs and entered the library. Sure enough, Trula was in the rare documents room with Jay. I would have to try to be chatty.

"Hi! Are you two making progress on your research?" I asked.

Trula appeared annoyed. "Jay is. Did he tell you about that fabulous woman who helped the war effort?"

"He did."

"Can you imagine being that brave? If, heaven forbid, Parker had been killed, I don't think I'd have had the fortitude to entertain spies, I would have cowered in my home without him."

"I was over checking on Gavin a while ago. He's a little grumpy about having to slow down and stay in bed. But Cindy's taking good care of him. I've heard so much lately about how close all of you were at the law firm."

"It was a very congenial group. Of course, that's why everyone is taking Hollis's death so hard."

"How is Parker holding up?"

"Hollis's death came as a huge shock to both of us. It took Parker a couple of days to recuperate. We're still not back to normal, though. We won't be until they arrest Cindy and we have a resolution. It won't bring back Hollis, but we need to be able to close the door on it. Right now it's hanging over everyone's heads."

I fibbed a little. "There's not much tying her to the murder."

"She hid those foggers!"

"She did. If only someone had seen her at the Habermans' house. I took Daisy for a walk after the dinner that night, but I didn't see her. Did you and Parker take a stroll?"

"We went straight home and didn't hear anything about it until the next day."

Jay began to observe me with an odd expression. I worried that I was being too obvious. "Pity. And now poor Angus. Did either of you know him?"

Jay's gaze shifted to Trula.

"I'd never heard of him before. Surely you don't think there's some connection?" She gasped. "Do you think Angus murdered Hollis?"

"It's a possibility," I said. "He knew about the bee problem."

"Everyone knew about that."

"I've never used foggers, have you? I wonder how they work?"

I heard a little intake of breath from Trula. "I haven't used them, either. I can't imagine having the kind of bug infestation that would require such dramatic measures. Kelsey must be a terrible housekeeper."

Well, rats! I wasn't getting anywhere with her. I left the library and headed home. As I passed Jay's house, I saw another casserole on his doorstep. It wasn't really any of my business, but it would spoil if it sat out in the sun.

I had just seen him at the library, so I knew he wasn't home. I walked up to the front door and realized once again that he kept his front drapes closed. I picked up the casserole just as Natasha drove by.

She whipped her car into an empty spot, parked, and ran up to me. "Now look, Sophie. I know that you're lonely. I fully appreciate that. But you have to stop pursuing the men I'm interested in. We've been friends for a long time. I cannot believe that you brought Jay a casserole."

"You will be pleased to know that I am not interested in Jay romantically. Nor did I bake this casserole. I just saw him at the library so I know he's not home."

"You're certain about that?" she asked.

I shrugged. "Maybe he walks faster than me and beat me here, but I doubt it."

Like a snake, her thin hand whipped out and tried the door handle.

"What are you doing?"

"Has he ever let you see the inside of his house?"

"No." I didn't mention that he tried to shake us the night the lights were out. That had been strange.

"I'm dying to get inside."

"Natasha, leave the poor man alone." I walked away.

"Where are you going?" she called.

"To wedge this into Kelsey's fridge. It was probably meant for her."

Natasha tried the door handle again. I wondered what

had happened to her big push for being queen of etiquette. I was pretty sure that breaking into locked houses was a breach of the worse sort.

I pulled Kelsey's key out of my purse and unlocked the door. The Habermans' house was eerily silent. I locked the front door behind me and headed for the kitchen. It took a little doing, but I managed to shove the casserole into the vegetable crisper. I stood back and stared at the contents of the refrigerator. What a shame that all that food would go to waste.

I filled a galvanized watering can and walked out to the back porch. I paused to check out the bee situation. The guy they had called must have done a good job. There wasn't a single bee buzzing around.

I walked around the corner to the rose trees. They were showing their unhappiness at having gone through such a brutal treatment. I hoped they would recover. I watered the impatiens along the side of the house and returned to the backyard. I was watering potted geraniums when I heard a crash next door.

Chapter 31

Dear Sophie,
My husband passed away suddenly. Am I required
to host a big repast at our home? I don't have the
energy to talk to all those people and play hostess.
Is it wrong of me to take my children to a quiet
family dinner in a restaurant instead?
    Widow in Whynot, Mississippi

Dear Widow,
The one thing etiquette demands is making every-
one comfortable. No one wants to upset or inconve-
nience the bereaved. If a quiet dinner in a restaurant
with your children is what you prefer, then by all
means do exactly that.
    Sophie

I dropped the watering can, dashed through the back gate, raced through the alley, and over to Jay's gate. I had to push it hard to open it. When I was able to wedge through the opening, I realized what the problem was. His backyard was a tangled mess of beautiful blooming perennials like black-eyed Susans, daisies, Russian sage, and coneflowers. No wonder the bees at the Habermans' had settled close by. His yard was a bee paradise. No one had mowed it in a very long time. An assortment of rusted gardening tools and empty flowerpots lay at rakish angles. I had a feeling that the two large pots he had brought to Kelsey's house for the roses had previously occupied what now appeared to be a newly empty space.

"Jay?" I called. "Is everything okay?"

A faint voice replied, "In here!"

I walked up on his back porch, which was littered with empty boxes and stacks of newspapers. The door to his house was open about one foot. "Hello?"

"In here! Hurry, Sophie!"

I pushed on the door gently. Like the gate, it wouldn't give any more. I peered inside. The backyard had been a warning of what was to come. Jay was a hoarder.

Squeezing to get through, I carefully stepped over a hodgepodge of stepstools, pots, and papers.

"Hurry up!"

"Natasha?" I asked.

"What is taking you so long? Jay could be home any minute."

"It's a little too late to worry about that. Where are you? Keep talking." I immediately regretted having said that.

"Did you know about this? I want Mars back. At least he's tidy."

I found her feet sticking out from under a pile of boxes and cushions that must have fallen on her. She wore short black boots. In the summer? I couldn't help laughing. It was just like the house landing on the Wicked Witch of the West.

I lifted each box and cushion and pitched each on top of

other junk until I could see her arms. I held out my hands and pulled her up.

We heard a sound at the front door. "Quick!" she said. "Let's get out before he finds us here."

The two of us slipped and slid on heaven knew what in our mad scramble to the back door. We pressed through the opening and closed the door quietly.

"Was it locked?" I whispered.

"Who cares? Come on!"

"We should leave it the way it was."

"Okay, yes. It was locked."

I reached around the doorknob and locked it before I pulled it shut. Natasha was already sprinting through the wild garden. I followed right behind.

We closed the gate and stopped to catch our breath.

Natasha leaned against the gate.

"How did you unlock the door?"

"There was a key over the top ledge of the door."

"Natasha! What would possess you to unlock the door and go inside?"

"He was so perfect. But I couldn't stand how secretive he was about his house."

I stared at her in horror. "Were you sneaking around the Habermans' side yard at night? Please don't tell me you're the one who knocked over the rose trees."

"All right, I won't tell you."

"Natasha! What is wrong with you?"

"I thought he might be entertaining Lavinia."

"Why didn't you clean up that mess?"

"I was going to, but you beat me to it. It doesn't matter. Now I know why he didn't want anyone seeing what's inside his house."

"And we're not going to say a word about it. Do you understand me?"

"Thank you, Sophie. You're such a good friend."

"Not for you, you doofus! For Jay, so he can save face. He will never know that we saw his secret."

"We ought to get him help. Like a backhoe to clean that mess."

"You're the one who broke into his house. You call someone who deals with hoarders and ask how we can help him without causing him any embarrassment."

She nodded. "It's the least we can do." Natasha walked away through the alley.

I returned to the watering can in Kelsey's backyard. When I was through, I locked the back door. Once again, I was overcome by the silence.

I strode through the downstairs rooms. Nothing appeared out of place. I climbed the stairs to the second floor and entered the master bedroom. The afternoon sun shone through the windows, warming the space. It was really quite lovely with soft blue walls and a busy blue on white fabric on the comforter. The dust ruffle matched it. Next to the bed was a cozy blue armchair covered in a velvety fabric with a luscious hand-knitted throw draped over the side. I reached out to touch the soft throw. It was mostly blue, but the yarn also contained shades of greens and purples. The knotted fringes touched the floor.

The scent of pesticides was completely gone. I gazed at the bed, full of fluffy pillows. Looking at it now, no one would ever imagine that someone had sneaked in and placed foggers next to it.

Cindy? Trula? Parker? I opened and closed the door to the bedroom. No squeaky hinges. A person could have easily entered without being heard.

I dropped to my knees, lifted the bed skirt, and peered underneath the bed. The angle of the sun helped me see without a flashlight. The hardwood floor was clean. Not a single dust bunny in sight. I was pretty sure that I couldn't say that about my own bed.

I lay there for a moment, thinking about someone starting the foggers, knowing full well that Hollis slept peacefully right next to them. The fumes must have wafted straight up to Hollis as he lay sleeping.

I sat up, my bracelet accidentally catching the fringe of the throw. As I untangled it, the sun caught on something I hadn't noticed before. A dragonfly earring whose colors shone in the sun but blended so beautifully with the colors of the throw that it would have been easy to miss it.

Chapter 32

Dear Sophie,
I met a guy whose house is beyond the norm of
messy or disorganized. I have watched hoarder
shows on TV, and that's where I think he's headed.
I really like him otherwise. How do I handle this?"
Want to Help My Honey in Chipmunk, New
York

Dear Want to Help My Honey,
Hoarding is a very sensitive matter. Do not simply
barge in and start cleaning up. You can talk to the
hoarder with empathy and try to understand it
from his perspective. Better yet, see if he'll talk
with a professional about the situation.
Sophie

Madison. There wasn't a good reason in the world for
Madison's earring to be caught in the throw next to
Hollis's bed.

Even if she'd been having an affair with Hollis, she'd

had the earring at the underground dinner. She could only have lost it there within the last few days.

Madison's earring must have snagged on the throw when she set the foggers. She would have been working in darkness and probably couldn't locate it.

Suddenly things began to fall into place. She'd been very close with the Habermans once. She might well have had a key to the house.

And she had probably been the one we interrupted when we walked Kelsey home when no one had electricity. Madison must have returned to look for her earring or the missing foggers.

Cindy's story made sense now, too. She was afraid Gavin had killed his dad. To protect him, she rushed to the Habermans' house, found the foggers, and removed them.

I couldn't help snickering just a little bit at the thought of Madison returning for the foggers and not being able to find them.

I left the earring hooked onto the throw. My fingerprints were on it now, of course, but it was probably better for Wolf to see it where it had been.

Locking the Habermans' front door behind me, I couldn't believe I had yammered on and on with Madison at the coffee shop. The whole time, she must have been thrilled that I wasn't on to her.

Mochie mewed and stretched when I walked into my own home. I called Wolf on my cell phone while opening a can of beef stew for cats. He didn't answer. I left a message for him on his voice mail.

I retrieved fresh red and yellow tomatoes from the garden. They were still warm from the sun. I sliced one into chunks, added strips of leftover flank steak and baby spinach leaves, and made a quick vinaigrette with sweet balsamic vinegar for my dinner.

By the time I finished, I still hadn't heard from Wolf. I called again and left another message. *"I found evidence today at the Habermans'. Left it in place for you to see. I still have a key to their house. Call me if you need to get in the house."*

It had been a long day and I felt like I had hiked from one end of town to the other and back. I settled into my little den with a good mystery and hit the sack early.

I woke to glorious blue skies in the morning. I was a little surprised that Wolf hadn't called. Maybe he had arrested someone for Hollis's murder.

It was still early enough to enjoy sitting out back in the garden. After a long shower, I threw on a sleeveless blouse and denim shorts with a comfy elastic waist. I fed Mochie Tuna Delight, which lived up to its name. It reeked of tuna and Mochie seemed delighted.

I made myself a large mug of hot tea, slid Mochie's harness on him, and carried them both out to the backyard.

Mochie was thrilled to prowl in the grass while I relaxed with my tea.

The gate creaked open. Mochie lifted his head from the scents in the grass. We watched as Fawn, a slender young woman, studied the back of my house. She clearly hadn't noticed Mochie or me.

She took a few steps into the yard, turned around, paused, and took a deep breath.

In as gentle a voice as I could manage, I said, "Good morning!"

She started in shock. "I thought I was being so careful, but I didn't even notice you."

She walked toward me. "Who is this?"

"Mochie."

Fawn bent to stroke him. I could hear him purring.

She looked up at me. "I talked with Bernie last night. He thinks pretty highly of you."

"We go way back. Could I get you a cup of tea?"

"No, thanks. I can't be here very long."

"Who are you hiding from?"

She slid into a seat. "Parker."

I sipped my tea and watched her.

"Bernie said I could be honest with you. But you should know that I'll deny everything."

What could I say? "Okay." She was clearly afraid of Parker. He seemed so harmless. What had he done to this poor woman?

"I was in a car accident six months ago. The people in the other car didn't have insurance and their little boy wasn't in a car seat. His medical bills were unbelievable. He's okay now, but they sued me for the cost of the medical care. It was crazy! If he had been in a car seat like he should have been, he wouldn't have been injured. My little boy was in *his* car seat and didn't get so much as a scratch. Anyway, the point is that I needed a lawyer, so I went to Parker."

She swallowed hard. "He agreed to let me pay his bill in installments. I thought he was the greatest thing ever. So sweet, so kind. Always checking to see how we were doing. And then the ax fell." Fawn looked away. "Parker came around and told me he could make my payments to him disappear if I would sleep with him. I threw him out of my apartment."

"Good for you! What a scumbag."

"The thing is that I have an incident in my life that I'm not proud of. I've worked hard to put it behind me. And if it came to light I wouldn't be able to get a job anywhere. It was stupid—I was running with the wrong crowd by a mile and stole from my employer. I left town to get away from my problem. Then I met my husband and had my little boy, Trevor. I'm a different person these days. I'd still like to pay back every penny that I took, but my husband got sick and died. I'm struggling to make ends meet. Parker found out about the charges against me. And now he's blackmailing me. But I set him straight. I saw his high-society wife at the underground dinner. And I let him know that if he presses me anymore, I'm going to tell her. I bet she wouldn't be happy to know about his behavior!"

"She would be mortified. I gather you didn't go to the police because of the charges against you?"

"What would happen to my baby? They'd sock me into jail and give him to strangers. I can't let that happen to him. He's everything to me!"

"Of course. I understand completely." It pained me to say it. Parker let Bettina think he was being kind to his clients by cutting their bills, when he was pressuring them into bed. Hollis must have learned the truth. Had Hollis confronted Parker? Maybe Gage had, too, before him.

"I think you're smart to avoid Parker. For the time being, anyway. Thank you for telling me what happened to you."

"You won't tell the police? Bernie said you wouldn't."

Ugh. Why was Bernie tying my hands this way? "I have to be honest with you, I think the truth will come out. Parker will be in a lot of trouble. If it's any consolation, I don't think you're the only one who is going through this."

When Fawn left, I changed into a skirt and slipped on some silver bangles. I walked down to Alex's office. He was just striding out the door when I arrived.

He pecked me on the cheek. "I'm on my way to court."

"Mind if I walk with you?"

"I would enjoy your company." We started walking toward the courthouse.

"So let's say I became your client."

"Uh-oh. What did you do?"

"Mmm, I don't know. Someone is suing me."

"For what?"

"I drove my car into their house."

"Were you drunk?"

"It doesn't matter."

"Are you kidding? Of course it matters."

"We're getting off track here. Just assume I need your brilliant legal expertise. But I struggle to pay your bills. So you propose a barter arrangement. You'll reduce the amount of money I owe you if I play hanky-panky with you."

Alex stopped walking and stared at me. "Is this some kind of weird game like I'm the cop and you're the chambermaid?"

"You play some strange games. I think it's the cop with the burglar, and the chambermaid with the duke. But you're missing my point. What would happen if you did that?"

"Well, I would lose my license to practice law, and you would have to find another attorney."

I smiled at him. "That's what I thought. Thanks! See you later."

"Sophie! Wait. What was that about?"

"I'll tell you later. Good luck in court."

I walked home slowly. I was in a pickle. If I told Wolf what Parker had been doing, even without mentioning Fawn's name, they would surely pull all of Parker's client records and ask questions. The trouble was that he probably was smart enough to hold some other sin over their heads. They might all deny everything, and Parker would get away scot-free.

Even worse, Parker's scam was a major motive to murder Gage and Hollis. If they found out, they would have notified the Virginia Bar. It would have brought Parker and the whole firm crashing down. Hollis and Gage would have had to leave and try to salvage what little respect they could.

But if Parker had killed Hollis, then what was Madison's earring doing on the throw in Hollis's bedroom? I didn't want to think that they had conspired to murder him. Had Parker used Madison? Had he convinced her to kill Hollis?

I didn't want Fawn's greatest fear to come true—her child placed in a foster home while she was in prison. But Parker had to be stopped.

Even when I was back at home making dough for chocolate chip cookies to put in the freezer, I wrestled with my conscience. If I told Wolf, Fawn would either run like Kelsey had, or she would have to deal with the consequences of stealing money from her boss.

Wolf showed up at my door when I was wrapping the dough in waxed paper. It was ready to be cut into cookies and baked when I needed them.

I motioned Wolf in and bit my tongue so I wouldn't say anything scathing. It had certainly taken him long enough to show up!

I slid the packages of dough into freezer bags.

"Could I make you some lunch?"

"No, thanks. But I'd take a cup of coffee if you have it. I was up all night working on a different case."

That explained the delay in responding. I could understand that. I poured us both a cup of coffee, the rich aroma filling the kitchen.

We sat down at the kitchen table, and with a heavy heart, I told him about Parker's scam on young women who had a secret to hide.

In all the years I had known Wolf, I had never seen him so spitting mad. His face turned a shade of red that I had never seen on him before.

"Who told you this?"

"One of his clients."

Wolf narrowed his eyes. "You're not going to tell me who it is? We'll need someone to testify. I can't just walk into court for a warrant without some kind of confirmation."

"Here's the problem. Parker was smart about who he targeted. I suspect all these young women did something in their pasts that they want to hide. That gave him leverage over them. Now they have moved on. Some of them are single moms who worry about what will happen to their children if they go to prison." I took a chance. "Is there any way you could wipe the slate clean on their past transgressions in exchange for their testimony?"

Wolf sat back and sipped his coffee. "We would have to take it on a case-by-case basis. If it's a misdemeanor, we might be able to work something out. But if it were murder, for instance, then that would be entirely different. I'm sure you understand."

I didn't like it, but I did understand.

We walked over to the Habermans' house. I unlocked the front door, flicked on lights, and led him upstairs to the master bedroom.

Even with the overhead chandelier on, it wasn't easy to see the earring. It took us a couple of minutes to find it.

"It was just dumb luck that the sun was at an angle that reflected the earring yesterday."

"You're sure this belongs to Madison?" asked Wolf.

"Madison was wearing a pair just like that at the underground dinner. She said they were a gift from her husband. It's true that someone else could have the same or similar earrings. I can't quite reconcile finding the earring here with Parker murdering Hollis."

Wolf nodded. "I'll follow up. Thanks, Sophie. You've been a big help."

After he left, I spent a few minutes watering flowers and making sure everything was in order before going home. Over my lunch of leftovers, I thought about Parker and how to get evidence on him. As I mused about his victims, it dawned on me that Kelsey may have been one. If Parker discovered that she was wanted for murder, he may have tried to blackmail her into bed, too.

The problem was getting someone to testify against him. Very briefly, I considered making up a legal problem and paying him a visit. But he would wonder why I hadn't gone to Alex. Hmm. I could invent something that I wouldn't want Alex to know.

But wouldn't that be some kind of enticement? I wasn't sure if it was legal. Parker was on the library board. Maybe I would see him in the evening.

In the afternoon, I walked down to see Alex again.

"Two visits in one day?" he asked.

"I want to be sure I understand the technicalities of attorney privilege."

"Okay."

"If I came to you because someone was suing me, but I happened to have committed a crime several years before, would you have to turn me in?"

"I'm under an obligation to keep your secrets."

"So then, let's say I want to be a witness in a case against someone else. Could you help me clear up my previous crime?"

"Depends on what it is."

"But you wouldn't turn me in?"

"Probably not."

"That's not very helpful."

"I can't help someone commit a crime, for instance."

"Okay. I'm going to send someone to you. Wolf seemed to think he might be able to cut her some slack."

"Thanks. What's her name?"

"Hmm, if she's not your client and Wolf comes asking you questions, then you might have to reveal her name."

"Sophie, you're driving me a little nuts here. Wolf can cut her some slack, but he doesn't know who she is?"

I grinned at him. "That pretty much sums it up. I'll let her tell you everything, if she decides to trust you."

"Sophie, don't forget there's a statute of limitations on most crimes. Whatever she did may not be a problem anymore."

"Except for murder, right?"

"She murdered someone?"

I said no, but I was thinking that Kelsey had.

I borrowed a sheet of paper from him and wrote a note to Fawn.

> *We desperately need a witness against P. The police cannot move forward without one. They may be able to help you with your previous problem. Please contact attorney Alex German. I can vouch for him personally. He will look into your issue and may be able to help you resolve it. Don't worry about the attorney's fees. You would be helping other women if you could talk to the police.*
>
> *Sophie*

I folded it in fourths and tucked it into my purse. "Thanks, Alex. If she comes in, I'll cover her legal fees."

His eyebrows raised. "That's a problem. But since you really want me involved in this, I'll see her pro bono, at least initially. If you don't tell me her name, how will I know it's her?"

"Oh, you'll know when you hear her story."

I walked around his desk and planted a big smooch on him. "Thanks, Alex."

As I walked out, he said, "Whatever possessed me to get involved with Old Town's biggest snoop?"

I waved to him on my way out of his office and headed straight to Fawn's apartment.

I let myself into the building and walked up the stairs. The neighbor's door flew open. She stood in her doorway, her eyes suspicious slits. She held her chin raised and crossed her arms over a sagging bosom.

I smiled at her and slid my message to Fawn under the door. "I'm glad Fawn has you to watch over her," I said, and hurried down the stairs.

I walked home leisurely, pausing to gaze in shop windows, but everywhere I looked, I thought of the murders. Would we ever know the connection between Parker and Angus? Or had Angus's death been unrelated to Hollis's?

At six o'clock, Alex showed up at my house bearing a giant bag of Chinese takeout.

He walked into the kitchen and set the bag on the table. "That was a fascinating client you sent my way."

"Oh? I thought you couldn't talk about clients."

"She asked me to tell you that she's in the clear. Her crime was a petit larceny, and the statute of limitations has already run. She's been worried about it because that idiot Parker lied to her and misled her into believing that someone would take her kid away."

"So you can talk about Parker?" I brought dishes, napkins, and chopsticks to the table while he took boxes of goodies out of the bag.

"I can promise you that Parker is toast."

"Iced tea or jasmine?" I asked.

"Definitely iced. It's too hot for anything else."

We sat down to eat. Alex wasn't a super chatty type, but he talked like crazy. "I'm stunned. I had no idea. In fact, it never would have occurred to me to be so heinous. It shows a totally evil side of him that I don't think any of us knew existed. He's twisted!"

"Trula is in for a big shock." I picked up a piece of spicy Kung Pao chicken with my chopsticks. "I bet the police re-open Gage's death. Don't you suppose Gage was on to him first?"

"Probably. Which proves that he's getting more and more desperate. No wonder Fawn is afraid of him. She has seen his dark side."

"Should I call Wolf and put him in touch with you?"

Alex grinned. "I already phoned him. He came to the office."

"So wheels are already in motion!"

"Thanks to you."

"No, I think we'll have to thank Fawn for being brave," I said. "Without her, nothing would go forward."

After dinner, I changed into a simple navy-blue sheath style dress and added dangling pearl earrings. If I was going to help the library with an event, I probably ought to look the part.

At eight thirty that night, I realized that the days were getting shorter. We had passed the summer solstice, and it was hard to believe that darkness would be falling a little earlier every day. I left the kitchen light and outdoor lights on, locked the doors, and set off with Alex.

"Are you sure you want to walk over there alone?" he asked. "I don't mind going with you."

"An escort? I don't think that's necessary. Parker doesn't know that we're on to him. It's Fawn who needs to be careful."

He squeezed my hand. "Call me if you change your mind." He turned off toward his home, and I headed for the library. I had walked about four blocks when I began to wonder if someone was following me. I made a point of walking on King Street, which buzzed with people and was well-lighted.

I stopped a few times and pretended to study store windows, but I didn't notice anyone suspicious on the busy street. I decided I was being silly. Besides, I now knew that Madison or Parker had killed Hollis. All I had to do was keep an eye out for them. Nevertheless, I stuck to busy streets.

It wasn't until I neared the library that I was certain someone was tailing me.

I dodged behind an open gate that was surrounded by a lush delicate cypress vine thick enough to hide behind. Pressing my back against a brick wall, I watched as someone scurried by. I was about to leave my hiding place when a second person rushed past me.

Either I was losing my mind, or something very peculiar was going on. I leaned to the left just enough to watch as they continued. Maybe they weren't following me at all. But now I was intrigued. What were they doing?

I left my hiding place and darted from shadow to shadow as I followed them.

The first figure appeared to stop and look back. I stopped, too, well away from the beam of the streetlight.

The second person darted to the side and waited until the first one continued on his way.

Trying to hide the light from my cell phone, I called Wolf's cell phone.

This time he answered. "Hi, Sophie. What's up?"

I whispered, "I'm on my way to a meeting. I thought I was being followed, but it turns out that someone is following someone else. It could be completely harmless, but I'm getting a little worried about them."

He took down our location and promised to send a squad car by.

I had barely slipped my phone back into my purse when

the first person appeared to turn right. The second person rushed forward. I picked up speed so I wouldn't lose them.

Although they were in a dark shadow, there was no mistaking that the first person reached out and dragged the second person off the sidewalk.

Nor was there any mistaking the chilling scream that followed.

Chapter 33

Dear Natasha,
I love the look of concrete planters. There's some-
thing very permanent and classic about them. But
my husband thinks plants won't do well in them.
What's the scoop on concrete?
Garden Lover in Concrete, Washington

Dear Garden Lover,
Concrete planters and urns do offer some benefits
besides their looks. Their weight prevents them
from blowing over easily, they last longer than a lot
of other materials because they don't rot or become
brittle, and the thickness helps the soil maintain a
more constant temperature.
Natasha

I ran forward, careful to slow as I neared the spot where I thought they were. I inched up and peered around the corner.

They were in an alley. One of them appeared to stand behind the other, strangling him with something. The second one was grabbing at his own neck, desperately trying to survive.

I looked around in a panic for something—*anything*—I could use to knock out the attacker. I spied a concrete urn overflowing with flowers just outside a gate. I tossed the plants and hoped I would be able to lift the heavy urn high enough.

It turned out that adrenaline really does help a person do amazing things. In an angry frenzy, I swung that baby up over my head, rushed forward, and let gravity take care of the rest. The urn came down on the attacker's head with a cracking sound so awful that I cringed. I hoped it was the concrete and not his head that made that sound.

He instantly released his grip and crumpled to the ground.

The other person fell, too, and lay there in a fetal position, hacking.

I grabbed my cell phone, which started to ring. It was Wong. I held my purse by the strap, ready to sling my bag at the attacker if he so much as raised his head.

"Wong!"

"Where are you? I'm cruising the street, but I don't see you."

I backed toward the sidewalk, never taking my eyes off the two people lying on the ground. The beam of car lights caught me, and the next thing I knew, Wong was standing next to me.

She flicked on her flashlight and walked forward. I went with her.

The beam lighted Madison Jenkins gasping for air with her hands on her neck. Not a foot away from her, Parker Dixon bled profusely from his head.

Wong called for an ambulance.

I knelt beside Madison. "Do you need help sitting up?"

She gazed up at me and blinked. "Sophie?" she rasped.

"Don't try to talk yet. Just concentrate on breathing."

I held her in my arms until the ambulance arrived. One EMT tended to Parker and the other checked out Madison.

When they asked what happened, I had to tell them the truth. "I hit him over the head with that." I pointed at the urn.

The EMT grimaced.

"He was trying to strangle Madison." I didn't want him thinking I made a habit of running around slamming urns on people's heads.

It wasn't until they were loaded into the ambulance that Wong's flashlight picked up the flash of a bloody knife on the ground where Madison had lain.

Wong looked over at me. "Does that belong to you?"

"Never saw it before in my life."

She bagged it as evidence. "This should be a heck of a story."

Wong was still shining her flashlight along the alleyway when Wolf arrived.

"There!" I shouted.

Wong backed up. "What did you see?"

"A chain."

The three of us studied the ground.

"Right there." I pointed at a golden chain that gleamed under the beam of the light.

Wong picked it up with a gloved hand and held it in the air for us to see. The ends had fancy clasps on them.

"I'd be willing to bet that chain belongs on a pricy purse that Trula can't find." I looked over at Wolf. "The weight-lifting chains didn't match the marks on Angus's neck, did they?"

"How did you know?" he asked.

"I'd bet this chain will be a perfect match."

Wolf gazed at me. "You okay?"

"Yeah, I'm fine. I might be a little sore tomorrow, though. That urn was pretty heavy."

"Do you know why Parker was trying to strangle Madison?" asked Wolf.

"If the chain matches, then Parker murdered Angus. But I have no idea why Parker was after Madison. Maybe she knew too much?"

"I'd better get over to the hospital," said Wolf. "Wong, can you give Sophie a lift home?"

I waved them off. "If it's not too late, I'm due at a meeting."

The story about Parker exploded through the rumor mill in Old Town the next day. My phone started ringing at seven in the morning and didn't stop. By eight thirty I turned the ringer off for some peace and quiet.

Of course, that didn't stop Nina, Mars, Bernie, and Francie from coming over and demanding confirmation.

Over coffee, frittatas, and a luscious fruit salad of summer berries with cantaloupe, I told them everything I knew. Mostly they were shocked about Parker.

"Maybe we should go over to console Trula," suggested Nina.

"Might be too soon," said Francie. "At the moment she must feel sort of shell-shocked. Who would ever have thought that mousy man would be so sick and devious?"

It wasn't until Wolf dropped by that we got the full scoop about the murders.

He sat down at the kitchen table with us and ate ravenously. "I've been up all night." He looked over at me. "Parker has a cracked skull."

I gasped. "Oh no! That's my fault."

"He was trying to kill Madison. No one is bringing

charges against you. You were defending her," said Wolf. "Besides, he'll be all right. He'll be in prison, but his skull will heal."

"In prison? So he murdered Hollis?" asked Nina.

Wolf gulped coffee. "Madison killed Hollis. Gage had asked Madison how she would feel if he left the firm. She knew something was wrong but he wouldn't tell her anything except that he was having a meeting with Hollis. She came to the conclusion that it was Hollis who was doing something wrong at the firm and that Hollis murdered Gage to keep his secret. Seems she told the police, but there wasn't any evidence. She thought Hollis was getting away with murdering her husband. Madison had a key to the Haberman house from the days when they were close. After the underground dinner she walked over there. She was lurking in the alley when she saw Kelsey leave, followed by Gavin. She let herself into the house, saw the foggers that Kelsey bought and set them off in the master bedroom in revenge for Gage's death."

"So she didn't know about Parker and what he was doing at the firm?" asked Mars.

"If we can believe her, she didn't know a thing about it. Parker picked his victims very carefully. He has lawyered up and he's not talking, but we think Gage found out what Parker was doing. Gage may have even confronted him and planned to tell Hollis. Angus made a very hefty deposit into his bank account the day after Gage died. If we follow the money, we're pretty sure it will lead to Parker."

"Parker hired Angus to murder Gage?" asked Mars.

Wolf took a deep breath. "That's how it looks. And it appears that Parker was paying Angus to spy on Hollis. Apparently, Hollis learned about Parker's unorthodox billing. We suspect that being a good guy, Hollis tried to give Parker a chance to give up his law license and retire. Before he stopped talking, Parker was highly amused by the fact that someone else murdered Hollis. He says he didn't know who did it, though. I think Parker imagined he was home free, except for Angus who would surely have testified that Gage's death was murder for hire."

"Then why was Parker following Madison last night?" I asked, sipping my morning tea.

"Madison thought you were getting too close to the truth. She was afraid that you would expose her as Hollis's murderer. Madison knew she'd lost her earring and was terrified that you would find it. Madison was following you last night, Sophie. That knife she was carrying was meant for you," Wolf explained.

I felt a little queasy. "I must have confused her when I ducked out of sight. But the knife was bloody . . ."

"She got a pretty good dig at Parker's leg when he grabbed her." Wolf downed his coffee.

"So that's why Madison lied about seeing Cindy running the night she set the foggers."

Wolf nodded. "She was trying to throw suspicion on Cindy."

I poured more coffee into his mug. "Did Parker tell you why he was strangling her?"

Wolf looked up at me. "He thought Madison was you. He meant to strangle *you*. Parker followed Fawn to your house yesterday morning. He knew it was only a matter of time before you knew the truth. Seems Cindy told him you would be attending the meeting at the library, so he waited for you and tailed you in the dark. You probably saved your life when you hid and let them pass you."

My friends looked at me in horror. Now I *really* felt queasy. But the one I felt the worst for was Gavin. He lost the only father he knew, one who had been good to him. And now when he learned the truth, he would know that his biological father was a murderer and a blackmailer.

* * *

After breakfast, we left the dishes in the sink. Except for Wolf, who had to get back to work, we all walked down to the waterfront and tied white cotton scarfs on all the benches. They looked very festive blowing in the wind. We didn't know if Kelsey was watching the live camera at that moment, but we all lined up and waved in case she could see us.

Kelsey returned that night. Nina, Francie, and I helped her clean out the refrigerator while we caught her up on everything that had happened.

"Madison?" asked Kelsey. "I never even considered her. And now I feel like such a dope for giving Angus a job as our handyman. I bet Parker set that up to get Angus inside our home. You can't trust anybody!"

Francie handed me another half-eaten casserole dish to empty. "We'll go through this again when they release Hollis and you can have a proper funeral service."

"Maybe this time people won't look at me like I'm a murdering vixen." Kelsey handed me a casserole. I dumped the contents and read the name on the bottom. *Lavinia Brown.*

"Maybe this time," said Nina, "we'll keep Natasha out of the way."

Kelsey laughed. "She *is* a little pushy."

I stacked clean casserole dishes on the dining room table and walked back to the kitchen through the living room. I stopped dead in the center of the room when I heard voices. I couldn't make out what they were saying, but someone was whispering. Jay's ghosts!

I hurried into the kitchen. Placing a finger over my mouth, I whispered, "Come into the living room."

They followed me in silence.

Francie was the first to speak. "Ghosts."

Kelsey frowned. "I heard them before I left. I thought they were Hollis's killers lurking outside. Where do you think they're coming from?"

"Was that a giggle?" I asked. Suddenly I had a sneaking suspicion that I knew where the whispers were originating. "Kelsey, have you got a flashlight?"

She retrieved one from the kitchen and handed it to me. I opened the door to the small side garden and walked to the base of Gavin's tree house. As quietly as I could, I climbed up the ladder. When my head reached the floor of the house, I aimed the light inside.

Gavin's friend Chadwick was necking with a pretty girl. They blinked and shielded their eyes when I shone the light on them.

"Do your parents know you're here?" I asked.

They sheepishly shook their heads and followed me down the ladder.

"Wait right here," I said. "Nina, would you phone Jay and ask if he can hear the ghosts in his house?"

She dialed his number and talked with him. "He doesn't hear them now."

I nodded to the kids. "Climb back up there and talk."

In seconds we heard the whispering.

Nina laughed. "Jay says the ghosts are back."

"Tell him to come over here," I said.

Minutes later, we introduced Jay to his two ghosts. He shook their hands. "You've been driving me batty. I must say that it's a tad disappointing that the ghosts of Revolutionary spies aren't chatting in my house. On the other hand, I'm relieved to know that I wasn't imagining things."

Chadwick and his girlfriend called their parents. We waited for them in Kelsey's kitchen, where the clean-up continued.

Jay pitched in, helping stack the casserole dishes. "Natasha paid me a visit today."

Uh-oh.

He bowed his head as if in shame. "She brought trash bags and wanted to clean out my house."

"I'm sorry, Jay. She can be quite obnoxious. I'm sure she meant to be helpful."

"After my wife died, I didn't want to be at home. Everything reminded me of her. I was devastated when I lost her. I even slept in my office some nights." He was speaking softly, and I could tell that he had loved her very much.

He finally looked up at me. "It's not like me. It's so awful that I just stay away. I live with my curtains closed so no one will know. Somehow, Natasha found out. It will be all over town in no time."

"Maybe you could talk with someone about it? A professional?"

"Could you help me? I want to clean it up, but it's so overwhelming that I don't know where to start."

"Of course. You have a lot of friends. We would be thrilled to help you."

The very next day, the entire neighborhood, except for Natasha, gathered at Jay's house. Bernie brought trucks, Kelsey brought beach music, and I brought trash bags. Gavin showed up on crutches with Chadwick and the cute girlfriend. They took the backyard under expert gardener Francie's direction.

Jay surprised me by wanting to rid himself of almost everything. I had expected him to hold on to much more.

Naturally, the murders were still a hot topic of discussion.

Nina, Kelsey, and I were working in the living room, which was turning out to be amazingly gorgeous under the clutter.

"So where did you go to hide out?" Nina asked Kelsey.

"To the mountains. I found a little place that rents out cabins. I figured strangers would be noticed around there if someone came looking for me."

"You really weren't hiding from Parker?"

"I didn't know who to run from. That's why I left. I was afraid to answer the door or even walk over to your place."

I tossed a stack of magazines into a trash bag. "Parker never propositioned you?"

"I probably have Hollis to thank for that. Once I met him, we were inseparable. Parker was probably smart enough to realize that while I fit his disgusting scheme, I would have ratted him out to Hollis."

The front door opened. I picked up trash bags to hand to Mars. But it was Trula who walked into the living room. For the first time in my life, I saw her dressed in jeans and a man's shirt with the sleeves rolled up.

We fell completely silent.

Trula walked over to Kelsey. "I'm so sorry about everything." Tears streamed down her face, marring her makeup. "I'm so ashamed of Parker. And I'm ashamed of myself for not realizing what was going on with him. I . . . I trusted Parker implicitly. How could I have been such a fool? I've been so rude and unkind to you, Kelsey. I thought you were a threat to my marriage. I saw how Parker looked at you. He hasn't ever looked at me that way. Is there anything I can do to make it up to you?"

I held my breath.

Kelsey reached out and hugged Trula. "I think you just did."

"So, Trula," I said, trying to change the subject, "did you ever work out Parker's ancestry?"

She wiped her face. "He comes from a long line of decent people. No spies, no historical figures, no one who owned or lived in a grand Old Town residence. I'll tell you what, though, they would be unbelievably ashamed of him now. Just like I am. The way he abused those women! And murder, too! I can't—" The tears began again. "I never imagined him being so brutal." Her shoulders curved forward. "How could I have lived with someone like that?" She swallowed hard and took a deep breath. "I was nothing but a bank account to him."

Trula had been through a lot in the last couple of days. I dared to ask her something I was itching to know. "Trula, why did you tell me you bought silver polish at the hardware store?"

She stiffened and her eyes grew large. Letting out a breath, she said, "Because I was ashamed that I had bugs in the house and needed a fogger."

I smiled at her and gave her a little hug. She was learning that she was just like the rest of us.

I hauled the trash bags out to the foyer just as Natasha and Lavinia Brown arrived. They jostled each other as they tried to be the first to the front stoop.

Lavinia gazed around. "Is Jay moving?"

Natasha gloated when she said, "I'm helping him overcome his hoarding problem."

That was a major exaggeration. The only impetus she had been was one of embarrassment.

"Hoarding?" Lavinia stepped inside with Natasha right behind her. I trotted out to the curb and handed Bernie the trash bags.

When I returned to the house, Lavinia and Natasha were squabbling about what color to paint the living room.

Natasha shook her head. "You're just like Sophie, you have no feel for what's trending. These walls should be minion yellow. All these antiques are passé. We'll bring in some mid-century modern and pale-lime accents."

Lavinia stared at her like she had lost her mind. "Colonial blue for the walls. And the stunning antiques stay!"

At that moment, Jay entered the living room.

Lavinia and Natasha descended on him, chattering non-stop. But he had eyes for only one person in the room. A gentle smile appeared on his face as he walked past Natasha and Lavinia.

Trula, her makeup horribly tear-stained, smiled as he approached her and took her hand.

There wasn't a doubt in my mind that a love match had bloomed in the library.

Recipes

Chocolate Truffle Tart with Strawberries

Crust

2 cups all-purpose flour
1 tablespoon sugar
⅜ teaspoon baking powder
½ teaspoon salt
7 tablespoons melted unsalted butter
⅓ cup very cold water

Preheat oven to 350. Place flour, sugar, baking powder, and salt in a food processor and pulse about four times to combine. While running the food processor, pour cooled melted butter into flour mixture slowly. Pulse several times. Add cold water while running. Pulse until it sticks together in small bits. Remove from food processor and press into ungreased tart pan.

Bake 18–20 minutes until it begins to pull away from the edge and is a light golden color.

Filling

1¼ cups heavy whipping cream
12 ounces 55% to 60% semi-sweet chocolate, chopped
 or a 12-ounce package of semi-sweet chocolate chips
2 teaspoons vanilla extract

Heat the cream until very hot but do not bring to a boil. Add the chopped chocolate. Stir until chocolate is dissolved. Pour in the vanilla and stir to mix. Pour into prepared tart pan. Set aside until cool. Refrigerate to set.

Topping

1½ pounds small strawberries
1 cup heavy whipping cream
⅓ cup powdered sugar
1 teaspoon vanilla

Wash and hull strawberries. Cut in half lengthwise. Place on top of the chocolate in a pleasing pattern. Beat the cream. When it begins to take shape, add the powdered sugar and vanilla. Beat until fairly stiff.

Pipe decoratively around the top edge of the tart. Place the rest of the whipped cream in a bowl and pass it when you serve the tart.

Italian Spritz

Ice cubes
3 parts sparkling wine (Prosecco or Cava)
2 parts Aperol (an orange aperitif)
1 part soda water
1 orange slice for garnish

Fill glass with ice cubes. Add sparkling wine, Aperol, and soda water. Garnish with an orange slice.

Piña Colada

1 cup pineapple-flavored white rum
1½ cups pineapple juice
¾ cup cream of coconut
¼ cup fresh lime juice
1 cup of ice
Pineapple and maraschino cherries for garnish

Place liquids and ice in blender. Blend until smooth. Pour into tall hurricane glasses. Garnish with a wedge of pineapple and one maraschino cherry.

Tomato Bacon Tart with Cracker Crust

Author's note: This crust is wonderfully light and delicious. However, it is very delicate and prone to crumbling. I'm very fond of it, but you may wish to substitute a sturdier crust.

2–3 tomatoes
½ teaspoon salt
4 ounces buttery crackers (if using Ritz, about 36
    crackers)
7 tablespoons butter, melted
1 plus 3 slices cooked bacon
6 ounces shredded mozzarella
1 garlic clove, minced
1 teaspoon thyme
1 tablespoon olive oil

Preheat oven to 375 degrees.
Spread out paper towels. Slice the tomatoes about ¼-inch thick with a very sharp knife. Lay the slices on the paper

towels. Set aside the ends of the tomatoes to use in a salad. Sprinkle with ½ teaspoon of salt.

Crush the crackers and mix with melted butter and one slice of bacon, very finely chopped. (You can do this in a food processor. Pulse the crackers with the one slice of bacon. While running, add the melted butter. Scrape the sides and run again.) Press into a tart form. Bake 5 to 7 minutes or until light brown.

Raise the temperature of the oven to 400 degrees.

Chop the remaining three slices of bacon. When slightly cooled, sprinkle half the bacon on the bottom of the tart. Sprinkle the mozzarella on the tart and spread to the edges. Sprinkle with the garlic and ¼ teaspoon of thyme. Place the tomatoes in an attractive pattern on top and sprinkle with the remaining bacon. Drizzle with olive oil.

Bake for 14 to 15 minutes.

Coca-Cola Cake

Note: If you would like to toast the ½ cup of pecans for the frosting, do so before baking the cake. If you don't have buttermilk, add ½ teaspoon of white vinegar to ½ cup milk and let stand a few minutes.

2 cups sugar
2 cups flour
1 cup butter
1 cup Coca-Cola
3 tablespoons cocoa powder
½ cup buttermilk
2 eggs, beaten
1 teaspoon baking soda
1 teaspoon vanilla extract
1½ cups miniature marshmallows

Preheat oven to 350 degrees.

Grease and flour a 9 x 13-inch baking pan.

Combine sugar and flour in a large bowl. Whisk well and set aside.

Mix together butter, 1 cup Coca-Cola, and cocoa in a pot. Bring to a boil, stirring occasionally. Pour over sugar and flour mixture and stir, blending well.

In a separate bowl, whisk together buttermilk, eggs, baking soda, and vanilla. Add to Coca-Cola mixture. Add marshmallows and stir well. (Note: The marshmallows will not melt.)

Pour into prepared pan and bake 35 minutes or until a cake tester comes out clean.

Frosting

Note: Frosting and cake should be warm when applying the frosting.

½ cup butter
1–3 tablespoons cocoa powder
6 tablespoons Coca-Cola
1 pound (1 box) confectioner's sugar
½ cup chopped pecans, toasted (optional)

About 10 minutes before the cake will be done, place ½ cup butter, 3 tablespoons cocoa, and 6 tablespoons Coca-Cola in a pot. Pour over the powdered sugar and mix well. Add vanilla and mix. Spread over cake while both cake and frosting are still warm. Sprinkle with chopped pecans.

Apple Coleslaw

⅓ of an average green cabbage
⅓ of an average red cabbage
2 crisp red apples (like Galas)
2 carrots
½ yellow onion
2 tablespoons white sugar
2 tablespoons dark brown sugar
2 teaspoons yellow mustard
½ teaspoon pink sea salt
¼ teaspoon black pepper
½ teaspoon celery seeds
½ teaspoon smoked paprika (or plain paprika)
2 teaspoons olive oil (one with a mild taste or other vegetable oil)
2 tablespoons apple cider vinegar
2 heaping soup spoons of mayonnaise (about ½ cup)

Peel the outer leaves off the cabbages, wash the cabbages, and cut off ⅓ of each cabbage. Cut out the big core. Shred the cabbage. (Note: Shredding is definitely easier with a food processor but can also be done by hand.) Leave the peel on the apples, cut in quarters, and cut out the core. Shred. Peel and shred the carrots and the onion. Mix cabbage, apples, carrots, and onion well in a big bowl.

In a small bowl, whisk together the sugars, mustard, sea salt, pepper, celery seeds, paprika, olive oil, and vinegar. Add the mayonnaise and whisk well. Pour over the cabbage and turn several times to spread evenly throughout.

Bourbon Garlic Flank Steak

¼ cup bourbon
¼ cup canola oil (or other high-heat friendly oil)
2 tablespoons apple cider vinegar
1 teaspoon smoked paprika
½ teaspoon salt
½ teaspoon pepper
4 garlic cloves, minced
1 flank steak

In a small bowl, mix together the bourbon, canola oil, apple cider vinegar, smoked paprika, salt, and pepper. Whisk briskly to blend. Stir in the minced garlic. Place the flank steak in as small a container (plastic bags also do the trick) as it will fit into flat. Pour the bourbon mixture over it. Refrigerate for at least 2 hours or overnight, turning once. (You can broil it sooner, but the flavors won't be as strong.)

Remove the meat from the refrigerator at least ½ hour before broiling. Line a broiler pan with aluminum foil and set the top on it. Alternatively, you can use any oven-safe pan with a rack over it. Place the meat on the pan. Broil at 500 degrees for approximately 4 to 6 minutes on each side. The amount of time will depend on the thickness of your meat. Use a meat thermometer to determine when it is ready. Flank steaks are best when red inside. When the temperature reads 120, remove to a cutting board and let it rest for 5 minutes before slicing. Slice thin, against the grain.

Funeral Potatoes

28-ounce bag of shredded hash brown potatoes, thawed
2 tablespoons butter
1 medium onion, chopped
3–4 cloves garlic, minced
16 ounces sour cream
10-ounce can cream of chicken soup
8 ounces sharp cheddar cheese, shredded
¾ teaspoon kosher salt
¼ teaspoon black pepper
½ cup Panko breadcrumbs
½ cup grated Parmesan cheese
4 tablespoons melted butter

Thaw shredded potatoes in refrigerator overnight.

Preheat oven to 350 degrees.

In a small skillet, melt the 2 tablespoons of butter over medium heat. Add the chopped onion and cook until translucent. Add minced garlic for 2 minutes, stirring with the onions. Remove from heat and set aside.

Pour the thawed shredded potatoes into a very large mixing bowl. Add the sour cream, cream of chicken soup, shredded cheddar cheese, salt, and pepper. Mix thoroughly.

Pour into a 9 x 13-inch casserole dish. Sprinkle the Panko breadcrumbs over top. Sprinkle the Parmesan cheese over top. Bake 30 minutes. Pour melted butter over the top. Return to oven and bake another 30 minutes.

A Day at the Beach Cocktails (or in the backyard)

Ice cubes (crushed or whole)
1 ounce vanilla vodka
1 ounce peach schnapps
3 ounces orange juice
3 ounces sweetened cranberry juice

Fill a tall glass with crushed ice. Pour in the vodka and the schnapps. Add orange juice and sweetened cranberry juice.

Make Your Own Ice Cream Board

You'll need one very large cutting board.

3 flavors of ice cream
3 kinds of cookies
3 fruits (slice if large like bananas)
1 or 2 toppings

Place scoops of each ice cream in its own separate bowl. Add them to the board, one in each corner and one in the middle. Add bowls with the toppings. Place the cookies in between the bowls of ice cream. Don't overload them. Groups of six to eight cookies are fine. Fill in the empty spaces with fruit.

Turn the page for a preview
of Krista Davis's next
Domestic Diva Mystery . . .

The Diva Sweetens the Pie

Coming May 2019
From Kensington Publishing

Chapter 1

Dear Sophie,
My new mother-in-law wins the local pie contest
every year. The recipe for her piecrust is top secret,
and his family makes a huge fuss about it. She and
her husband are coming to visit my hubby and me
for the first time. Hubby says a pie is obligatory.
Each of her other daughters-in-law bakes a pie for
her visit. I'm terrified! What do I do?
Newlywed in Coward, South Carolina

Dear Newlywed,
Bake a cake. There's no point in competing with
her, and a cake will last longer than a pie, anyway.
If someone comments on the missing pie, tell your
mother-in-law that you're eager to learn how she
bakes her wonderful pies that everyone raves
about.
Sophie

Daisy, my hound mix, stopped walking abruptly. I thought she had picked up the scent of a squirrel in the night air, but then I heard rustling in the bushes. In a split second, I was face-to-face with Patsy Lee Presley, and both of us screamed like we were under attack. Daisy barked, which added to the drama.

Wide-eyed, as though she were horrified, Patsy Lee took off running like a woman in her fifties who didn't get much exercise.

My heart still pounding, I sucked in a deep breath. It wasn't long ago that someone had meant to harm me. I guessed I was still wary and a little jittery. The truth was that the streets of Old Town, Alexandria, Virginia, were safe at night. I often walked Daisy after dark, enjoying the lights glowing in the windows of the historical homes that lined the streets.

Now that the momentary shock was over, I wasn't certain it had been Patsy Lee. I had never met her before, but I had seen her on TV many times. Patsy Lee Presley was the current darling of the TV cooking world with the number one show. Sweet as the pies she baked, she was slightly chubby, and watching her show was like a visit from a favorite doting aunt. Patsy Lee was due to be in Old Town on Friday for the pie festival, so it could have been her. But what was she doing hiding in bushes and running around like she was afraid?

I looked back in the direction she had gone, but she had disappeared. Whoever that woman was, I hoped she had the good sense to call the police if she was in trouble.

The next morning I told Nina Reid Norwood and Officer Wong about it while we rolled out dough in Tommy Earl Felts's class on pie baking. Nina, my best friend and across-the-street neighbor, unwisely added too many drops of water to her dough. I watched as it became sticky and unmanageable, but decided it wasn't my place to say anything. After all, Tommy was teaching the class.

Nina frowned at me. "Why isn't your dough sticking to your hands like mine?"

Wong glanced at her. "Mercy, Nina! Dip your hands in the flour, honey."

Wong focused on her own dough, which looked perfect to me.

"I'll check the log to see if anyone called in last night," she said. "It was probably some married woman sneaking home after a rendezvous with a boyfriend. Not to put Patsy Lee down, but a lot of women still wear their hair real big like she does. It could have been someone else."

Tommy Earl approached our group. "Bless your sorry little heart, Nina." Tommy gazed at the sticky lump in front of her, and patted her on the back. "Why don't you go to the mixer and try again? I don't think that's salvageable."

Tommy nodded approvingly at my pie dough. "Did I hear you talking about Patsy Lee?"

"I thought I saw her in Old Town last night. Do you know her?" I asked.

He snorted. "I taught her everything she knows."

"You did not," Wong scolded him. "On the show Patsy Lee is always talking about her grandmother, from whom she learned how to cook and bake. She was just a tiny thing when she started cooking. So young that she had to stand on a chair to reach the countertop to work next to her meemaw."

Tommy laughed aloud. "Is that the story she spins? Have you ever seen this meemaw on her show?"

"Good grief, Tommy," said Wong. "Patsy Lee is in her forties. Meemaw would probably be in her eighties."

Tommy lowered his voice and said, "Patsy Lee is so far into her forties that she has rolled over into her fifties. And

Meemaw doesn't come on the show because she has a receding hairline, a five o'clock shadow, and her legs are too fat to wear a skirt."

Tommy had done a fairly good job of describing himself. I couldn't help grinning.

Wong's eyes narrowed. "Are you saying there is no Meemaw?"

"I guess she had a couple of grannies, most people do." He shrugged. "But when *I* met Patsy Lee, she couldn't crack an egg without breaking the yolk."

Tommy moved on, pausing to talk to Nina about the dough she was carrying back to our workstation. She sidled in next to me and plunked her dough on the table.

"The secret to a perfect piecrust"—Tommy paused to build up suspense—"is vodka. I find drinking it helps *me,* but a splash in your dough will prevent too much gluten formation. There are other important factors, like keeping the ingredients as cold as possible, but the vodka is helpful because it makes the crust flaky."

Nina licked the spoon she had been dipping into the lemon filling for her lemon meringue pie.

"You won't have any filling left for your pie," I whispered.

"That's okay. You didn't think I was actually going to bake anything, did you?" she whispered back to me.

Officer Wong shot us a dirty look. "Shh!"

Nina had made fun of me for participating in the class. I had baked plenty of pies in my life, but piecrusts could be tricky. Tommy was a pro, and I figured I would pick up some tips. He baked pies for a living and sold them at Sweet as Pie on King Street in Old Town, Alexandria. Rumor had it that people drove an hour across greater metropolitan Washington, DC, just to buy Tommy's pies. At Thanksgiving and Christmas, they had to be pre-ordered because he couldn't fill all the requests.

He roamed the room as he spoke. The buttons on his short-sleeved white chef's jacket strained a bit against the pressure of his stomach. I could relate. I had my own difficulties maintaining the weight I would like to be.

Wong giggled when he stopped to praise her dough. "I'm so thrilled to be in your class. My grandmother was an expert pie baker. I wish I had paid attention to her techniques."

Was she flirting with him?

Just as he had described, his hair had begun to recede, but he was taking it in stride and wore it brushed back off his face. He smiled at her and the little crinkles at the outer edges of his brown eyes deepened.

African-American Wong, who attributed her name to the wrong husband by a long shot, wasn't wearing her police uniform today. Her hair waved to just below her ears in a cut that was shorter in the back and longer in the front. One sassy curl dropped on her forehead.

I looked a little closer. She had taken a lot of care with her makeup today. The buttons on her shirt strained a bit, not unlike those on Tommy's jacket. The two of them could be cute together. Nina nudged me, and I suspected she was thinking the same thing.

While the pies baked, Tommy drifted through the room, engaging all his students. When he reached Nina, he asked, "Is it true that you're judging the pie-baking contest?"

Nina turned as red as the cherry filling I had cooked for my pie. "That's why I'm here. I thought I should have a feel for all the work that goes into baking a pie."

Tommy stared at her and appeared confused.

"She has an amazing palate," I offered.

Wong looked over at us. "What's that supposed to mean? I like food, too, but nobody asked me to judge anything."

"I mean that Nina has the ability to taste flavors that

the rest of us miss entirely or barely notice. If someone in this class sliced her fruit on a cutting board that was used to mince garlic last night and was thoroughly washed afterward, Nina would still taste the garlic when she ate the fruit."

"I've seen contests like that. They blindfold people to see who can recognize the flavors or textures," said Tommy. "Well, Ms. Nina Reid Norwood, I apologize for doubting you. I guess there's more than one way to judge a pie."

"I hope you entered in the professional category," I said.

"You bet. I can't talk about it in front of a judge, though." Tommy winked at us.

"You're so cute. But it's not a problem," Nina assured him. "The pies won't have any names on them. It will be a blind tasting."

Tommy smiled. "Good to hear. I wouldn't want to be disqualified." He moved on to the next group.

An hour later everyone except Nina went home with a pie. The class was a small part of the Old Town Pie Festival, which was scheduled to commence in earnest the following day.

Nina offered to carry my pie as we neared my house. She took deep breaths. "Do you think there are calories in what a person sniffs?"

"I'm almost positive there are. I know I weigh more every time I leave a bakery."

As we approached my house, we saw a man peering in the window of my kitchen door. He cupped his hands around his eyes and leaned against the glass to see better. I could hear Daisy barking inside the house.

Chapter 2

Dear Natasha,
My daughter loves to bake fruit pies and we love to
eat them. But she makes such a mess of my oven! I
have to clean it every single time she bakes because
the bubbling juices always run over the pie pan.
Fastidious in Elderberry Pond, Pennsylvania

Dear Fastidious,
Tell your daughter I said to always place a rimmed
baking sheet underneath the pie to catch any juices.
Problem solved!
Natasha

"I've got your back," muttered Nina. "I'm dialing 911 now, just in case."

The man must have heard us approaching. He pulled away from the door and flushed with embarrassment at being caught.

"Put your phone away, Nina. I know him."

"Which one?" she asked.

"What?"

She pointed at a man who sprinted around the corner and disappeared.

"Who was that?" I asked.

"I didn't get a good look at him."

We walked toward my kitchen door.

Roger MacKenzie was wearing his trademark bow tie with a seersucker suit and looked completely comfortable in spite of the sweltering summer temperature.

"Roger, did you see a guy hanging around here?"

"Have you got yourself an admirer, Sophie?" he teased.

"Seriously. You didn't see anyone?"

"Darlin', I have got a lot on my mind. I can't say I saw a soul. But I'm sure glad that you're home. Disaster has befallen me." He clasped his hands over his chest as though our mere appearance had solved all his problems.

I had a hunch I knew what they concerned. Roger was a pastry chef who was sponsoring a weeklong PiePalooza event for home cooks and pie fans. But Roger wasn't an event planner, and while he had done a lot of things right, he had also been overwhelmed by the amount of work and planning that went into an event. Pie fans from around the country had signed up for the baking classes he offered. Over the last six months Roger had called me to ask questions. In the beginning I heard from him once a week. The number of calls increased with his level of anxiety as the date of his event grew closer. For the last month, he had phoned me daily.

He sucked in a deep breath, and touched the spots just over his eyebrows with three fingers of each hand as though he was doing some kind of relaxation technique. "Amy Wellington Smith has shingles." He lowered his hands and reached out to Nina. "Roger MacKenzie, pleased to make your acquaintance. Do you think shingles is a reasonable excuse? Twenty-four people have signed up for her class, Taming Beastly Berries. I think she should slap on some thick foundation and fulfill her obligation to her students."

He ran out of breath and stared at the two of us. I had a very bad feeling that he wanted me to agree with him.

I unlocked the door and invited him into my kitchen, where Daisy pranced with glee at our return, her long ears flapping. "From what I hear, shingles can be very painful. We have some excellent pie bakers in Old Town. Maybe one of them could fill in for her," I suggested, watching Nina set the pie on top of the island in my kitchen. She glanced at me and pulled a knife out of the drawer.

"It needs to set up, first," I said. "Otherwise the filling will run all over."

Nina frowned at me, but she promptly refrigerated the pie.

"Have any of *them* written a book on pie baking?" Roger asked rather haughtily.

He had high expectations. "Patsy Lee Presley is in town—"

He cut me off. "She's already scheduled to teach Avoiding the Shame of a Shrinking Crust, on Tuesday, and Blackbottom Pie Doesn't Mean Burned, on Thursday. Amy Wellington Smith's class was also on Tuesday, at the same time as Patsy Lee's."

"What about Tommy Earl?" asked Nina. "I can vouch for him. He's an excellent teacher."

Roger's lips pulled tight. "Ohhh, I don't think so. His pies are delicious, I'll grant you that. But Tommy Earl is notoriously unreliable. Such a pity. He's so talented, but I know better than to hire him. I wish Nellie Stokes were available. That woman knows how to bake!"

"What's wrong with Tommy Earl?" asked Nina.

Roger didn't say a word, but he cupped his hand as though he was holding a glass and tipped it toward his mouth.

"Are you sure?" I asked. It wasn't as though I spent a

lot of time with Tommy Earl, but I had ordered plenty of pies from him for events and he had never let me down. "I've never had a problem with him."

"Trust me on this," grumbled Roger. "It's well-known in baking circles. Ask anyone in the business. He must have some great employees who cover for him at his shop. Sophie"—Roger gazed at me with sad eyes—"Can't you help me out? Could you teach the classes?"

"Me? Good heavens. I just took one of Tommy Earl's classes. I'm not a pie pro by any stretch of the imagination. Not even a little bit. And I haven't published a cookbook." Whew. That would get me off the hook for sure.

But Nina exclaimed, "You should! I would buy it."

She wasn't helping. "Why don't you come to the Old Town Pie Festival tomorrow? A lot of professional pie bakers will be entering their pies in the contests there."

"I would sleep better if I had someone scheduled in the slot for Tuesday." He eyed me again.

Well, there was nothing I could do about that.

Nina said, "I find melatonin helps me."

I bit my lip to keep from giggling. "I'll keep an eye out for an appropriate baker tomorrow."

Roger no longer looked quite so crisp. He thanked us before leaving and dragged away like a disappointed child. I let Daisy out in my fenced backyard.

When I returned, Nina asked, "Can we try your pie now?"

"Not unless you want to see the Horror of the Runny Filling play out right here in my kitchen."

"Why do pies take so long?"

Her question was rhetorical. Nina knew that fillings had to set, although she probably wouldn't have cared. She would have scooped up the oozing filling with a soupspoon and declared it delicious.

"Besides," I said, "don't you think we'd better check on

Bernie? The pie festival is a big undertaking. He could probably use some extra hands."

When Daisy returned, she was panting and headed straight to the water bowl. I added a couple of ice cubes to her water to make it super cold. Her nose wet, she sprawled on the floor as if she was trying to cool off. The August heat was brutal, but the weather was supposed to cool off dramatically for the weekend.

I didn't feel guilty about leaving her at home when we stepped out into the humid heat again. We had only trudged one block when I asked, "How would you feel about an iced coffee or tea?"

Nina moaned. "Anything with ice in it would be welcome."

We stopped at Moos & Brews, relieved to be in the air-conditioned café while we ordered.

Nina checked the time. "Ugh. I am officially over the hill. I'm too old to drink real coffee after noon. I'll have a decaf iced caramel latte."

I ordered a plain iced coffee with a scoop of vanilla ice cream, which I knew would melt into my coffee in less than a minute once we were outside.

We were slurping the remains through biodegradable paper straws as we approached the park, where banners for the Old Town Pie Festival already fluttered in the gentle breeze.

"Francie is going to be mad that she missed this."

My elderly neighbor was a hoot, and had she been home, she would surely have attended the pie festival. "I don't think she'll be too upset. I'm sure she's having fun with her sister. How many women their age go on an African safari to photograph animals?"

So many people surrounded Bernie that he was barely visible. He had been the best man at my wedding. Bernie's sandy hair was perpetually mussed, and his nose had a kink in it where it had been broken, possibly twice. Foot-loose, Bernie had traveled the world before settling in Old Town, Alexandria, Virginia, and taking on the management of a restaurant for an absentee owner. To our astonishment, he had a flair for the business and The Laughing Hound had become one of Old Town's most popular eateries.

But today, mellow Bernie was being yelled at by one of our friends.

"For your information"—Natasha pulled her shoulders back and held her chin high—"I grew up in the country, and no one knows pies like country cooks. And why are *you* in charge of the festival, anyway? English people don't know anything about pies."

Bernie had listened politely right up until she said that part about the Brits.

In contrast to Bernie's just-rolled-out-of-bed mussed hair, not a single hair on Natasha's head dared stray out of place. She wore an admittedly elegant cream-colored suit in spite of the ninety-five-degree weather and unbearable humidity. Natasha fancied herself the Martha of the South—except she wasn't. Knowing her penchant for wreaking havoc, and given the chaos she caused the previous year, Bernie, who was in charge of the pie festival this year, had pointedly omitted Natasha from the event arrangements.

The two of them didn't get along at all. Natasha resented Bernie for not bowing to Her Highness's whims, and Bernie was unimpressed by Natasha's constant self-serving demands. A confrontation had been inevitable. I had expected kindhearted Bernie to relent, but then Natasha had to go and offend the Brits. I held my breath.

Connect with Us

Visit us online at
KensingtonBooks.com
to read more from your favorite authors, see books
by series, view reading group guides, and more.

for sneak peeks, chances to win books and prize packs,
and to share your thoughts with other readers.

facebook.com/kensingtonpublishing
twitter.com/kensingtonbooks

Tell us what you think!

To share your thoughts, submit a review,
or sign up for our eNewsletters, please visit:
KensingtonBooks.com/TellUs.